PHOENIX DU ROSE

The Hana Du Rose Mysteries
(Generation Z)

K T BOWES

Dedication

Sometimes these acknowledgements come easily and at other times, they can hold up publication.

I owe so many of you my thanks for your support, your input and your guidance, and it can be difficult to single out anyone in particular. This book was produced during the dark days of lockdown and Covid 19, and it was born into a different world from the one in which I began writing it.

I wrote of Phoenix's experiences in the bush when I couldn't venture more than a kilometre from home. And her conversation with her father at the end of the novel is poignant, because I still can't visit mine in the UK.
Nobody will come out of this experience unscathed. We're not the same people who retreated to our homes and cut ourselves off from the rest of the world.

We won't be unchanged, but perhaps we'll be more appreciative.

So, this novel is for you, wherever you are and however you're getting through.

Kia kaha. Be strong.

Psalm 119:114

"You are my hiding place and my shield; I hope in Your word."

WOULD YOU LIKE TO BE PART OF IT?

I'm a believer in 'try before you buy.' There's nothing worse than forking out your hard-earned cash on a doozy and regretting it. If you'd like to join me on my writing journey, you can pick up 4 free eBooks by joining my mailing list at ktbowes.com

1

SUMMER BLUES

"Please, can I speak to Wiri?" Phoenix held her breath and waited for the reply. She disguised her voice, so the hotel receptionist didn't recognise her. She didn't want her father to hear she'd called and wonder why.

"He isn't here right now. Please, can I take a message?" The woman's clipped voice cut across the kilometres.

Phoenix's heart clenched tight in her chest. "No, it's fine thank you. I'll ring back later." The fake Scots accent borrowed from her maternal grandfather wilted. It had proved difficult enough to access the telephone in the first place without having to go back for a second attempt. Phoenix hung up the receiver and glanced around the sparse office. She stifled a sob.

She'd spent the entire year canvassing her parents for permission to attend the holiday camp. Asking them to come and fetch her after one night seemed like the worst failure imaginable. Her mother hadn't enjoyed towing the horse trailer along the narrow lanes which cut through the dense bush. Phoenix had wanted to play a grown up role with temporary freedom from her eighteen-year-old cousin's overbearing influence. Then at the first sign of trouble, she sought

Wiremu's help as a reflex. Her shoulders slumped. Perhaps she couldn't manage without him. She wished she hadn't tried. The urge to grab her rucksack and escape on her horse, played around the edges of her consciousness. She needed to speak to Wiri first, regretting how they'd left things and certain he'd offer his customary reassurance.

Phoenix crept to the window and peered through the smudged glass. The campers sat in a huddle around the campfire with the leaders dotted among them. Their faces flickered, reflecting the flames which united youth and age beneath an orange hue. The girls from her cabin sat together, testing the newness of their relationship and trying to bond. Mosquitos and night flies hummed in the glow, taking the opportunity to dive bomb anyone not wearing insect repellent. Phoenix turned the door handle with care to avoid the irritating squeak. Dusk covered her movements as she crept from the office and slipped out onto the deck. The steady rumble of conversation returned to her in snatches of words and half-finished sentences. Laughter sounded as someone's marshmallow caught fire and a flurry of movement found the stick owner losing their trophy beneath a stamping boot.

"Don't do it again, Sharon," one of the camp leaders complained. "You're doing it on purpose now."

Phoenix slid sideways, her palms pressed against the weather board wall. She reached the end of the building and skipped down the stairs. Executing the turn she'd planned at the bottom step, she prepared to re-join the campfire huddle with the excuse of having visited the bathroom.

"Hey." The whispering male voice took her by surprise and Phoenix jumped and squeaked at the same time. She missed her footing on the bottom step and tumbled to her knees. Grit and small stones grazed the skin. Pressing her palm over her mouth muted the hiss of pain.

"Sorry, I didn't mean to scare you." His tone sounded apologetic. Slipping from the shadows, he offered Phoenix his hand. She gripped the bony fingers and tried to salvage some of her dignity once on her feet. "What were you doing in the office?" he demanded. Keeping his adolescent voice low caused the baritone pitch to waver. "I heard you using the phone. You know we're not allowed any technology, so what's important enough to break the rules?"

Phoenix swallowed. It seemed an impossible task to stop the words from tumbling free. She shook her head, not trusting herself. "Nothing," she lied. The dual actions of rule breaking and lying made her feel dirty, so she opted for misdirection to appease her horrified conscience. "Nothing important."

The unexpected misery consuming her since her arrival burned the space between her eyes with the effort of holding it in. Used to venting to a mother who listened, Phoenix sensed the dam cracking from twenty-four hours without empathy.

The teenager frowned. "It looked like more than nothing to me," he said. "I figure if the good girl among us is rule breaking, it must be serious." His brown eyes held the promise of understanding and Phoenix wavered. Her lips parted in a dismissal, but her problems had other plans.

"I wanted to speak to my cousin," she admitted. "It's complicated." She swallowed and gnawed on her lower lip. "It's not important." A sense of extreme relief accompanied the realisation she'd stopped herself blurting everything to a stranger.

He nodded, giving Phoenix time to sort her thoughts back into their relevant boxes. Tall for his age, he wore his hair hanging over his face like curtains as though he spent his life hiding. "You're Phoenix," he said and took a step forward. "I'm Kirwan."

"I know." Phoenix frowned. "You got told off on the first night for smoking."

"Yup." Kirwan pulled a lighted cigarette from behind his back. His easy smirk spread into a grin. Not much wider than a cocktail stick, he'd rolled it with expertise to conserve tobacco. "Busted. I'm glad they didn't find my whole stash, or I wouldn't last until the end of the week."

Phoenix wrinkled her nose. "But it stinks," she said. "How can you stand to put that muck into your body?"

Kirwan frowned and deep furrows appeared in his forehead. "It's the only thing I have," he admitted. He nipped the end of the cigarette between finger and thumb, blowing on the stub to cool it. Then he pushed it into the front pocket of his jeans. "Waste not, want not," he said. "Are you gonna tell?"

"No!" Phoenix took a step back. Logan Du Rose's daughter knew better than to squeal to the authorities about anything. She shook her black curls with more emphasis than she intended.

"You didn't answer my question about who you were phoning." Kirwan patted his pocket as though afraid the cigarette stub might already have disappeared.

Phoenix sighed. "My cousin," she admitted. "I want to go home."

"After one night and a day?" Kirwan's head jerked back on his neck. "Aren't you enjoying it here?"

Phoenix shook her head. "It's not what I thought it would be like." Her voice lowered to a whisper and disappeared in a sigh.

Kirwan shrugged. "So, you're phoning the cousin you wanted to get away from? Must be bad."

Phoenix turned her head towards the sounds coming from the campfire. The sudden urge for confession had abandoned her. "We should get back," she said. Her fingers writhed in front of her tee shirt.

"What, to roasting gluten free marshmallows over the fire?" Kirwan scoffed. "And not being allowed to swear for an entire week?"

Phoenix smiled and the action felt genuine. Kirwan's colourful dialogue had got him more fines in the single game of Capture the Flag than he would ever finish paying. If the game had involved real money, he'd be bankrupt before the age of sixteen. "I should have come with a friend," she admitted. "I thought it sounded great. But he got called away at the last moment and couldn't come."

"Boyfriend?" Kirwan raised a dark eyebrow and Phoenix's cheeks turned pink. Her fingers writhed and she shoved them behind her back to hide their betrayal of her discomfort.

"No, he's my pastor," she said. Her tone became defensive. Burning pink cheeks disclosed the monster crush she'd had on Sam since junior school. It had survived his marriage to a local woman and the birth of his own child. But his veneer of the perfect man had lost some of its shine when he informed her she'd be attending the camp alone. Empty words and a pat on the head told her she'd be fine.

Phoenix squared her shoulders to make the thread of disappointment lose its grasp. "Do you like it here?" she asked, only half interested.

"Hell no!" he replied. "I'm only here so my foster family can go on holiday without me." His fingers fluttered over the comforting outline of the cigarette in his pocket. "I'd rather stay here than spend a week listening to them complain about how much extra it cost them to take me with them. They only foster me for the money."

Phoenix gaped and her eyes widened. "That's horrible!" she whispered.

Kirwan gave her a rueful smile. "Welcome to my world," he said. His nose wrinkled. "I lived with a nice family for a while, but I messed it up, as usual. The mum caught me wagging school and I got mad and put my fist through the bedroom door. The social worker wouldn't let me stay there after that."

"There you are." A woman rounded the corner and raised a blonde eyebrow overlaid with thick brown pencil. It gave her a look of perpetual surprise. Kirwan's lips curled into a sneer at the sight of the girls' leader. A blush crept up Phoenix's olive neck, prickling the soft skin as it flooded into her cheeks.

"I fell, Tina," she gushed, pointing to the scuff marks in the dirt. "Kirwan helped me."

"Oh." Tina's head jerked back on her neck and her sharp features softened. "Are you okay?"

Phoenix nodded and bent to brush the dirt from her knees where they'd struck the baked earth. Lines of blood streaked her palm in the half light from a dirty overhead bulb. "It's nothing," she said, adding as much dismissal into her voice as she dared. "I didn't look where I was going and tripped."

"I bet she's had worse injuries falling off horses." Kirwan smirked and Phoenix couldn't tell if he meant to help or hinder her.

"Come to the office and I'll get the first aid box." Tina wagged her fingers and turned her body towards the stairs. She halted and frowned. "Where were you going?"

"I went to the bathroom," Phoenix said. The crafted lie seemed to stick in the back of her throat. Her lifetime goal of impressing Sam with a persona of kindness and honesty drifted further out of reach. She sighed and stared at a tuft of sun scorched grass between her ankle boots.

"Did you go to the bathroom too?" Tina's blue eyes narrowed and she regarded Kirwan with a look hard enough to convey her thinly veiled disdain. Phoenix held her breath. Tina's inference hung over them, the unasked question forming a guillotine above their heads.

Kirwan snorted. "No, Tina. We didn't go to the bathroom together. Just say what you mean." He jerked his head towards the dense tree covering beyond the cabins. "I went for a smoke."

Phoenix swallowed as Tina's jaw flexed and then set into a firm line. "You can't smoke here." Disgust entered her tone and Phoenix pursed her lips. Standing with Kirwan gave her an alternate view. No one had spoken to her with as much dislike as Tina conveyed in a single sentence to Kirwan. Phoenix was Sam's prodigy, arriving at the camp with a reference and a verbal pedigree. Kirwan came on sufferance; to suffer and be suffered.

Kirwan jerked his chin up, perhaps in acknowledgement but more likely intending to disarm Tina. "I'm an addict," he said. "Sorry." He didn't sound sorry, but his words had their desired effect. Tina nodded and her expression softened.

"Grant brought nicotine patches if you're interested in quitting," she said. "I know he already caught you once. But you can't keep smoking in the bush. It's a fire hazard."

Phoenix resisted the urge to dart a sideways glance at the raging campfire floating sparks and flakes of lighted marshmallow into the tinder dry bush. She tamped down the debate rising in her chest and clamped her tongue between her teeth to keep her objections inside. Growing up on her father's mountain, she knew the risks of fire in the vegetation. One spark took on a life of its own. It would blacken a whole section of bush within minutes, chewing through it like a child eating popcorn at the movies. Her paternal grandparents had both died in a house fire the night before she was born.

The sense of injustice rose and refused to remain contained behind her gritted teeth. The words popped out before she could stop them. "What about the campfire?" she demanded. "My father won't allow any fires on our property."

Kirwan's gaze tracked towards her. Behind the veil of scorn, Phoenix detected a flicker of appreciation. Tina huffed. She jabbed an index finger at a hose pipe running from the boys' bathroom shed and disappearing under the office. It reappeared on the other side and snaked around the edge of the fire pit. "Grant set the hosepipe up, so they're ready if it gets out of hand," she bit. "We know what we're doing."

Phoenix opened her mouth with an instant objection. The pipe wouldn't work without the tap turned on at the source and she saw from the handle it wasn't. Someone would have to remember to run across and turn it on in an emergency. The slight shake of Kirwan's head halted her and she licked her lips in confusion. She felt like a marionette controlled by his force of will. A heady sensation of fear sent off cloudbursts in her brain.

"I'll get you some antiseptic for that cut," Tina said. She jogged up the steps to the office without looking back and the door handle creaked beneath her fingers.

Hearing a low snicker, Phoenix glanced up at Kirwan and caught the smile spreading across his lips. His dark eyelashes lowered in mischief, giving him an attractive, cheeky appearance. "Nice distraction technique, Phoenix Du Rose. She forgot to punish me now." His grin grew wider and he cocked his head. "Maybe we can help each other?"

Despite herself, Phoenix smiled before following Tina up the steps.

2

JUDGE NOT

"**Y**ou need to watch that boy." Tina opened a rusty first aid tin and leafed through a collection of sticking plasters and bandages. She pulled one out and measured it for size against the oozing cuts on Phoenix's knees.

"Watch him do what?" Misery lowered Phoenix's voice and made her deliberately obtuse. She sat on the desk and swung her legs, trying not to stare at the telephone in the corner. A tattered ordinance survey map covered a cork noticeboard above the desk. Someone had taped the two halves together long enough ago for the glue to leach through and turn it yellow. Phoenix studied the map, tracing the sweep of the coastline and yearning to follow the wavy contours home.

Tina raised a blonde eyebrow, perhaps doubting the girl could be quite so naive. "He's nice enough," she conceded. "But he's trouble. Mind you don't get pulled into something you can't escape."

"Like what?" Phoenix persisted. She pursed her lips, knowing her mother would have rebuked her about then. Her father would have given her 'the look' and it would have proved more than enough to silence her. "How can he be trouble and nice at the same time?"

Tina frowned. She ignored the grimace of pain on Phoenix's face as she exercised her revenge, spreading iodine over the tiny cuts with cotton wool. "I can't give you specifics. Let's just say he's had a rough start in life. Time will tell if he's able to carve something better for himself or end up disappointing us all."

Phoenix hissed as Tina dabbed at her knee with a fresh piece of dry gauze. She spoke through gritted teeth, writhing beneath the pressure of the sticking plaster Tina slapped over the joint. "How can he carve something better for himself? He needs help to change his circumstances. Isn't that why he's here?"

Tina blinked and her cheeks flushed enough to reveal her discomfort. Built from solid stock, her skin appeared pink and downy like a peach. She cleared her throat. "Yes. We'll pray for him. Gus is great at steering people in the right direction." Her eyelashes fluttered as she said the camp leader's name with a hushed reverence.

"But what about practical help?" Phoenix slid from the desk and straightened her shorts. Escaping iodine left a brown rivulet along her shin and stained the top of her sock. "My mama calls it a leg up. She helps lots of people get back onto their feet." Names and faces drifted across her inner vision. So many people owed their change in circumstances to Hana Du Rose's generosity and Logan Du Rose's tolerance. She thought of her father's dead pan expression and missed him. Her gaze strayed to the telephone again. "I want to call home," she blurted. "My parents will help Kirwan."

"It doesn't work." Tina didn't look up from her task. She sorted the various plasters into size order within the tin.

Phoenix held her breath. She'd used the phone less than ten minutes earlier. "Can I try?" she whispered. "My Poppa is sick. I'd feel better if I could speak to my mama."

Tina shrugged and Phoenix stole across the creaky floorboards. She grasped the receiver in sweating fingers and lifted it to her ear. Her fingers poised over the buttons, the numbers obscured in the semi darkness. Nothing. Swallowing, she depressed the large button occupying the space where the receiver usually sat. Her ear filled with the sound of dead air. "I don't understand," she hissed. "Why isn't it working?"

"It's intermittent." Tina bent and jiggled the connection where the wire met the socket. "Our cook phoned her husband yesterday, but I tried to call home earlier and it wouldn't work."

Phoenix replaced the receiver and picked it up again. She lifted it to her ear and willed it to recreate the dial tone. Still nothing. Exasperation made her clumsy as she dumped it in the cradle. An uncharacteristic flare of temper made her want to slam it over and over again. "Don't the leaders have mobile phones?" she snapped. "How can you call for help in an emergency?"

Tina shook her head. "Technology is banned from this camp. We've never had an emergency, but Grant has a contingency just in case."

"What contingency?" Phoenix's voice rose. She ached to go home, back to the mountain and her family. And Wiri. She needed to speak to Wiri. Things had gone wrong between them and she wanted to put it right.

"It doesn't matter what contingency," Tina said with a chuckle. She snapped the lid on the first aid tin and settled it back inside the desk drawer. "He's the head leader and he's got one. That's all you need to worry about young lady." She jerked her head towards the door, telling Phoenix without words she needed to leave. She complied, dragging her feet with her shoulders locked in a slouch. Tina patted her arm with a meaty hand. "Cheer up," she joked. "It might never happen."

Phoenix sat on the fringes of the group gathered around the campfire. Misery dimmed the sounds of laughter and the flickering firelight, leaving her mulling over her fight with Wiri and subsequent exit. Her head gave an involuntary shake at the weight of her thoughts and she covered her eyes with her hands. She'd made an idiot of herself with him.

"Phoe is crying!" The shrill voice split the airwaves and the laughter ceased. A small hand landed on Phoenix's sore knee and another patted the small of her back.

"No, just smoke in my eyes." Phoenix released the lie and another section of her conscience withered. She'd never lied so much in her life as she had in the previous half an hour. She dropped her hands and blinked at the boisterous flames licking the stones surrounding the fire pit. A sparking campfire in the bush during the heat of summer; she imagined Logan's frown at the idea. "I'm fine." She bestowed a generous smile at the tiny girl to her right and forced herself to wrap her arm around the slender body. Kylie beamed up at her, desperate for acceptance and blossoming beneath its attainment. Phoenix frowned as another child edged nearer on her left. The palm's owner continued to pat her back. "Thank you." Phoenix's smile looked more genuine as she wrapped her other arm around the girl to her left. Carrie cuddled closer as though wanting to disappear into Phoenix's armpit.

Phoenix nodded to Grant across the dancing flames and he smiled at her. This was why she'd gained entry to the camp, as a leader and mentor for the younger girls. Sam had sung her praises from the depths of his parish in the Waikato, pulling strings and making coherent arguments for why a fifteen-year-old could attend as a junior leader. Then he'd pulled out at less than a day's notice and left her rudderless and alone, fending for herself among strangers.

Someone produced a guitar and the singing began. They belted out the usual favourites until a string snapped. A series of groans followed. The singing had given Phoenix a lightness of spirit and reminded her of home and her father's skill with the guitar and local waiata. "Let's sing 'Tūtira mai ngā iwi,' Phoenix suggested. Shyness gripped her as all eyes turned to stare at her.

"I don't know it," the guitar player confessed. The young man's eyes crinkled at the edges. "I should though. Can you teach us? I'll mend the string for tomorrow night."

Phoenix swallowed and nerves stole her voice. Kylie reached forward and gripped her hand. Blonde curls drifted across her eyes as she sheltered behind her fringe, staring up at Phoenix with adoration. "I know it," she whispered.

So, they sang. The first verse wavered on the breeze until others picked up the tune. Many realised they did know parts of the familiar waiata and joined in the chorus. 'Tūtira mai ngā iwi, Tātou tātou e.'

"What does it mean?" Suspicion back lit Tina's eyes, propaganda making her believe Māori worshipped other gods. She didn't want Phoenix hailing damnation on the nice Christian camp without permission. Phoenix channelled her father's cultural confidence into her answer. "It means, 'Line up together, people, All of us, all of us. Stand in rows, people, All of us, all of us. Seek after knowledge and love of others - everybody. Be virtuous. Stay united. All of us, all of us.' That's what it means."

"Oh." Tina's head jerked back in surprise. "So, like a Christian song, then?" She nodded with approval, her bleached hair bouncing as she spoke. "I didn't realise." Phoenix saw the non-verbal communication she sent to Grant and the confirmation from his raised eyebrow.

"Yes, I guess." Phoenix ground her teeth against exasperation and clutched the girls closer to her body. Kylie squirmed and she realised she'd gripped them too hard. "My father says the prejudice is unfounded. The missionaries and government representatives told lies about us to the English queen. We've never worshipped other gods, just Atua, the creator. We revere our ancestors, but they were real people." The facts rolled off her tongue from within easy reach at the forefront of her mind. She'd heard it often enough from Logan Du Rose. Her father possessed mana, the inexplicable sense of power and authority afforded to a few worthy individuals. In that moment of challenge, she felt his strength and wondered if she might possess it too.

Tina snorted and Phoenix's bubble of righteousness burst in her chest. "That's not true," the older woman sneered. "They definitely worshipped heathen gods." She rose and removed Phoenix's right of reply and in that moment, she hated her with the passion of Logan Du Rose.

3
THROUGH THE BARRICADES

Phoenix awoke to the sound of scratching outside her cabin. She lay awake for a while, thinking about the effort involved with climbing from her bunk to locate the culprit. At least it stayed outside on the deck, not interested in coming inside the bunk room. She sighed, imagining the mayhem a furry intruder might induce. Getting up would involve finding her boots and an inevitable trip to the bathroom, but the sound of a twig breaking alerted her to the presence of something larger than a mouse. Her mind switched to concern for her horse and she forced herself to a sitting position. The notion of worrying about Mikaere seemed ridiculous even in her head. The black and white gelding bred from her father's favourite mare showed no fear of anything. Logan had helped her train Mikaere herself, teaching her tricks she didn't know existed. The result was that only he or Phoenix could catch or ride her horse. The other stable hands avoided him for what manifested as an unpredictable nature. Or demon possession.

Phoenix stretched her arms above her head and touched the low ceiling above her bunk. She knew she wouldn't go back to sleep. Mikaere didn't need her to check on him, but the thought of his company caused a yearning in her soul. She decided the walk to the paddock and back might help her get to sleep. Hanging from the top bunk to avoid the creaky ladder, she dropped to the ground with a dull thud. Unable to locate her ankle boots in the dark, her bare feet padded across the cabin. Carrie's discarded hair clip made a painful pin cushion as Phoenix passed her sleeping form. She hissed in pain and resisted the urge to strangle her while she slept.

The handle squeaked as Phoenix pressed down on it and despite her best efforts; the door groaned inward. She held her breath and paused for a moment. Kylie turned over with a sleepy snort and settled onto her other side to face the wall. No one else moved. Phoenix continued to pull the door wider and slipped through the gap. Closing it behind her proved even more difficult and the volume of the creak seemed louder, reverberating off the trees surrounding the clearing. She released the handle with a sense of relief when no one challenged her.

"I'm just going to the bathroom," she whispered to herself, practising her excuse if she should run across a leader on night duty. The thought got into her head and she realised she needed the bathroom for real. A mouse skittered from beneath a silver fern as Phoenix walked across the campground. She clutched her chest in fright and her other hand muffled her squeak of fear at the sudden movement. She paused to catch her breath and released a sigh of relief as the tiny body scampered in the other direction. Changing her trajectory from the track leading to the horses, Phoenix walked to the bathroom.

A dim night light burned in the hut, still enough to attract hundreds of flying bugs which circled the dirty bulb in a maniacal dance. Phoenix used her forearms to shield her head from the bigger moths as she ducked into a stall. The flushing of the toilet disturbed two cockroaches and a lost toad from the cubicle next to hers. Born and raised in the bush of north Waikato, Phoenix grew up with the night creatures. But she shared her English mother's appreciation for a clean bathroom and a comfortable, bug free bed. If her father felt disappointed that the baby birthed at the top of a lonely mountain should show such distaste for its multi legged inhabitants, he never said.

Phoenix washed her hands, wrinkling her nose at the light brown tinge in the water. Exiting the bathroom, she paused on the threshold. A possum scratched around the campfire looking for scraps of marshmallow amid the remnants. It sat on its haunches in the moonlight and closed its eyes to savour a pink sugary treat.

Phoenix froze as she heard it again. The sound of twigs breaking. The noise echoed, the sharp sound alien amid the muffled blanket of the bush canopy. She worried at her thumbnail and contemplated looking for the leader on night duty. She wished she'd paid more attention earlier when Grant announced where to find them in case of an emergency.

"I could scream," she whispered to herself. Her reason batted away the ridiculous thought as soon as it rose to the fore. She imagined the chaos she'd cause, only to identify another possum feasting on food waste. "I came here to find my independence," she hissed. "It's time to put my money where my mouth is."

Phoenix pointed her reluctant feet towards the track leading to the paddock where the horses grazed when not working. The moonlight picked up sticks and sharp stones which threatened her bare soles. She'd grown up barefoot and trod the tracks as though wearing shoes, the skin hardly registering the obstacles. Halfway along the track she noticed a cigarette butt and her shoulders slumped. Readying herself for an argument rather than a battle, Phoenix picked up the butt and held it between finger and thumb. "Bloody Kirwan!" she complained. She imagined her father's disgust at the easy desecration of his beloved whenua, Phoenix padded further along the track in search of the perpetrator. The moon slipped behind a low cloud and left her relying on instinct to find her way. The occasional snap of a twig made her turn as an eerie sensation crawled up the back of her neck.

Air left her lungs in a whoosh as a hand snaked around her mouth. Her body shifted backwards at speed. She landed on her backside amid a clump of low growing ferns and the hand released her mouth. A foot dug into her thigh and a heavy leg kept her pinned to the dusty earth.

Kirwan's eyes stared into hers, his pupils wide. He extracted himself and scrabbled around to face her. As Phoenix's lips parted to protest, he slipped his palm back over her mouth. His other hand gripped her wrists together in her lap. "Shush!" he hissed. "Don't let them hear you."

Phoenix gasped and the inhale took with it the scent of nicotine. Freeing one of her hands, she pulled his fingers away from her mouth. "Who is it?" she demanded. "Are they after the horses?"

4

CAPTURE THE FLAG

Phoenix sat on the beach and hugged her shins. Her heels dug into the iron rich sand. "We should do something," she hissed.

"No!" Kirwan flopped down next to her, smelling of cigarettes and cheap deodorant. "It's not our business."

"But those people must be suffering!" Phoenix exclaimed. She turned to him, her grey eyes wide and filled with storm clouds as she searched his face for some shred of humanity. "Why did you tell me if you mean to just ignore them?"

Kirwan shrugged, "I wish I'd kept it to myself." He spun in the sand to face her. "I wanted to stop you blundering into a situation that could get you killed." He pulled his knees into his chest and mirrored Phoenix's stance. The tide licked at the shore with growing tendrils of white surf. "They're refugees," he said. His Adam's apple bobbed as he took a deep swallow. "I saw them arrive. A fishing boat anchored in the bay on our first night here. Two men brought the people ashore in a dinghy." His dark hair flopped into his flecked hazel eyes as he tilted his head to face her in the silvery light. "They had a dog with them, but they tied it up on the beach. The refugees were too afraid to walk past it."

Phoenix shook her head. "At least they're all grown-ups," she said with a sigh. "Children would make more noise and complain about being hungry and bored." She glanced down at her watch. The hands shaped the imprint of four o'clock in the morning and she stifled a yawn.

Kirwan released a tired laugh. It held no mirth. "There are two children," he stated. His shoulders bowed as though the world rested its head on his delicate teenage bones. "A baby and a little girl." He paused as though considering his next words. "We can't do anything. It's not our business. These people paid money to come here. If we call the authorities, they'll send them home. These aren't people who just fancied a trip to New Zealand. They're hiding in a barn in the middle of nowhere. They're running away from a war."

"But it's wrong!" Phoenix released her legs and dug her toes into the black sand. Despite the late hour, it still contained the day's warmth. Flying bugs nipped at her arms and the cool air created prickles which ran up and down Phoenix's bare limbs. "It's not okay to smuggle people into New Zealand. We can't just ignore it." Her honesty metre hiked towards critical as conflict budded in her chest. She pressed a hand over her lips as though willing herself to keep the refugees' secret despite herself. Phoenix held her breath. Fear slipped a hand around her neck in an unwanted caress. "We can tell an adult," she pressed. She sounded earnest. "Let's tell Pastor Grant. He'll tell us what to do."

Kirwan shook his head and his eye roll expressed his dismissal. "You've no idea how the world works," he said. "You've grown up on your lonely mountain, surrounded by family and privilege. I bet your stomach never burned with hunger. Has Child Services ever dumped you in a family that doesn't want you there? You know nothing, Phoenix Du Rose. And if you tell anyone about this, I'll make you sorry." Kirwan stood and sand kicked up in his wake. His footsteps sounded heavy as he walked away, leaving Phoenix alone on the beach.

She watched his lanky frame disappear beneath the bush canopy. The click of a lighter created an orange bloom in the darkness, followed by the red glow of a cigarette. Phoenix pulled the slender cigarette butt from her pocket and sighed. "Thanks for nothing, Pastor Sam," she hissed under her breath. "If you were here, you'd tell me what to do." He'd given a weak reason for pulling out of the camp and abandoning her, citing a bogus sounding excuse. He seemed so keen when he presented the junior church leaders with the pamphlet for a summer horse camp. Four had signed up straight away, dropping out one by one until only she and Sam remained. Phoenix remembered the frisson of delight which had heralded the realisation. She'd relished the opportunity to be alone with Sam. Then he'd pulled out without enough notice for her to do likewise.

Phoenix squeezed her eyes closed at the memory of her altercation with Wiri. He'd found her crying in the feed barn and sat down next to her on the hay bales. Older than her by three years and two months, he'd wrapped his muscular arm around her shoulders and tugged her into his side. He'd listened to the reason for her distress and frowned, a familiar dimple etching itself into his cheek. "I think it's for the best," he'd said, his voice just a whisper. "It seemed cute how you adored him as a kid, but you're not a child anymore and he's a married man. I'm glad he isn't going."

Phoenix inhaled and pulled away from him, his voicing of her thoughts casting a filthy pall over her reverence for Sam. "That's disgusting!" she breathed. "I'd do nothing to hurt his marriage!"

Wiremu Du Rose's handsome face creased into a series of sad lines. They pulled his grey eyes into narrow slits. Lifting a hand, he brushed his thumb across her lips and sighed. "Stop running from me, Phoe," he whispered. "Sam's a smokescreen. We both know that."

Phoenix had squeezed her eyes shut. They'd trodden a tightrope for far too long and she sensed Wiri's urgency increasing with every touch, every surreptitious caress. They'd ignored their mutual attraction forever, skirting it like a spectre within their familial relationship.

"You and I need to acknowledge what's between us and face the music." Wiri had turned with classic Du Rose stealth and brushed his lips across hers. His fingers pressed against the back of her head and she'd tasted spearmint and tangy aftershave. A fire lit within her belly, leaving her shaking and confused as she parted her lips and allowed him to deepen the kiss. It felt right and yet so wrong. Wiri pulled away and dropped his arm, standing up and facing her. He looked rattled as he stuffed his hands into his pockets and the action hunched his broad shoulders. "We're inevitable, you and me," he'd said with more confidence. "I'll speak to Uncle Logan."

"Don't!" Phoenix's teeth ground in her jaw. "Don't you dare!"

Wiri's frown pulled his eyebrows into a line. He'd turned and strode from the barn without another word, leaving her crying on the hay bale. He didn't help her load Mikaere into the trailer the next morning like he usually did and he didn't say goodbye.

Pain squeezed Phoenix's heart at the thought of his suffering. She squeezed Kirwan's cigarette between her fingers and flakes of tobacco scattered over her legs. The urge to speak to Wiri surfaced again and she got to her feet in the sand. Daylight streaked the sky with yellow highlights as she faced the narrow track back to the camp. The disintegrated cigarette remains fell to the ground, buried beneath the sand as Phoenix turned. She'd apologise to Wiri and promise they'd talk when she got home. Then she'd tell him about the refugees. He'd know what to do. But first she needed to communicate with the outside world.

5

SCAVENGER HUNT

"Tell me about your family," Phoenix said. She flicked a blade of grass from her leg. The teenagers watched a group of the younger children having a riding lesson. Rough post and rail fencing separated the arena from the grazing paddock. The riders had already worn away the scrubby grass burned by the summer sun and dust puffed around the horses' hooves as they dragged their feet. Phoenix tensed as the mare Kylie rode shied at a fluttering leaf. "Heels down, tighten the reins and stop flapping your legs!" Phoenix called. The leader taking the lesson glanced across at Kylie and her eyes widened in alarm.

"I don't have a family," Kirwan growled. "There's nothing to tell."

Phoenix gave an encouraging smile to Kylie as the child struggled to gather her reins and regain her precarious seat. "Sit your bum heavier in the saddle," she shouted. Kylie's attempt at shifting her weight into her backside seemed imperceptible but made enough of a difference for the horse to slip back under her control. "Good girl!" Phoenix called and Kylie's lips parted in a grin.

"You're good at that," Kirwan commented.

Phoenix shrugged, pushing away his compliment with an ease of practice. "I wanted to be helpful," she admitted. "It feels like they don't really need me."

Kirwan snorted, snatching Phoenix's attention from the riders. "Welcome to my club. I'm not sure anyone ever needed me." Phoenix listened for any trace of self-pity in his tone. She heard none. He seemed resolved to his lack of importance, content in the belief he was neither wanted nor needed in any sphere of his life. She resisted the urge to cover his truth with empty platitudes. Kirwan gave a tired smile. "What about yours? Tell me about your family."

Phoenix sifted through potential sentences in her head, each falling short of the mark. Kirwan's question made her suspicious. He'd already commented on the integrity of her family. She wondered if he asked through a genuine spirit of camaraderie or because he sought information to confirm an already formed opinion. "What do you want to know?" she replied, couching her answer with another question.

The teenager frowned. "It's not a hard one," he replied. Scorn rippled through his tone. "I'm just curious about how the other half live."

Phoenix rolled her eyes. "It sounds like you're trying to trip me."

Kirwan shook his head in denial. "I'm not, I promise. Tell me about your cousin and why things are complicated."

His words reactivated the pain and Phoenix snatched a clump of grass from the ground next to her. Wiremu Du Rose appeared in her inner vision, the hurt in his eyes reinforcing her desperate need to speak to him. Her lips burned with the renewed sensation of his forbidden kiss. The voice in her head told her she couldn't be what he wanted. She couldn't be what he needed. They were destined to cause disappointment. Her father would kill them both and bury the bodies. "I don't want to talk about it," she whispered. "It's private."

"Sounds intriguing." Kirwan's long fingers reached for the discarded blades of grass which Phoenix had torn up by the roots. He sifted them, regarding each blade with more than a passing interest. "I know you want to talk about last night. But we can't do anything about it. You understand that don't you?"

"I don't see why not." Phoenix turned her body, so she faced him, her palm resting on the ground between them. "It's wrong! Why are those people trapped in the barn? We need to get help!"

Kirwan frowned and pressed his fingers over her lips. Her stunning grey eyes widened above them. "Keep your voice down!" he snarled. "You have no idea who's involved or who might be listening right now. They will have paid a fortune to come here. They'd rather hide in a barn than dodge bullets at home. The people running an operation like that can make you disappear the second you become a threat. Stop behaving like an idiot and listen to me. We are not getting involved and that's final."

Phoenix narrowed her eyes and glared at him over the top of his hand. "You're not the boss of me," she hissed, her words sounding muffled and distorted from behind his finger. "I can do what I want!" Her plan to ask for his help accessing the office phone faded to nothing.

Kirwan withdrew his hand and shook his head. He rose in a fluid motion, his legs unfolding and his spine remaining stiff and unyielding. "Then you're on your own," he snarled. His light jacket made a swishing sound as he walked across the paddock towards the camp.

Phoenix watched him clamber over the gate which kept the horses in the riding arena. His long legs helped him cover the ground quickly and she compared his physique to Wiri's before correcting herself. Her cheeks flared pink. "I am on my own," she repeated. "And I hate it."

As Kylie's balance on the horse wobbled, Phoenix got to her feet and walked across the arena. She approached the leader taking the lesson. Apprehension slowed her steps. "Amy, would you like me to help Kylie?" she asked.

The woman eyed her with suspicion before releasing a shrug of indifference. "There's no need. All these kids signed to say they're intermediate riders." She jerked her head towards the assortment of horses and ponies circling her. "I bought the steadiest horses from my riding school. We're fine thanks."

Phoenix paused and spun in a circle. A few of the girls rode with confidence, but others sat like sacks of potatoes in the saddle. Kylie and another girl from her cabin appeared terrified, hanging on to clumps of mane for dear life. The wildness in Kylie's eyes communicated her terror to the horse. Her mare responded with jerky movements before planting its hooves and ignoring the windmill actions of Kylie's feckless, flailing heels.

Ignoring Amy's look of irritation, Phoenix strode across the paddock to where Kylie's horse had buried its muzzle in a clump of grass at the edge of the arena. It tore off sizeable chunks despite the metal snaffle impeding its chewing. "Tighten your reins, Kylie," she called. The child gave a weak tug on the leather and the horse flexed the muscles in its neck, determined to continue lunching. But its body language altered as it sensed Phoenix's approach, knowing by her demeanour she meant business. At a click of her tongue the mare lifted her head at speed, grass spilling from either side of her mouth. She continued to chew while hurrying back onto the track and joining the group. Phoenix fell into place next to Kylie as her horse followed the others around the oval. Someone had used weed killer to mark the route. Battered white cones designated eight points around the wonky arcs. Faded black marker pen showed the letters.

"I want a turn on the forehand and a steady walk from A to C." Amy slapped a riding crop against her jeans. The ride turned in obedience, the lead horse familiar with the drill. Phoenix put herself on the near side, so she could observe instructions from Amy while helping Kylie.

"Shorten your reins, Kylie," she said, infusing kindness into her tone. At the fluttering of the girl's fingers, Phoenix turned her body to help her while her feet continued pacing along next to the horse. She gathered up the leather reins hanging like a washing line along the horse's shoulder and fitted them into Kylie's fingers. "Hold your hands like this," she said, demonstrating the correct way of gathering up the reins. "Thumbs stay on top and let the reins feed between your ring fingers and your pinkies. Holding them this way stops you from yanking on the horse's mouth and causing damage to her lips. It gives you a lighter touch and allows you to communicate with her. Think of the reins as an electric current between you and your horse. You can tell what she's thinking and ask her to work for you. They're not handlebars." Phoenix smiled up at Kylie and saw relief flood the child's face.

"What do the letters mean?" Kylie demanded. She jerked her head towards the cones. Her blonde brows furrowed into a frown as she twisted her fingers through the reins and tried to mimic Phoenix's demonstration.

Phoenix shrugged. "There are lots of theories based on history. They're easy to remember if you learn the rhyme."

"What rhyme?" Kylie got her fingers sorted and grinned at her accomplishment.

Phoenix paced alongside her. "All King Edward's Horses Carried Many Brave Fighters." She placed her palm against the mare's neck to steer her right as Amy divided the riders by even or odd number. It caused a bottleneck by the C marker and chaos as one horse kicked out at another. "How old are you, Kylie?" Phoenix asked, distracting her as the riders bunched ahead of them.

"I'm seven," she replied.

"How much riding have you done?"

Kylie's cheeks flushed pink and she avoided Phoenix's gaze. The slightest shake of her head told Phoenix she'd lied on the camp's entry form.

"Amy thinks you're an intermediate rider," Phoenix whispered. "I don't understand why you let her think that."

Kylie swallowed and lowered her voice to little above a hiss. "I needed to get on the camp. They wouldn't take beginners. I thought I might be okay."

"They held a beginners camp last week." Phoenix frowned. "Why not come on that one?"

"Because Sharon's on this one!" Kylie raised her voice. "We had to come together!"

Phoenix glanced across at Sharon's posture on the bay mare. Heels down, hands together and thumbs on top, she posted up and down to the beat of the mare's lengthened trot. Phoenix breathed out through her nose and kept hold of Kylie's loose rein. A boy behind lost control of his horse and it walked its snout straight up the backside of Kylie's. He gave a squeak of dismay as Kylie's horse kicked out, almost unseating them both.

Sally, the redheaded girl from Phoenix's cabin dropped her reins in fright as her horse backed away from the trouble. "I can't do this!" she cried. "It's too hard."

Phoenix grabbed the reins of both horses and pulled them away from the track. Turning, with a horse on either side, she led them towards Amy in the centre of the arena.

"Please don't tell?" Kylie begged. She punctuated her plea with a tearful sniff.

Amy fixed her hands on her hips and glared at Phoenix. "What are you doing?" she demanded. Brandishing her riding crop, she waved it towards her. "They need to get back behind the rest of the ride. We're getting ready to canter in a minute."

"These two are having a little trouble," Phoenix stated, downplaying the extent of their incapacity. Conflict budded in her chest as she sensed herself getting offside with Amy in her efforts to fix the kids' difficulty. "The horses won't behave. I'll take them into the paddock next door and help them, so you can continue teaching everyone else." Channelling her father's natural authority and not waiting for an answer, Phoenix led Kylie and Sally towards the gate.

6

HI HO SILVER

It was worse than she'd imagined. Logan Du Rose had ensured his children grew up in the saddle and she couldn't imagine a life in which riding wasn't second nature. It didn't take a genius to see that neither Kylie nor Sally had ever sat on a horse. She marvelled at how they'd got up there at all. "Stand here," she ordered, lining them up in front of her and releasing the reins. "We need to do some groundwork first, so you're more confident." She bit back the truth at the last minute. They needed to do groundwork, so they stopped looking like terrified victims anticipating a zombie attack. And she'd noticed Sally hadn't fastened her riding hat properly. "I'll help you dismount and then we'll run through the exercises."

Phoenix ignored their grumbling and stood next to Sally. She rested her hand against the horse's cheek piece to stop it snaking its head towards the grass. "Lean down, so I can clip your chin strap into position," she commanded. Sally bobbed forward and Phoenix fixed her hat. "Right, quit your stirrups and dangle your legs," she ordered. "Then dip forward while keeping your left hand on the pommel of your saddle." Stepping close, she touched the front of the saddle as it rose to crest the horse's shoulders. The little girl performed an awkward bow and looked more like she wanted to puke than dismount. "Now, throw your weight forward and slip your right leg back over the saddle. You can use your momentum to slide down to the ground. Bend your knees to take the impact away from your ankles."

The girl frowned and Phoenix waited for the familiar challenge. "Can't I use the metal thing like a step?" she asked.

"No." Phoenix shook her head. She repeated the same sentence she'd given hundreds of tourists at her father's hotel. "You're not a cowgirl. It overbalances the horse. Keeping your foot in the stirrup when you dismount is a sure way to dig your horse in the gut and find yourself dragged back to Auckland." Sally twisted her lips and pouted. Phoenix sensed her scrabbling for a distraction.

"I don't snore," she declared. Her gaze flicked to Kylie. "Make her get off first. She snores real loud."

Phoenix smiled. "I think the others in our cabin might disagree about who snores the most," she said.

Sally grinned and her pupils dilated. "I'm ten," she volunteered, in that beautiful pre-teen innocence. "I'm the oldest out of us two. Make her get off first."

Phoenix's mood lightened as she slipped into familiar territory. Teaching others to ride felt as natural as breathing. It fed her sense of authority and infused her with bulletproof courage. "Right, Sally," she said, suffusing determination into her tone. "Seeing as you're the eldest, you can show Kylie how to do a proper dismount."

It wasn't a pretty descent, but it wasn't tragic either. Somehow, Sally landed upright and in one piece. Phoenix tugged the horse's reins over its ears and handed them to her. "Keep hold of these while I help Kylie. Don't drop them or he'll put his foot through them and then we'll have a problem."

Kylie worked hard to achieve elegance, dismounting with gymnastic precision but overbalancing at the last second and finding herself on her backside. To her credit, Sally didn't laugh at her.

"Never mind," Phoenix urged as Kylie's face creased into an embarrassed snarl. "I've lost count of how many times I've done that." She helped Kylie up and handed over her horse's reins.

"Right," she said, "let's lose the saddles and bridles and switch them for head collars. I'm giving you a crash course in horsemanship 101, Logan Du Rose style."

Phoenix worked with the children until the sun morphed into a scorching ball of yellow. She got them leading their mounts with confidence, stamping their feet and flinging their arms wide when the horses became pushy or disrespectful. They did some light lunging on a long rope and gained understanding of the different gaits, what they looked like and how the horses moved from one to another. By the end of the session, the horses had become more attentive and the children had lost their terror. The minutes blurred into hours and Phoenix had just tacked both horses and got the children mounted, when Tina called to her from the paddock gate.

Sally looked at her watch and gasped. "We missed lunch!" she exclaimed. "We didn't hear the bell."

Kylie's face curled into an expression of misery. "I don't wanna stop!" she begged. "I'm not hungry."

Tina climbed the gate and walked across the paddock. Phoenix held her breath and waited for the rebuke. It didn't come. Tina smiled. "Perhaps Phoenix should have been our instructor," she said, raising an eyebrow at the girls. "You looked like you were having fun."

The children nodded and relief flooded Kylie's face. "Phoe's the bestest teacher," she gushed. Sally nodded in agreement and Tina smiled.

"Great. Let's settle the horses and go back to camp. The others are eating, but I saved food for you guys. Gus set the games up and then we're going back to the beach for a swim."

Untacking the horses took little time with an extra adult and Phoenix showed the children how to brush the dust from the horses' coats. "They aren't as sweaty as usual," she said, helping Sally pull the curry comb across her horse's flank. "Today, they did more thinking than moving."

The saddles and bridles stowed back in the makeshift tack shed created from a shipping crate at the edge of the paddock. Tina closed the door behind them. Phoenix checked the tap and the pipe taking water to the troughs. The water level looked high enough to last until the end of the week.

The girls skipped ahead to retrieve their lunches from the kitchen. Tina hung back, her forehead furrowed. "Thanks for doing that," she said as Phoenix stood upright. "Amy's fuming. She said they couldn't cope. Grant needs to investigate how such poor riders got onto the camp."

Phoenix shrugged. "I shouldn't bother. Maybe they just needed to be here." Mikaere stuck his beautiful head over the fence and whinnied for attention. Phoenix ruffled his forelock and shook her head at the warning roll of his blue wall eye.

"He has an unusual colouring," Tina commented. She lifted her hand but pulled it back again as Mikaere's lips made jerky grabbing motions. "Has he always been vicious?"

Phoenix wrinkled her nose. "He just likes to assert his authority. My father says his dam was always the same." She kissed the end of his bristly nose and turned away, following Tina along the narrow path back to the camp.

As they reached the wide grassy circle flanked by the cabins, Tina halted and frowned. "You're not what I expected." She lowered her voice. "I think I've misjudged you. I assumed you were a little rich girl playing 'rough it' for a week. But you're not, are you?"

Phoenix swallowed and fought the biting retort her father's genetics provided. She fixed a serene smile on her face and kept silent. It occurred to her she didn't care what Tina thought of her. It was just a week of her life and she'd bring a little colour and happiness wherever she thought needed it.

Phoenix used her free time after lunch to exercise Mikaere. She kept him in a paddock adjacent to the other horses; close enough for him to see them, but not near enough to kick. Despite the hours of work which went into him and made him an affable, willing companion for her, the gelding's genetic code infused him with unpredictability and the need for domination.

Phoenix sat on the uppermost fence rail and whistled to him as he grazed. His head shot up and she felt him connect to her. After a moment's hesitation, just to make his point about who was really the boss, he shook out his white mane and turned his forelegs in her direction. "Come on boy," Phoenix called. "We don't have all day. Haere mai. Haere mai."

Mikaere picked up speed and ambled across the paddock. His jaw continued to chew the last chunk of grass he'd snagged as he heard her approach. Sunlight danced across the rippling grey muscles and played over the black dapple on his flanks. He'd been Sacha's last gift to the Du Roses before she disappeared. Logan's favourite mare had accepted her exile from the stable yard with good grace. She'd become a hazard to anyone without Du Rose blood in their veins and her behaviour left Logan no choice. He'd turned her out on the mountain with a retired herd and somehow, she'd fallen pregnant in her dotage. It remained a mystery, as no stallion with Mikaere's colours called the mountain home.

Sacha had visited their garden with her swollen belly and then with her colt. After she'd weaned him, she left her foal with Logan and never returned. Phoenix called the colt, Mikaere, after Michael the loyal angel of God. It suited him. Aloof and forbidding like his dam, Mikaere played second fiddle to no one. He bonded with Phoenix and tolerated her on his back, but he retained enough of his own identity to scare off any other would-be riders. It took two vets, four stock hands and a tranquiliser gun the day Logan decided to stop the blood line continuing. He'd trained the horse but suffered more frustrations with Mikaere than with all the hundreds that preceded him. Mikaere proved the only creature on four legs who forced Logan Du Rose to admit defeat.

"Come on Grumpy Knickers!" Phoenix called. Mikaere gave a long snort of disdain and shook his mane. His tail swished behind him, projecting the impression he didn't care and would arrive in his own time. He paused before Phoenix and lifted his muzzle to sniff her face, scenting her and searching for the key to unlock the inner tameness behind the beast facade. Phoenix scratched the whiskery chin and hopped down from the fence. Ignoring all the rules of horsemanship, she tucked herself under his neck and wrapped her arms around his wide shoulders. The scent of horse filled her nostrils, dust, grass and summer sunshine. Phoenix released the sigh building in her chest, able to breathe for the first time since her argument with Wiremu. "Everything will be okay," she promised herself.

7

AWAY

Phoenix lunged Mikaere in a tight circle, pushing him from walk to trot and back again. He tolerated the indignity, first with feigned irritation and then indifference. When Phoenix released the pressure of the rope clipped to his nose band, he slowed and then halted. He turned his body to face her, his head drooped in relaxation and he gave a slow blink. "Right then," Phoenix sighed. She approached him with confidence, allowing him to view her through the brown eye on his left. She patted his neck and then switched sides, seeing his opposing blue eye give a slow blink. "Always greet both sides of a horse's brain," she recited out loud, hearing her father's advice running on a loop in her head. Mikaere snorted and shook his mane as though agreeing. Phoenix had assessed his movements as she lunged him and he showed no sign of overnight injury or pain. She ran a curry comb over his body and down his legs. Pulling a hoof pick from her back pocket, she checked each hoof, nudging him so he knew when to lift his feet.

They both jumped at the sound of footsteps hitting the hard earth, Mikaere jerking backwards with a snort. Phoenix rose to see

Kirwan striding across the next paddock. "What are you doing?" she called. "I thought Gus wanted help with the games."

"Yeah." Kirwan shrugged and his features creased into a scowl. "But maybe I'm sick of being used as a babysitter." He changed direction and leaned his forearms on the top rail of the fence. The camp horses edged nearer like a crowd of curious onlookers to a road traffic accident.

Phoenix frowned. "Isn't that why you're here? As a leader or helper?" She adjusted Mikaere's head collar and draped the lunge rope over his withers. His skin crawled against the alien sensation, but he turned at her touch and followed her to the fence.

"Nice horse." Kirwan jerked his head towards Mikaere. "Yours?"

"Yeah." Phoenix smiled. Her father's gift always brought pleasure, unless it was bucking her off or dumping her in a ditch. She lined Mikaere against the fence line and climbed onto the top rung. Her long legs swung over his withers and her backside settled across the bony ribs either side of his spine.

"You're riding like that?" Kirwan sounded surprised and his dark eyebrows curved upwards into mirrored arcs. "With no tack?"

"Yeah." Phoenix shrugged. "His gear is in the shed, but we're only going for a quick run. I can't miss dinner because my girls are on duty."

Kirwan twisted his body to survey the gathered horses behind him. "Can I come?" he asked. His mood seemed to lighten and Phoenix bit back her instant refusal. She opted instead for an excuse.

"It'll take ages for you to tack up," she countered. A glance at the burning sun gave her a time stamp on the day.

"I'm not a beginner!" Kirwan snapped. The ominous cloud settled back over his head as he strode towards the tack shed. "My social workers have been parking me at summer camps since I could walk. There's very little I can't do." He pressed the code into the padlock holding the door closed and wrenched the prongs apart. Phoenix sighed as he disappeared inside the metal shed. A series of clanks sounded as he chose a saddle and bridle. His presence antagonised her, though she didn't understand the reason behind it. Other than the fact they sparked like sandpaper and matches.

Phoenix utilised the time it took for Kirwan to tack his chosen mount and join her on the dusty track surrounding the paddock. She put Mikaere through his paces, halting, backing up and warming his muscles. Kirwan sat in the saddle with ease, but his English riding style made her turn aside with a smirk. He'd clamped a riding hat onto his head and he lifted an index finger and pointed at Phoenix's curls. "You should wear a hat," he stated. "In case you fall."

Phoenix tugged at the cord around her throat and lifted the cowboy hat onto her head. "There you go," she replied, injecting sarcasm into her tone. "Happy now?"

"I don't care," Kirwan replied. He smirked and sent his horse in the other direction, easing into a steady trot as a warmup. Phoenix breathed out a sigh of exasperation and turned Mikaere towards the gate.

"Have fun, Mark Todd," she called. "I'll see ya later." She reached the gate and leaned down to release the metal catch. The sound of drumming hooves sent Mikaere's head rising with a snort and she almost pitched forwards along his shoulder.

"Where are you going?" Kirwan forced his horse between Mikaere and the gate.

Phoenix sat up with a hiss. "None of your bloody business," she snarled. "Get out of my way." As a last-ditch attempt at salvaging her dignity, she pointed at the dirt. "You didn't pick her feet out, ass-hat!"

"I did," Kirwan growled. "You didn't watch me tack. You've no idea what I did or didn't do, Miss Fancy-pants Du Rose." He edged nearer the gate, blocking Phoenix's exit. Rage lit a torch in her belly. She needed to escape, to canter through the bush to the beach and just stand in the sea with the surf lapping over Mikaere's hooves. It ate at her like a biogenic drive; necessary. Lifting the rope off Mikaere's withers, she urged him backwards. He kept his feet moving until she dropped the rope and then responded to its pressure against his neck. He executed a perfect turn and moved from standstill to canter like any talented stock horse.

Phoenix felt the wind in her hair and the cord pressed against her throat as her hat flew backwards to settle between her shoulder blades. She aimed Mikaere's giant hooves at the fence and saw the top rail disappear beneath them. He landed in the bush on the other side, faltering a little and righting himself within a few strides. He battled his way through the undergrowth, content to pick his own footing as Phoenix twisted her body to look behind her.

Kirwan swore and fumbled with the gate catch, bending his tall body so his rounded, velvet hat obscured his face. Phoenix imagined the swearwords coursing from his lips and the thought pressed a smile to her lips. Mikaere found the track and turned onto it as the tang of salt and surf hit their nostrils. Then he dug in and they picked up speed, leaving a cloud of dust for Kirwan to follow.

8

FATAL ATTRACTION

Phoenix rode Mikaere along the water's edge, smiling when he paused to paw the sand and kick up the surf. Droplets speckled her bare legs and the ankle boots she wore to ride. With no one to impress, she let her feet dangle and relaxed her seat. Mikaere's muscles bunched beneath her as he played and she trusted him to step through the waves wherever he wanted. The ocean scent filled her nostrils and relaxed her knotted sinews and tendons.

Laying the lunge rope across her thighs, Phoenix raised her arms above her head and stretched. She arched her spine and the delicate bones cracked as she lay back against Mikaere's body. Her hat slipped sideways and the brim dug into her shoulder. The breeze stirred her hair and the sleeves of her tee shirt and the thin fabric of her shorts allowed her to feel Mikaere's hard ribs beneath her. Mikaere's ears flicked back and forth, the sense of companionship both safe and familiar.

Their peace shattered as the sound of drumming hooves increased in volume. The sand vibrated beneath them.

Phoenix used her stomach muscles to sit up and groaned at the sight of Kirwan pelting towards them. He stood in the stirrups, his long legs straight and his heels pointing towards the earth. His chest bowed low over his horse's neck as the mare extended her stride into a flat gallop.

Mikaere jerked backwards in the surf and rose onto his hind feet in a lazy arc. Phoenix slapped his neck as his front hooves cut into the sand on landing. Her inner thighs ached with the effort of moulding herself to his body and not falling. "Idiot!" she hissed, lifting the rope and opening it out to the left, forcing him into a tight circle. She dug her left heel into his ribs to drive him into the turn. He tossed his head and resisted, desperate to join the chase and run ahead of the approaching mare.

Kirwan's torso rose and he sat heavy in the saddle as he reached Phoenix. His mare slowed with enthusiasm, her ears forward and her gaze fixed on Mikaere's spinning body. A grin broke across the teenager's lips. "Race ya!" he called. The mare snorted as he stopped her turning into the surf and drove her back onto the sand. Mikaere stopped spinning and Phoenix sensed herself losing control of him as he hauled on the rope. Common sense told her not to play Kirwan's game, but his exhilaration infected her with the need to run. With a whoop of joy, Phoenix flicked the rope against Mikaere's neck and released the heel pressing against his near side. He lurched from the surf with a bound fuelled by excitement and flattened his ears against his neck. Then he lurched for the fleeing heels of Kirwan's mare.

It all turned to crap about three minutes later when Mikaere showed off by jumping a piece of driftwood. Not just any piece of driftwood either. Immaturity led him to punch far above his weight and the tree trunk, escaped from a distant forestry work site, made an unforgiving opponent. Phoenix held her breath and squeezed her thighs together as the gelding veered towards the hulk of rotting wood. Taking off too late, he performed a strange cat jump which would have dislodged even Phoenix's capable father. The jerky motion threw Phoenix up and forward at the same moment Mikaere's head lifted. She smashed her face into his corded neck and the pain in her nose blinded her for long enough to miss retrieving her seat before landing. A moment of nothingness followed as she became airborne. Mikaere's hoof beats sounded muffled as he collected himself and continued galloping up the beach. Phoenix's head hit a protruding branch as she landed, knocking the remaining sense from her brain.

She lay on her back, the damp sand sending its cool fingers to chill her spine. Phoenix kept her eyes closed, her brain running copious mental checks of her faculties and then her limbs. An ache crept upwards from her left hip and spread throughout her torso, culminating in an irregular pounding in her head. Her arms trembled like jelly as she flexed them enough to push herself to a sitting position. Running a tentative hand across her face, she winced against the roughness of sand as she spread it across her left cheek. Her nose felt painful, but not broken. Seeking fingers dug into her hair, locating a growing lump behind her left ear. Slick blood coated her fingers as she pulled them away.

"Nooo!" she groaned. Hauling herself upright, she noticed the sound of cantering hooves. Thinking of Mikaere's stupidity made the blood pound in her forehead and she stumbled towards the surf. A shout and running feet sounded behind her as she bent to her knees in the shallow sweep of water and cupped her hands. The cold saltwater stung the cut, but she repeated the action. The cool Tasman delivered relief from the throbbing and the blood diluted against her tee shirt until it showed as little more than a pink stain against the light fabric.

"You okay?" Kirwan sounded puffed. "I couldn't catch your horse." Concern knocked the hard edges from his voice and he knelt next to her in the water. "Let me see," he demanded. Cupping his hands either side of her head, he inspected Phoenix's face.

"Bloody horse," she groaned, cursing Mikaere through the mixture of gritty sand and saltwater in her mouth. "Sometimes I hate him."

Kirwan blinked and released her cheeks. She expected him to reiterate the need for a riding hat, but he didn't. Instead, he lifted her curls to sight the cut behind her ear. "The blood makes it look worse," he concluded. "It's a minor cut and a big bruise. I bet it hurts." He withdrew his hand from her curls and picked off tendrils of loose, damp hair which stuck to his fingers. "Geez, never rob a bank. You'll leave enough hair DNA for a conviction." His lips made the joke, but the sentiment stayed away from his eyes. Hazel irises sparkled in the sunlight, filled with concern.

Phoenix nodded, screwing her left eye shut as the action sent a dart of pain into it. "Ouch!" she hissed.

"We should get you back to camp." A tram line formed between Kirwan's dark brows as he frowned. "Let Tina check you."

Phoenix made a sound like a snort. She loosened the cord of her hat from around her throat with trembling fingers. "I'd rather chop my head off, thanks."

His expression lightened. "Know what you mean. We should tell someone anyway. In case you get concussion and die in the night."

"Cheerful. Thanks so much." Phoenix blew out a breath. She looked at her filthy tee shirt and wrinkled her nose. Attempts to brush off the black, iron rich sand made it worse, grinding it into the creases and highlighting the bra beneath it.

"Don't do that." Before she could stop him, Kirwan seized the fabric. He slipped a hand inside Phoenix's tee shirt and pressed his palm flat. The other hand brushed at the black sand, leaving wet trails. Phoenix stared at his expression, seeing only concentration in the way his top teeth gripped his lower lip. He brushed a clear patch and nodded in satisfaction. Then he glanced up into Phoenix's face.

"Oh." He gulped and she saw the moment he registered what he'd done. His hand withdrew from inside her shirt, the backs of his fingers coasting over her bra and the soft swell of her breasts. His pupils dilated as he looked for an appropriate sentence to excuse himself. Kirwan floundered and then laughed, his fingers resting over her hips. "I want to say sorry," he breathed. "But I'm not." His gaze raked her face, his pupils huge in his dark eyes. "I'm not sorry at all."

Phoenix felt his grip increase over her hips, the pressure matching the sudden drop of Kirwan's torso. Their lips bumped together as the surf swirled around their knees. The peak of his riding hat dug into her forehead. He tilted the angle of his head and before she could object, his hands switched to the back of her neck, forming a gentle cup as he deepened the kiss. Phoenix's stomach dropped as though she fell again. This time, she didn't hit the sand with a bone crunching thud, but her heart soared as though it never wanted to re-enter her chest cavity.

The surf grew more insistent, tugging at her knees and trying to unbalance her. A fleeting thread of consciousness told her the tide obeyed her powerful father's whims just like everything else. Resentment stirred against all things Du Rose and she reached her fingers up to grip Kirwan's forearms, reluctant to break the kiss.

The intimacy left Phoenix breathless and ragged. It screwed with her body far more than the unanticipated fall, producing emotions and endorphins she couldn't control. The fall paled in significance next to the kiss as she started down the track of commandment breaking. Her fingers slipped beneath Kirwan's tee shirt, contacting hard muscle and an unexpected covering of chest hair. She pushed her palm across it, liking the prickling sensation of hair against her wet hand. Kirwan groaned and his exhale filled her mouth as she drank in the essence of his maleness. His tongue performed a lazy arc around hers, inviting it to learn the dance steps of passion.

Then the bloody horse intervened, saving her modesty and channelling her father's ire. Kirwan let out a yelp of pain and shot backwards, covering Phoenix in salt spray and black sand. Mikaere stood in the water, the lunge rope dragging through the surf like a snake. The tide snatched at it and tossed it around his hooves with enthusiasm. Closing his mismatched eyes and snaking his neck, he pulled his lips back to reveal sharp yellow teeth. Kirwan rubbed at his left biceps and scrambled away from another painful rebuke. He got to his feet, swearing and cursing as his jeans clung to his calves and dripped salt water into his boots. Mikaere took another tentative step forward and snatched a chunk of Phoenix's hair. Waving her hands, she batted his face away, gratified when he jerked his head up and released her curls without pain. She knelt in the deepening water with her fists balled at her sides, counting to ten as her mother taught her. Then she eyeballed the gelding with as much restraint as she could muster. "You're ruining my life!" she snarled.

Happy with the outcome of his interference, Mikaere turned his bulk in the water and plodded back to the safety of the beach. Lifting his tail high, he released a burst of gas loud enough to summon the camp for assistance. Then he dropped a splatter of green muck guaranteed to send Phoenix squealing out of the surf as his gift floated towards her.

9

CONSEQUENCES

"I'm amazed your horse came back," Kirwan commented as Phoenix reached the beach. She turned to see Mikaere nibbling grass from the sand bank. Kirwan's horse tried to follow, backing up at speed at the sight of Mikaere's hind leg lifting in threat.

"Of course, he did. Where's the fun in causing mayhem if you don't stick around to see the damage?" Phoenix leaned forward to scoop another handful of water over her cut. Kirwan had avoided pressing it when he kissed her. She sensed it was more through accident than intention. Embarrassment flushed her cheeks as she contemplated how close they'd come to taking it further. Once she'd stepped over that line, she couldn't go back. Antagonism flared in her chest as she sought to re-establish her dignity. Rinsing her hands and wrists, she stood up straight. "You look like an idiot," she commented, wiping her mouth with the back of her hand. A shaking finger pointed at his riding hat.

Kirwan frowned and released the chin strap. It dangled along the line of his neck. "Not as stupid as you on your back in the sand," he scoffed. Their safe equilibrium returned; Phoenix the obedient girl and Kirwan the rebel. But his lips curved upwards in a smile.

"No one could have stayed on through a bad jump like that. Not without a saddle, anyway." He wiped his salty hand against his soaked jeans and reached forward, running his index finger along Phoenix's upper lip. She blinked at the tickling sensation which danced across her skin. Her body betrayed her, demanding more of the addictive sensations and carrying her towards conflict and misery. She held her breath for a moment as the surf tugged at her ankles. Kirwan leaned forward until the peak of his hat bumped her forehead. He paused a beat and as Phoenix waited for his lips to brush hers, he pulled away, his face impassive. "If you're okay, it's time to get back," he commented. "Tina should look at that cut."

Backing away from her, he tramped through the foamy tide to his horse. He collected the reins and mounted without difficulty, his right leg moving in a smooth arc across the saddle until he settled between pommel and cantle. Phoenix stood in the water, her brows drawn into a frown. Her hair swirled around her head as the sea breeze brought it to life. "What a dick!" she breathed, acknowledging the effect his near kiss had created. She stamped from the sea, her boots making squelching noises against the wet sand.

Mikaere came to her whistle and she used the fated piece of driftwood to give her enough height to vault onto his back. The long lunge rope had grazed her fingers where she'd held on while falling. Phoenix wrinkled her nose as she looped it around his neck and let the leather end hang down against his shoulder. Sand coated her dark shorts and added itself to the loose hair sticking to the damp fabric. Her tongue clicked against the roof of her mouth, telling Mikaere to move on as she lifted the rope in her left hand and gave it a gentle tap against his withers. He responded by lifting his head and moving in the direction Phoenix's body pointed. Kirwan fell into line behind them and they left the beach in silence.

They travelled for ten minutes before Kirwan spoke, his throat clearing disturbing a kereru settling nearby. It lifted into the air, its metallic green wings and white vest forming a stark contrast in the speckled sunlight of the bush. "Steady," Kirwan said, soothing his horse as she spooked. Then he repeated the question Phoenix had ignored. "Were you looking for the barn?"

Phoenix ground her teeth and sighed. She half turned to face him, leaving Mikaere to pick his way along the track. "No," she replied. "I felt cooped up and needed to escape." Her brows knitted, annoyed she hadn't thought of the refugees at all in the last few hours. "I'm not sure I could find my way there alone."

Kirwan nodded. "Good. Rocking up there on horseback is a terrible idea. They could have cameras set up or worse."

"Worse?" Phoenix's voice rose in a question. "What kind of worse?"

"Traps." Kirwan ran a hand across his face, the chin strap still dangling along his neck. "When people grow weed in the bush, they fortify the area with things to stop anyone nosey enough to trespass. Maybe the traffickers did the same."

"Like what?" Phoenix rested her palm on Mikaere's flank and twisted her body.

"Guns with tripwires connected to the trigger. Tree bark laced with poison. Metal traps hidden in the undergrowth that will sever your leg. Stuff like that."

"For real?" Phoenix's eyes widened. "And you think they might have hidden things like that around the barn?"

"Could have." Kirwan sighed. "Where there's money at stake, people will do anything to protect it."

Phoenix turned to face the track again and her brain worked through scenarios. She discarded the solutions one at a time. "Is that why you won't help the refugees?" she asked, her tone accusing. "You're afraid."

Kirwan growled and Mikaere's ears flicked back and forth. Phoenix had always imagined the horse would defend her against an overzealous stock worker on her father's mountain and he'd proved his jealousy on the beach. "If you're not afraid, then you should be," Kirwan snarled. "Unless you're stupid. Always a possibility."

Phoenix slumped on Mikaere's back and he shook his mane as though asking if she was okay. "Bit late dude," she sniped at the horse with sarcasm. "You kinda missed that boat."

As the track widened, Kirwan pushed his horse next to her. Mikaere's ears flattened against his head in protest and he snaked his neck, though he didn't employ his sharp teeth in rebuke. "I don't want to argue," Kirwan said. His brown eyes glittered beneath a shaft of sunlight. "You're the only person who speaks to me in this stupid place. It's a nice camp for nice kids leading nice lives. I shouldn't be here and everyone knows it."

Phoenix smiled and released a snort of mirth. "Are you kidding me? Haven't you met the girls in my cabin? Half of them are in the care of the state and the other half are a long way from being labelled nice. If you stopped hanging around the fringes and breaking the rules, you might make a few friends."

Kirwan grinned and clamped his teeth over his lower lip. The corners of his eyes crinkled in genuine amusement and his burst of laughter echoed around the bush. "Where's the fun in that?" he demanded.

10

THE SISTER CODE

Phoenix left Mikaere in the paddock and jogged back to camp. Kirwan stayed to untack his borrowed camp horse and to run a curry comb over its sweating flanks.

"We were looking for you, Phoenix." Tina sounded suspicious and Phoenix fixed a light expression on her lips.

"I told Grant I was taking my horse for a run along the beach," she said. It seemed no minor feat to keep the wooden smile on her face as Tina glared at her.

"Did you go alone?" Tina's tone sounded threatening and took Phoenix by surprise. She swallowed and opted for a partial truth.

"No, I told you. I took Mikaere with me." Before Tina could probe further, Phoenix made her escape. She sought the girls from her cabin and found them already seated in a circle waiting for her.

"Kylie's got a bellyache." Sharon rolled her eyes in a petulant display of exasperation. Phoenix turned her gaze to the young girl in the corner.

"Is that true, Kylie?" She asked. "Do you want me to take you to see Tina?"

Kylie's eyes rounded and she shook her head with emphasis. "It's not that bad. It'll disappear soon."

Phoenix frowned and studied her, searching for the source of the lie. "I don't mind. I'll come with you."

Kylie shook her head again and her blonde brows drew into a line. Her rosebud lips pursed into a sneer. "I said I'm okay!" she bit.

The other girls gasped at the disrespect in Kylie's tone. Sharon's lips parted as though to rebuke her. Phoenix shook her head. Instinct told her there was more to the refusal, but a lack of experience paralysed her and left her without a solution.

"Is that blood on your neck?" Sharon shifted enough to lean sideways and inspect Phoenix.

She replied with a dismissive wave. "I fell off Mikaere on the beach. I'm fine." Phoenix gritted her teeth, a familiar morbid hatred of her own polluted blood surfacing. She tamped it down with practice and snatched her Bible from the spare bunk above Lexi. Her cabin deputy raised an eyebrow which Phoenix ignored. Lexi waggled her eyebrows and offered a surreptitious grin as though she knew Phoenix hadn't gone alone. She pursed her lips, but the smile remained as an irritating shadow.

The girls settled down to their study. They read the selected passage and planned for the discussion scheduled for after dinner. Lexi squinted up at the sheet tacked to the back of the door. "Who's leading tonight? Please tell me it's not Gus."

A collective groan ricocheted around the cabin as Carrie bobbed up to confirm it. His prose filled messages seemed verbose and lost in translation. "I never know what he's trying to say," Carrie grumbled. From Auckland, she possessed a wide face and round body. The suitcase filled with packets of instant chocaholic gratification which her mother had hidden under her bed before leaving, betrayed a love of junk food. The ensuing weight problem had sapped Carrie's confidence and set her on a journey of self-deprecation and obstinacy.

"I think Gus is hot," Sharon stated. All eyes turned to her in surprise. She shrugged her shoulders and grinned. "What?" she demanded. "I like men with big tummies and shaggy black beards." The room burst into raucous laughter and Phoenix found it difficult not to join in as she glanced across at Lexi for assistance. Common sense told her she wouldn't get it, even before she asked.

Her deputy looked up from the bottle of fluorescent green nail polish and gave a nonchalant shrug. Then she continued to plaster the lurid colour onto her nails. The room stunk from the chemical scent and Phoenix sensed Tina would hold her responsible for the girls' intoxication.

"I love Kirwan," a little voice piped. "I think he's hot."

As though she had imparted something akin to murder-lust, a gasp ricocheted around the room. Everyone stared at Kylie, but Sharon took up the cause. "You can't like Kirwan!" she protested. "We all agreed last night. Nobody can have him."

Phoenix stared around the angry faces in confusion. "What's wrong with Kirwan," she demanded.

"Wrong question." Lexi sighed and screwed the lid on the nail polish. "You're meant to tell them he's not a possession and nobody can own him."

Phoenix glared at her deputy with poorly veiled anger. "Thanks for that," she growled.

Carrie tossed her blonde hair and pouted. "We all like him. I like him, Sally likes him and so does Sharon. But it's the sister code. We can't all have him, so no one can." Carrie glared at Lexi as though drawing battle lines. "No one."

Sally sat next to her and nodded her head with vigour. Short red curls shivered with the action. "We agreed," she said, fixing her gaze on Kylie. "We shook hands. You were in the bathroom."

Phoenix watched as Kylie's face crumpled. The child gripped her stomach as though the disappointment had reminded her of the physical pain.

"Remember the rules, girls," Phoenix chided. A flush spread from her chest to her neck with the hypocrisy of her words. "No relationships between campers. And yes, Lexi's right. You can't argue over him like he's a toy."

The girls gave a collective groan, masked by the sound of Bibles flipping back open. Phoenix asked Carrie to read the last question in the study book, conscious of her reddening cheeks and the duplicity with which Kirwan's remembered kiss burned her lips.

For the hundredth time, Phoenix wished she'd never heard of the damned camp.

11

DISPOSABLE

"Y**ou need to stop doing that.**" Phoenix stood with her hands on her hips, darting a furtive glance towards the kitchen. The woman taking on the role of camp mother watched them through the window slats. Her hands moved as she washed the massive saucepans used to cook pasta for dinner.

"Doing what?" Kirwan sulked on the deck, his hand caressing the pocket where he kept his cigarettes. The outline of his lighter pressed through the fabric. He scuffed his feet in the dirt and ceased the motion of his fingers, which betrayed his overwhelming craving. He placed his palms either side of him on the deck and leaned back, the last rays of sunlight kissing the stubble sprouting on his cheek.

"Keep sabotaging the meetings!" Phoenix hissed. "Gus wants you sent home. I heard him."

Kirwan dedicated more effort to his expression of indifference and Phoenix almost fell for it. "Why do you care? Will you miss me, Du Rose?" he demanded, his lips loosening into a sarcastic smile.

"Yes, actually," Phoenix retorted. She'd spoken, intending just to keep him at the camp, but the truth of her words took her by surprise. If Kirwan left, she'd always wonder what became of him.

Besides, she'd slide back into the loneliness of the first twenty-four hours. And she'd think too much about Wiri again.

Kirwan swallowed and straightened his shoulders. Courage flooded his stance, more obvious because Phoenix hadn't noticed it lacking. Bravado had covered the gap and the difference looked striking. Kirwan flicked at a chunk of bark blown onto the deck. "I didn't mean to sabotage anything," he said, his tone soft. "Sorry."

Phoenix snorted. Her palms remained on her hips but her grip tightened. "Really? Ooh, let's deal with the tough subject of sex before marriage and why God doesn't want us to do it."

Kirwan pursed his lips and a line showed across his nose as he wrinkled it. "Yeah. Okay. Maybe that wasn't the best reply."

"No. 'Oops, too late,' wasn't something the older girls needed to hear." She gnawed her lower lip and looked away as a series of pictures moved through her inner vision. Kirwan naked. Kirwan kissing another girl.

Phoenix swallowed, the sound loud enough to embarrass her. Her mind strayed towards wondering what it might be like losing her virginity to him and she shut it down with a stamp of her foot. "Just think about what you're saying in front of the campers!" she snapped. Needing to put space between them, she strode towards the cabin and the jewellery making exercise Tina had organised. She looked over her shoulder as she let the door close behind her and caught Kirwan staring at her. His eyes narrowed to slits and his full lips possessed a predatory smile. He'd scented her confusion and Phoenix hated both him and herself in that moment.

Wiping her hands on her shorts, she faced the group of bowed heads and surveyed the beads trickling outward from the circle like a flood. She kicked off her boots and then wished she hadn't as the vibrant orbs rolled towards her.

"Kylie dropped the whole container," Sharon announced. She bobbed her head up from the circle and frowned.

Lexi drew her legs up to her bottom and slumped back on the bunk. A bottle of bright pink polish produced a chemical haze around her head as her fingers forced the brush to dance in long strokes across her thumb nail. "Kylie hasn't moved," she commented. Her gaze flicked to Phoenix and she rolled her eyes. "I think someone likes to blame someone else."

Phoenix peered around the group to look for Kylie. The child sat on the bunk behind the girls, her spine pressed against the wall and her head bowed. She watched but didn't take part as they scrambled around the floor after escaping beads. Phoenix beckoned her with curled fingers. "I need help, Kyles," she mouthed. She wrinkled her nose at the fine thread and fiddly beads, truth in the statement. She hated delicate work of any kind, not blessed with the dexterity required for crafts.

Kylie scooted from the bed and picked her way across the floor. She winced and lifted her foot, finding a glittery bead stuck to her sock. Rolling it in her fingers, she skirted jutting arms and legs as the other girls gave chase to the bouncing, sparkling orbs. She settled her bony bottom on Phoenix's knee as soon as she'd sunk onto a mattress. "The girls in the other cabin are making chocolate biscuits," she said. Her nose wrinkled in disgust at the short straw they'd drawn. "Why can't we do that instead?"

Phoenix bounced her feet and Kylie pitched around in her lap, the cross expression dissipating. "It's our turn later in the week," Phoenix confirmed. "They can do beads while we scoff cookies."

Kylie's fingers rolled the bead in her right hand. Her left thumb slipped between her lips and Phoenix ignored the primeval urge to do the same. Her fingers twitched and she shoved them beneath her thighs to avoid embarrassment. It worried her she might do it in her sleep.

"I'm making a necklace for Gus," Sharon announced. She seized a length of thread and stood in the centre of the circle. Someone flicked a bead and it skittered across the floor and hit Phoenix's bare toe. Chancing a glance at Lexi, Phoenix saw the merest shift of an eyebrow as Lexi loaded nail polish onto her big toe. Sharon stood like a Maypole as the girls swirled around her feet. Spotting a bead she wanted, she jabbed a finger in its direction and waited for someone to hand it to her.

"I'm making a bracelet for Kirwan." Kylie's voice rang out, muffled by the thumb in her mouth. A collective gasp split the air.

"You can't!" Carrie's whine set the tone for the session. "We all agreed."

"I'm making him one then," Sally commented, defiance in her tone. She gritted her teeth and her jaw set in a line.

"Me an' all," said Sharon. "He can have mine."

Carrie huffed and puffed and glared at Kylie. Phoenix watched as the child grinned around her thumb, her lips shiny with saliva. Devilment surrounded her and Phoenix pursed her lips and kept her laughter contained. She imagined Kirwan with bracelets strung from wrist to shoulder and the thought both amused and irritated her at the same time.

Phoenix persuaded Kylie to select beads from the mess on the floor. The girls' efforts had added fluff from under the beds to the bead box and Phoenix decided Lexi could return it to Tina at the end of the session. She'd done little else apart from paint black stripes over the pink polish and make the girls high on the solvent fumes. Kylie collected the beads in the rolled bottom of her tee shirt. She retrieved enough for Phoenix to make a bracelet. "Come on," she insisted. "Your mum might like one. Don't you have a mum?"

"I do." Phoenix sighed and lifted the elasticated thread. She held it to the light to find the end and slipped a tiny silver heart over it. "Mama doesn't like jewellery much. Dad has bought her heaps over the years, but she won't wear it. Says she's too afraid of losing it." The bracelet twirled in her fingers and she swallowed, realising she'd subconsciously started making it for a particular recipient. It became even more precious as she gazed on it, the weight of giving it to him dragging on her heart.

"Where might she lose it?" Kylie asked. She shifted her bony bottom on Phoenix's knee and caused her to drop the next bead.

"Dunno." Phoenix examined the ratty end of the thread. "I think I need my eyes testing."

"She might lose it in the car," Carrie chimed. "Or the waste disposal in the sink. That ate my mum's engagement ring. Glug

glug." A titter of laughter followed and Carrie beamed. Her pale cheeks pinked with pleasure. "Glug glug," she repeated, but no one laughed a second time.

"She rides a lot with my dad," Phoenix said. She pursed her lips and stabbed the end of the thread at another silver heart. "And she works in the museum more nowadays since Will passed."

"Passed what?" Kylie asked.

"Passed the sauce." Carrie sought to recapture her role as the cabin clown. She glowed beneath the attention.

Phoenix winced. "Passed away. Died." She held her breath in an effort not to cry. Gruff and inhospitable to the rest of humanity, Will had adored Wiri, Phoenix and Mac as though they belonged to him. They had, in a way. Descended from similar branches of the fearsome warriors who arrived in Kawhia, they'd shared blood and DNA. Their whakapapa intertwined at the root and tied them together. Family. Whānau. The unbreakable bond.

Kylie leaned sideways and pressed her rosebud lips to Phoenix's temple. She said nothing else as though relying on her childish sense of solidarity to convey a shared sympathy. Phoenix swallowed and her hands shook as she pushed another silver heart onto the wiry thread. "Put other things on too," Kylie urged. She unfurled the fingers of her right hand to reveal coloured beads. "Mix them."

"I'm good." Phoenix threaded another silver heart and then another. Deep down, she doubted she'd ever find the courage to give it to the intended recipient. Another silver heart and then another slipped on until the elasticated thread bulged like a thousand-dollar bauble fit for a millionaire's glitzy wife. Phoenix knotted the end and shoved it into her pocket.

"Let me see!" Kylie demanded, but Phoenix shook her head.

"It's no good," she lied. But it was. It represented a perfect analogy of her life; her heart fractured and split in too many directions to count. Silver and shiny on the outside with a fake, plastic centre. Phoenix shrugged Kylie from her knees and rose, the silver hearts digging into her thigh through the pocket lining. "Tidy up time," she said, her tone definitive. "Collect all the beads and the cord together into the container. Then give it to Lexi. She'll take it across to Tina and let her know we're on our way to set up for dinner. Phoenix glared at Lexi. She hadn't moved from her slumped position on the bed.

"Can you tie my knot?" Kylie asked. She clamped the two ends of her bracelet in her fingers and dangled it in front of Phoenix's face. Every colour of the rainbow hung from the thread and Phoenix imagined Kirwan's reaction. She worried he'd reject the gift and by implication, the child. Her heart hammered in her chest with the need to fix it, to run the scenarios in her brain and divert the trouble elsewhere. Nothing emerged as a solution and the knowledge floored her. She always knew what to do. They all came to her, Wiri, Mac and her mother. Wiri called her The Fixer.

Phoenix gaped down at Kylie and her fingers shook as she hid them behind her back. "I can't do it," she breathed. "I'm rubbish at knots. Ask Lexi or Sharon."

Kylie gave a snuff of irritation, but Carrie stepped in to save the day. Only she didn't. The elasticated thread pinged from her fingers during the final strengthening of the knot and the beads shot in every direction. Carrie winced. "Shit. Sorry," she gasped.

Horror crossed Kylie's face, replaced by fury. With a glare of pure rage at Phoenix, she strode from the cabin and slammed the door behind her. The girls stared at one another in the ensuing silence. Sharon shrugged. "She gets like that," she announced. "My mum wanted to adopt her but my dad said no. Because of her temper. As soon as we get home, the social worker is coming for her. They're sending her back."

"Sending her back where?" Lexi asked, her tone soft.

Sharon bent to retrieve the fallen beads. Instead of threading them again, she dropped them into the container. "Dunno," she replied. "Back where she came from I suppose." She jerked her head towards the empty bunk where the girls had stored their suitcases and extra supplies. "That's what happened to Mandy. She should have come back the same as last year but she got adopted. Her new family didn't want her to come." Her nose wrinkled. "We're friends on Facebook.

She's got her own pony now. Kylie won't get a family like that. She's too high maintenance."

Phoenix swallowed and another shard of her heart broke off like one of the silver beads. Sharon's words rolled off her tongue, fresh from the adults she'd overheard. Phoenix couldn't speak, an unfamiliar sense of hopelessness filling the space where her optimism should have been. Kylie, Kirwan and the refugees' lives were a bigger problem than she could fix alone. As Sharon's chunky fingers dumped the beads back into the container and the elasticated thread into the dustbin, Phoenix knew the word that described their plight.

Disposable.

12

TO SEEK AND SAVE THE LOST

Lexi walked the girls to the kitchen to set up for dinner. Phoenix stayed in the cabin and remade Kylie's bracelet. She strung together the eclectic beads in a random order, hoping they matched Kylie's decorative original. A lump rose into her throat without warning and she fought to push it away, the sense of overwhelm nipping at her psyche. Her fingers performed the delicate task with frustration and for the first time in her life, she resented her need to fix all the broken things. The responsibility bowed her head low over the detested task as her fingers fumbled with the writhing elastic cord. The sad realisation trickled its poisonous truth into her mind; not everything was fixable. The brand of optimism redolent of her great grandmother, Phoenix Du Rose, wilted on the stalk and caused her shoulders to slump as she tied the last knot. Then she flopped back onto the mattress.

Her lips moved in prayer. "I can't do this," she confessed. "Kirwan and Kylie are too broken. I can't even think about Wiri without shame and fear. There's a group of refugees in a barn in the middle of the bush and these girls are nuts."

The door creaked and Phoenix turned her face towards the sound. Kirwan smiled from the doorway. "They are nuts. You got that right. Who are you talking to?"

Phoenix's spine stiffened. "How long were you standing there?"

Kirwan shrugged and stared around the room. It looked neater than the others and didn't stink of wet dog like the boys' cabins. When his gaze tracked to her, his pupils grew large enough to obscure the flecked hazel of his irises. "I just heard you say the girls were nuts."

The air left her lungs and Phoenix's chest sagged. "I was praying," she said, her voice sad. "I can't do any of this. Why did Sam think I could?"

"Because you can?" Kirwan framed it like a question and edged nearer. Phoenix froze as he sat next to her on the mattress.

"What are you doing?" Her gaze flicked to the door and back to his face. Fear licked her spine from pelvis to crown. "Boys can't come into the girls' cabins!" She nudged his thigh with her fist and tensed, waiting for Tina to burst in weighed down by Grant's massive, leather bound Bible and order her stoned for fornication. Phoenix pushed herself backwards on the mattress but found her hip pressed against the wooden foot board.

"They're all busy," Kirwan stated. He turned sideways and stretched out his right hand to touch her hair. A coil from Phoenix's ponytail bounced against his fingers and he caught it and held it up to the light. "Red," he breathed. "There's red in your hair."

"My mama has red hair," Phoenix whispered.

From the moment of entry, Kirwan had wound a spell over her and she couldn't seem to break it. Like gold gossamer threads woven by a spider, it moved and shifted in the dappled light from outside, pinning her in place and holding her still. Kirwan raked her face for something and paused, but his body continued to tip until his lips almost touched hers. His fingers dropped the curl and stroked her cheek, their tenderness revealing more of his nature than he realised.

Phoenix held her breath and her body seemed to light up from the inside, a flame searing her innermost parts until they burned. It took her by surprise and she gasped. Kirwan's breath caressed her cheek. The fingers of his other hand picked up her bunched right fist and massaged it until it unfurled. The action felt sensuous and indecent, splaying her fingers wide until Kirwan's slipped between them like jigsaw puzzle pieces. Kylie's bracelet hung between them, a barrier sent to thwart them.

"Where's Phoenix?" Tina's shout came from just outside the cabin, her tone sounding angry.

Lexi's shouted reply came from a distance, backed by the clatter of crockery. "Kylie's bracelet broke. She's mending it."

The mattress shifted as Phoenix bolted upright and turned towards the door. A protest of pain issued from the cut behind her ear. She gaped as Tina burst through the gap and the door hit the bunk behind it. "You need to come and help!" Tina snapped.

Phoenix swallowed and dared to turn her head. A dent in the mattress greeted her, but no sign of Kirwan. She lifted Kylie's bracelet and winced. "I remade it." Her voice sounded feeble. She jerked her head towards the open container of multicoloured beads interspersed with lint and dust bunny fragments. "I'll take it all back now."

Tina's eyes widened. "I don't care about the bead making!" Her voice rose to a screech. "Kylie's missing."

13

INVISIBLE

Phoenix crouched in the semi-darkness and lifted the silver fern frond upright with her fingers. It bent at an odd angle, the main stem fractured at the halfway point. "She went this way." The surety in her voice drew a nod from Kirwan and Grant. Lifting her torch, she shone it in the direction she imagined Kylie running.

"Thank the good Lord you can track," Grant gushed. His voice sounded breathy. "Do you think she's heading for the ridge? It's a sheer drop. She could pitch over it before she even knows it's there." Shaking fingers lifted his baseball cap and he wiped his sweating forehead with his other hand.

Phoenix winced. "I don't know the geography of this reserve. A map would have been helpful."

Grant released an enormous sigh and nodded. "Sorry." He lifted a walkie talkie to his lips and depressed the button. "Big Fish to Holy Joe. Big Fish to Holy Joe. Over?"

Kirwan's eyes widened to the size of saucers and he coughed to cover the laugh bubbling from his lips. Phoenix turned her face away, keen not to join his attack of inappropriate giggles in such a serious situation. She clamped her teeth over her lower lip and bit down, curious to know who used the moniker, Holy Joe.

Gus' voice crackled through the receiver, the words sounding disjointed and ghoulish in the dusk. "Holy Joe to Big Fish. Go ahead." Phoenix glanced up at Kirwan. His shoulders shook and his eyes glinted with tears in the moonlight filtering through the bush canopy.

"Can you send Prayer Warrior on the dirt bike to our position with the OS map from the office?" Grant stared down at the handset as Gus repeated his question.

"Go ahead, Big Fish. Are you there brother?"

Kirwan made a peculiar whale sound. He interspersed it with a gagging noise.

"Oh." Grant lifted his spectacles and peered at the buttons on the walkie talkie. "I forgot to press the button when I spoke." He repeated his request. "Can you send Prayer Warrior to our position with the OS map from the office?" He fumbled the handset and dropped it in the bushes. The reply sounded muffled. Kirwan staggered to a nearby kauri trunk and bent double. He looked like he might vomit. Phoenix rolled her eyes and remained in her crouched stance. She trained the torch on a gap in the supplejack and spotted a dusty footprint. Grant continued his fight with the walkie talkie. "Yes, over. Sorry, sorry."

"Where are you, Big Fish?" Gus sounded annoyed. "How will Prayer Warrior find you in the dark?"

Kirwan had almost recovered, but the question sent him into paroxysms of laughter. "Tell them to follow the star," he snorted, his witty answer fuelling his mirth.

"I'm surrounded by morons," Phoenix breathed. She rose and took a wide step, landing next to the jagged imprint of a training shoe. Two dents marked by more crushed ferns revealed the place where a young girl had fallen and landed on her knees.

As Big Fish argued with Holy Joe about where on the map they were, Phoenix progressed her search and continued alone. She cast her torch beam around in a wide arc. "Kylie?" She made her tone sound soft and supportive, though the insects biting and sucking the blood below the hem of her shorts made her want to scream in frustration. "Kylie? Are you hurt? Come out. I'm getting bitten alive. You must be itching your skin off by now."

The sound of leaves rustled ahead of her and a sense of certainty percolated her mind. It conveyed the heady rush of relief into her heart. "I re-made your bracelet." Phoenix paused and closed her eyes. Hauling Kylie from a bush by her hair seemed inappropriate though tempting. Heavy tread behind her heralded Kirwan and Phoenix tensed. His arms wound around her waist and he rested his chin on top of her head. A memory of Wiri doing the same thing flashed through her mind and guilt rippled from her stomach to her chest. Though Wiri's hands hadn't loosened her tee shirt from the waistband of her shorts or pressed warm fingers over her sensitive ribs to cup the soft buds of her breasts.

Phoenix shuddered and took a step towards the rustling bush. She needed to disconnect from the teenager before he undressed her and she let him. His caress lowered and he matched her movement, though the sensation of his palms smoothing her flat stomach sent shivers through her innermost core. He pressed a soft kiss to her neck in the darkness. The beam of her torch lowered by degrees until it created a cream arc along the ground.

Undergrowth crunched behind them and torch light bounced off the canopy overhead as Grant crashed through the supplejack. Phoenix tensed, Kirwan's spell broken "Stop," she whispered. "He'll see."

Kirwan's breath warmed her skin as he drew a line along her collarbone with his lips. "Live dangerously," he growled.

Phoenix gave herself a shake and stepped away in a jerky movement like a marionette. Embarrassment flushed her skin and she swallowed, grateful that the darkness hid her confusion.

The bush ahead rustled and a small voice issued from it, the tone petulant. "You're blinding me!" Kylie complained.

Phoenix froze as fear beat through her veins. She held her breath and waited. Her skin cooled without Kirwan's palms and she agonised over what Kylie might have seen. A firm hand cupped her shoulder and squeezed through her tee shirt. "It's all good," Kirwan whispered, sounding certain. "You had the torch pointed right at her." His voice rumbled low and confidential as he drew Phoenix into his conspiracy. He moved in front of the torch beam and she heard Kylie gasp.

"Who's that?" the child exclaimed. "Is it an angel?"

Phoenix frowned until she understood what Kylie saw; Kirwan back-lit by torch light. Her heart rate returned to a less painful thud in her chest as Kirwan took a few tentative steps towards the bush. "It's Kirwan," he called, his tone nonchalant. "You coming out tonight kid? The bugs are eating me alive."

"Kirwan!" She sounded intoxicated as she repeated his name. He'd assumed the role of hero and the child revelled in his attention. "You came especially for me?" Kylie scrambled from the bush, her face filthy and her jacket stained. She ignored Phoenix.

"Oh, praise the Lord!" Grant crashed through the undergrowth and bumped into Phoenix, almost sending her sprawling. "Oh, young lady, you've had us all worried!" He spoke to Kylie, the kindness of his tone tempering the rebuke clothing his words. Phoenix watched as Kylie hurled herself at Kirwan, allowing him to lift her off her feet and carry her over the supplejack. He grinned at Phoenix, the conquering hero. She narrowed her eyes in reply, her brow furrowing as he showed no sign of registering her pique. Wiri would have understood the coded message hidden behind the simple action. He would have hastened to highlight her role and get her the proper recognition. Not for the first time, Phoenix missed him with a physical ache and confusion took a firm stronghold in her heart.

Unacknowledged and forgotten, Phoenix followed Grant and Kirwan back to camp. Tina appeared ten minutes before they arrived. She rode an ancient dirt bike which looked like it had seen better days. Rusty mudguards hung from coils of Number 8 wire and blue smoke belched from the exhaust. She carried the ordinance survey map in her teeth like a retriever, puttering along behind the group as though integral to their triumphant return.

Kylie rode on Kirwan's back, her cheek pressed against his shoulder and a satisfied smile lifting her lips.

14

PRAYER WARRIOR

"**I** almost wet myself when I saw Prayer Warrior on that dirt bike." Kirwan sank onto the makeshift wooden bench hewn from driftwood. Phoenix braced herself as it shifted beneath her. The fire crackled to itself as flames danced in search of another sacrifice. She fed its need, leaning forward to lay another smooth log over its core.

"Hail conquering hero." Her tone sounded lacklustre and she sat back to watch the flames eat.

"What?" Kirwan frowned, his brows a grim line highlighted by orange shards in the firelight. He flapped his hand in front of him. "The kid? She just saw me first, is all. I told her you tracked her."

"Liar." Phoenix breathed the word and he heard her, shifting closer so their shoulders touched.

"Yeah." His irises sparkled. "I'll tell you any lie you want if you promise to stop being dirty at me."

Phoenix closed her eyes against his pragmatic answer. "You're a chameleon," she concluded. "Shifting shape and colour to match whoever you're with at the time."

Kirwan jerked his head back and then nodded. A smile lit his lips. "That's fair." He glanced behind him at the darkened buildings, the kitchen empty and the campers asleep. Only Grant's cabin showed a soft light escaping beneath the ragged curtains. A mischievous glint stole across Kirwan's dark irises. His kiss took Phoenix by surprise and she lost valuable rejection time. When he slipped his tongue past the sentry of her lips, she knew she'd missed any hope of escape. His tenderness seemed mismatched against the force of his personality and the brusqueness of his speech. "You've bewitched me, Phoenix Du Rose," he whispered. His teeth nipped at her lower lip. "I can't think straight when you're around me."

Moral sense robbed her of a calm reply and she shifted back to put suitable distance between them. "I think it's the other way around," she replied, her tone scratchy. The fire crackled and spat and Kirwan studied her with his forearms resting over his thighs. He didn't try to move closer, perhaps aware of the prickles of self-protection rising from her bones.

Sounds issued from Grant's hut and low laughter followed. Kirwan turned his head to watch the light change in the window as silhouettes moved behind the flimsy fabric. "Leader's meeting," he said. "Probably praying for the kid's divine deliverance." He leaned back with a sigh. "It beats their usual treadmill of praying for my soul." A sarcastic snort punctuated his sentence.

"What's wrong with your soul?" The question surprised them both, Phoenix frowning as she realised she hadn't meant to ask it.

"What's right with it?" Kirwan sounded sad. "Is that why you keep freezing me out, Phoenix? Because I'm a no hoper."

Phoenix's lips parted and she shook her head. She knew before she said it that her reply sounded lame. "It's not that."

Kirwan exhaled through his nostrils, a loud, haughty sound reminiscent of Mikaere's temper tantrums. "I guess you'll go home and Daddy will pick a suitably rich husband for you. How many perfect kids do you want, Phoenix? Five? Ten?"

Her entire body stiffened as Kirwan pressed on a sore. Pain radiated out from her chest in a wide arc and pulsed with enough force to wake the campers. Phoenix ground her teeth together so hard, it seemed doubtful they would ever part in a smile or a kiss again. "Go away." The words sounded strangled and filled with something sinister, an agony with otherworldly origins.

Kirwan started and his gaze held genuine concern. "I'm sorry. I didn't mean it."

"Leave me alone!" Phoenix's legs moved as though wooden, the tendons and sinews formed from thin string as she rose in a jerky movement. A stick dropped from her lap as she stepped away from the warmth. The cool air at her spine touched her soul like fingers of ice.

Phoenix backed up until she could escape without Kirwan touching her. A pall of misery fell like a familiar shroud as her reality infected her thoughts as well as her blood. The effort to explain left her in a haze of pointlessness. Her heart pounded in her chest, sending the treacherous blood through her veins to blind her eyes with skipping lights and black spots. Balled fists hung rigid by her thighs as she stalked across the campground to her cabin. She couldn't explain her decision to never have babies to a boy looking for a quick hook up for a week. It wasn't worth her energy.

"Miss Du Rose!" The title sounded formal and stilted in the natural surroundings. Recognising Tina's voice, Phoenix forced her body to turn. A glance at the fire showed no sign of Kirwan. He'd done one of his famous disappearing acts again. "I hope you weren't planning to leave the fire in that state?" Tina framed it as a question, but it was more of a statement. She stepped off the porch in front of Grant's cabin and settled her hands over her hips.

"I wanted a cardigan," Phoenix lied. "The fire is almost out, but I can damp it down if you think it needs it."

"Of course, it needs it." Tina's pencilled eyebrows knitted into a thin line. She glanced back at the lighted cabin behind her as a burst of laughter excluded her from the missed joke. Her head shook and her blonde curls bounced in the fading glow of the fire. Phoenix cringed as her heavy footsteps closed the distance between them to continue her tirade. "Someone growing up in the mountains should know how little sparks can create great bush fires. I'm surprised at you."

Phoenix inhaled through her nose, a slow, calculated process aimed at blocking the series of screams she would release if she breathed out yet. Tina continued to stare at her, waiting for a cue to slice off her pound of flesh. "I left Kirwan sitting by the fire," Phoenix asserted, aware of her gritted teeth hindering the words' exit.

Tina turned to face the fire and her eyes narrowed. "I don't see him," she stated, and the scream rose back into Phoenix's throat. "You know the rules; last one by the fire puts it out." She jabbed a finger into Phoenix's chest. "And that's you. Don't blame others for your shortcomings."

"Yes, Miss." The words grated free of Phoenix's lips and she pointed her feet towards the fire. But Tina hadn't finished.

"You need to follow the rules, Phoenix. Don't abandon the fire again." Tina glanced at a chunky digital watch on her wrist. The numbers glowed green in the half light. "It's late. You should have gone to bed ages ago." She blinked as though answering her own question. "Why aren't you coming to the leaders' meetings?"

Phoenix held tight to the stab of exclusion as she repeated Gus' attempt at a tactful dismissal. "I'm too young. You talk about confidential matters. It's best I don't come."

"Oh." Tina frowned and her nose wrinkled. "I guess. If your pastor friend had come, we could have let him mentor you. Maybe next year."

Each step cost Phoenix as she walked back towards the dying flames and spitting embers. To her chagrin, Tina followed. Her gimlet eyes studied Phoenix's actions as she picked up the metal bucket containing spring water and doused the fire. She'd meant to dribble the liquid, but anger caused her to tip the entire contents on the flames. Superheated vapour spat at her shins to leave angry red spots on her skin. Phoenix blinked against the external pain and married it to the inner turmoil so she could fight both instead of splitting her defences.

"Thank you." Tina sounded satisfied but her expression showed otherwise. She rested her weight on one leg and tilted a little backward, as though surveying Phoenix through a different lens and seeking clarity. "Grant said you found Kylie," she stated.

Phoenix gave a sharp inhale, the acknowledgement both welcome but unwanted from this quarter. "It was nothing," she whispered.

Tina's face broke into a smile and she nodded. "You and I are very alike," she said, her voice soft. "We have to fix broken things. It's in our nature. We get no thanks, but we do it anyway." She reached out and rested her hand on Phoenix's shoulder. Twin reflections of the half moon glittered in her irises. "Perhaps leave Kirwan to the professionals." She lowered her voice to a whisper. "There's nothing you can do for someone like him. I've tried to help more kids in my lifetime than you've had hot dinners. He won't change. He enjoys having no rules or boundaries. You can't help everyone. Put your energies into those who deserve it."

Phoenix's head jerked on her neck, a strange wobble which Tina read as agreement. Her wooden limbs walked her to the deck of her cabin and she kicked off her boots beneath the narrow porch. Then she carried them inside with her. Possums skittered around in the tree canopy and a morepork called from high up as it searched for dinner. The door clicked shut behind her and Phoenix leaned her body back against its rickety structure. A vile swearword danced in the periphery of her mind, one her mother had banned from their house years ago. She hissed it anyway, satisfaction shrouded by the dirty sensation it brought. Her rational mind told her there were worse things in life than being likened to Tina, but as she changed into her pyjamas in the cabin's darkness she couldn't think of a single one.

Phoenix pushed her boots under the bottom bunk, climbed up the ladder and snuggled into her sleeping bag. Thoughts of Wiremu Du Rose pressed to the forefront of her brain once her muscles stilled. To her surprise, she drifted into a heavy sleep, though the hounds of hell chased her in her dreams and Kirwan drove them at her with a smile.

15

DUCK-DUCK-GOOSE

Phoenix woke with a start, her sharp inhale prevented by something over her mouth. She gasped and lashed out with the heels of her hands, hearing a hiss as she contacted an angular chin.

"Stop!" The whisper sounded close to her face and she stilled. His breath smelled of minty toothpaste overwritten by nicotine from a recent cigarette. "I feel bad about this afternoon." Kirwan rose on tiptoes to reach Phoenix's bunk. He released his hand over her mouth. "I'll take you to the barn. You can check the refugees."

Triumph bloomed in Phoenix's chest. Tina had it all wrong. Kirwan showed subtle signs of redemption in his risky mission to summon her. She nodded as excitement sent a faint tremor into her fingers. She expelled him from the cabin and slipped a fleece over her pyjamas. Wood smoke wafted into her nostrils and reminded her of home. Again, Wiri's spectre rose to dog her steps as she slipped from the cabin and closed the door behind her.

Clouds obscured the slip of moon as Kirwan led Phoenix from the campsite. He jerked his head at her bare feet and raised his eyebrows. Phoenix shrugged to show she couldn't find her boots in the darkness. Scrabbling under the bottom bunk had left her empty-handed, though she knew she'd find them straight away on her return. He moved off the deck like a fox, making no sound.

They skirted the hut he shared with Grant, Kirwan taking her on a circuitous route towards the bush. "Grant is on night duty, but he's snoring," he whispered, his lips curving upward into a mischievous grin. "I slipped a little something in his hot chocolate."

Phoenix followed, her heart flooded with the conflicting emotions of fear and indignation. Drugging an adult reached beyond her experience and she wanted no part of it. But another voice in her head justified Kirwan's actions if it helped the refugees. She readied herself to rain a hail of fury on anyone who stopped her on her mission. Commitment and loyalty had won the battle in her heart, her effervescent spirit not yet jaded enough by the world to lose its energy. Her powerful father had invested much time and effort into sheltering his children from the wickedness of humanity, but she'd seen it at the camp. This was her summer of reckoning.

Kirwan refused to speak to her as they crept through the bush. Though she pointed at the dirt path which would have made the journey easier, he shook his head and pursed his lips. When she reached out and tried to steer him towards the track, he grabbed her elbow and spun her around to face him. Leaning close, his whisper tickled the shell of her ear as he rebuked her in a hissed undertone. "We do this my way, or we don't do it at all!" His eyes narrowed. "And leave no trace for someone else to track."

Phoenix started in fright as the task loomed bigger than them both. In her fantasy of rescue and redemption, she had thought only of her own heroism. The reality proved something different. Kirwan's ridicule of her family setup and her reliance on her father came home to roost. She wished with all her heart that she could contact Logan Du Rose and call upon his might and influence to help her. She contemplated disobeying Kirwan and leaving a trail, but she'd brought nothing with her and feared the traffickers' ability to follow her clues back to the camp's innocent inhabitants.

Kirwan forced her to walk over fern fronds and supplejack vine. It snatched at her legs and tripped her too many times to count.

Phoenix tried to take stock of her surroundings, wondering if she might make the journey alone at some point and free the captives herself. But every tree looked the same in the darkness and no ready landmarks caught her eye.

Kirwan moved with easy stealth like a hunter in his element. A glimpse at the determination in his face caused Phoenix a moment of fear as she wondered if she'd walked into an elaborate trap. Kirwan reached for Phoenix's hand but she resisted his touch, readying herself to run if needed. She saw Kirwan's brow knit into a series of lines as he sensed her reticence. The moon moved behind a cloud and sheltered his true intentions beneath shadows. Low-lying supplejack snatched at Phoenix's ankles and unable to extract herself, she fell to her knees with a grunt.

Kirwan dropped next to her, shoving the back of her head so her face landed at the roots of a low growing fern. He clapped a hand over her mouth and froze. Phoenix wriggled in protest and the pressure of his fingers increased. "Shut up or I'll leave you here!" he growled. "I knew you couldn't cope." His rebuke fired up her sleeping determination and she resisted the urge to bite his fingers. His palm tasted of soil and deodorant and Phoenix waited for him to remove it from her mouth. "Stay down!" Kirwan hissed. "The barn is through the trees. Can you see it now?"

Phoenix rose enough to follow the line of his finger. A faint light showed, muted but still strong enough to glow from between a stand of wide kauri trees. Kirwan kept his hand on the back of Phoenix's neck. She nodded to show she'd recognised the barn from their first visit and understood his caution.

"They're checking on them, see!" His voice held a note of victory. "There are two men. I told you they wouldn't starve them. Those refugees came here of their own free will."

"Then why are they locked in the barn? Why don't they run?"

Kirwan shrugged. "Perhaps they're getting ready for the next stage of their journey."

Phoenix abandoned her imagined role of saviour. She nodded and settled onto her bottom amid the bush debris. Everything seemed futile against the might of experienced traffickers and she decided to reach Wiri somehow. Or her father. They'd know what to do.

Tapping Kirwan's arm, Phoenix motioned back the way they'd come.

"Not yet." His breath brushed her ear. "It's too dangerous."

Phoenix sighed and settled on the ground. The intrinsic dampness of the bush affected her limbs, causing a clammy cold to seep into her bones. She pulled her fleece closer, hoping they wouldn't have to wait too much longer to return to the campground and the fetid warmth of her cabin.

After a while, Phoenix groaned, her legs stiffening from remaining fixed in one position for too long. She fidgeted. "Can we go yet?" she grumbled.

Kirwan's sparkling eyes reflected concern. "Keep still!" he hissed. "They'll hear you."

Phoenix tuned in to the sound of male voices as they drifted on the breeze. She closed her eyes, listening to their lilting cadence as she searched for distinguishing features. Her keen ears picked up a South Island accent in one man, but nothing else of note. The cool night air attacked the tender skin of her thighs beneath her pyjama shorts and her body rebelled by shivering and shaking until her teeth made an audible chatter.

"I want to go back." Her whispered admission of defeat received a frown from Kirwan and a shake of his head. "I need to leave. I'm cold."

His gritted jaw signified his anger. "If we move now, they'll hear us."

"I'm sorry," she began as another round of shivering racked her slender frame. Her voice rose by accident and Kirwan's eyes widened to glinting crystals in the moonlight. He froze at the sound of movement coming through the bush in their direction. Helplessness sped across his face. He covered Phoenix's mouth with his hand again.

A black shape burst from the undergrowth with a low growl. Teeth bared, it ground to a halt and planted its legs in front of them.

Its mouth parted, ready to give away their hiding place with a bark. Phoenix scrambled in the dirt, unused to dogs and clueless about its intentions. Kirwan released his hand from Phoenix's mouth and scrabbled at something in his pocket. The dog released another low growl and edged closer, saliva dotting the rough fur coating its chin. The peeking moon cast shadows over its brindle and white coat. Phoenix held her breath and waited, closing her eyes against the expected attack.

Kirwan's frantic fingers searched, dragging something crumpled from his fleece. His elbow dug into her ribs as he moved. Phoenix watched open mouthed as he extracted a wrapper, pulled a piece of ham from between two slices of bread and threw it at the dog. The hound caught it in mid-air and stopped growling. The meat disappeared in a single gulp. Kirwan followed it with the empty bread. Again, the dog caught and swallowed without effort. Its growl changed to a pitiful whine and it watched Kirwan with hopeful anticipation.

"Keep still." Kirwan leaned sideways and whispered into Phoenix's ear. "Don't get eye contact with it. I think it will be okay. It's someone's pet."

Phoenix lowered her gaze as instructed, her brain registering the sight of the GPS collar strapped around the dog's neck. It looked more like a hunting dog, but she didn't want to ruin Kirwan's confidence by telling him her thoughts. The dog issued another whine and a second sandwich disappeared down its throat. Kirwan didn't bother to separate the pieces, watching with amusement as the dog caught the food and swallowed in a single, fluid motion.

Shouts issued from beyond the glow and the dog glanced back towards the voices. Its ears twitched, betraying an inner conflict as it hankered after more food while knowing it should obey its master. Shouts sounded again, the words indiscernible and shrouded in irritation.

Laughter followed, accompanied by mocking. "Have you lost that dog again?"

Someone chuckled and the first voice replied in anger. "Idris!" Twigs snapped in the undergrowth. "Get back here!"

The volume of noise near the barn intensified as the man set out in search of his absent dog. Phoenix froze and snatched at Kirwan's elbow. "He'll find us!" she hissed.

Kirwan nodded, his mind working overtime as he ran through scenarios. Phoenix saw him shake his head as though disregarding several of them before deciding on a suitable plan. Pulling a hunk of chocolate cake from his other pocket, he unwrapped it and dropped it into his palm. Crumbs cascaded over Phoenix's legs. Kirwan held out the cake, lengthening his arm. The dog dropped to its haunches and crawled along the ground on its belly. As it drew closer, Phoenix pulled her knees up to her chin in terror.

The dog ventured near enough to almost lick Kirwan's fingers. Its eyes widened as he lifted his hand and threw the cake through the trees in a magnificent cricketer's lob.

The dog turned and fled after the cake, wading through the undergrowth with excited barks.

"Idris!" its owner yelled, irritation turning to anxiety. "Come here, boy. What have you found?" Running footsteps headed towards the teenagers and Phoenix tried to recall an emergency prayer Sam once taught the Sunday school. It evaded her, leaving only a stream of burble in her head.

Kirwan snatched at Phoenix with an outstretched arm, tipping her sideways and hurting her neck as he flung her downward into the undergrowth and covered her body with his. She landed with her ear against his chest and felt his rapid heartbeat thudding through her cheek.

Phoenix held her breath and waited for discovery. Every nerve ending fired a warning filled with alarm. Kirwan kept his arm around her neck, pressing her head against him. He didn't cover her mouth and Phoenix experienced a flash of gratitude as frightened puffs of breath seemed all she could manage.

The dog gave an excited yap as it found the cake. It snorted like a feral pig as it inhaled the chocolate treat. Its owner found it hunting the remaining crumbs and torchlight danced overhead in the tree canopy just metres from the teenagers' hiding place. The man gave a sigh of relief.

"Idris!" he exclaimed. "What have you found?" The dog's answering whine changed as the man gripped its collar and constricted its throat.

Another voice sounded louder and a light tread accompanied it. "What's he doing?" the man demanded. "You're making enough noise to wake the whole camp."

"Sorry. Idris found a possum track. He's back now."

"What's he eating?" The other man sounded doubtful. The dog grunted again as its owner pulled it closer to examine its face.

"It looks like chocolate," he groaned. "Dogs shouldn't have chocolate."

"I'm not surprised. There are kids everywhere. We couldn't have picked a worse time to do this."

The dog's owner released a sigh like a growl low in his throat. "It's what the boss wanted," he said. "It's not our job to ask questions. Let's clear up and leave before all those kids wake. The last thing we need is them stumbling across us."

Footsteps rustled through the undergrowth, punctuated by the sound of the dog's sharp cough as it regurgitated cake crumbs. "This is the last camp apparently. Then they'll close up for the winter and we can do what's necessary. I don't like this thing. It's riskier than last time. We're running out of water. The tank collecting the rain from the roof is almost empty. I know we're in a drought, but I think there's a leak. These refugees need to disappear. And fast."

The teenagers remained in hiding for another twenty minutes by Kirwan's watch before daring to relax. "Let's get back," he whispered, his lips close to Phoenix's ear.

She pushed herself upright, all complaints about the cold forgotten. Her eyes flashed with determination as her goal renewed itself. "No way!" she snapped. "You heard those men. They'll kill them. We're here now. I want to see the refugees. Maybe we can set them free."

16

DOING THE RIGHT THING

"You're joking, right?" Kirwan baulked, his eyes widening and his olive complexion looking bleached in the moonlight.

"I want to see the refugees," Phoenix demanded. Her voice rose enough to make his body tense next to hers. "We know they haven't set traps by the way they crashed around looking for the dog."

"No!" Kirwan hissed. "It's too dangerous!"

Phoenix possessed the wrong genetics for obedience. She'd begun crawling before he could stop her. Once in sight of the barn, she paused, overestimating her ability to move through the bush without creating a disturbance. She relished the bush skills her father had taught her; laborious hours spent staring at marks on the ground. Hoof prints, footprints and items he laid there to test her. Phoenix squinted at the ground beneath her, almost sensing his disappointment.

But the traffickers hadn't bothered to cover their tracks either. It appeared they shared an arrogant overconfidence. It sounded like they'd hidden people in the barn before without detection. Perhaps many times.

Kirwan didn't follow. Phoenix found herself alone as she traversed the barn in the darkness. No sound issued from inside and no lights showed through the slats. On the beach side of the wooden structure, Phoenix's exploring fingers discovered a crack wide enough to peer through to the interior. She placed her eye against the narrow aperture and waited for her vision to adjust to the darkness inside the musty space.

At first, she spotted nothing. Then she drew her head back with a gasp. A hand covered her mouth as she fell backwards, her bottom landing in the dirt.

"Happy now?" Kirwan growled. Phoenix shoved his hand away long enough to sit up and turn towards him. Her shock was reflected in his eyes as Kirwan blinked and leaned closer in alarm.

"I saw an eyeball," she whispered. Kirwan's eyes widened further until they looked too large for his face.

Phoenix shook her head and waved a hand to emphasise her point. "No, it's attached to a face. Someone looked back at me through the gap."

Curiosity got the better of Kirwan, enough to send him scrambling to peer through the crack on his knees. He froze at whatever he witnessed on the other side and then Phoenix heard him begin a slow conversation.

"What's your name?" he whispered. He turned to Phoenix and slapped at her leg, alternating between slapping and beckoning her to his side. Phoenix scrambled onto her knees and joined him next to the crack between the wooden slats.

"I can't see," she protested, her voice rising. Kirwan placed his hand over her mouth again.

"For goodness' sake, woman!" He growled. "This is dangerous enough without you making it worse. Do you want those guys to come back and find us?"

Phoenix shook her head, her eyes wide above Kirwan's fingers. He released his hand and she issued a whispered apology. "Ask them where they're from?" She moderated her tone to avoid Kirwan's ire.

He nodded and pressed his eye to the crack. He repeated Phoenix's question and she held her breath while he waited for an answer. Then he turned to her, the whites of his eyes glinting in the moonlight. "Syria," he replied.

"They're illegal." Phoenix sat back on her heels. She felt the blood leave her face as the problems unravelled before her. "We need to tell someone," she concluded.

Kirwan glared at her in the moonlight. He shook his head from side to side, forming a silent accusation. "Of course, they're bloody illegal," he snarled. "You knew that. Do you think they'd hide out in a barn in the middle of nowhere if they'd come through customs and immigration?"

"We need to do the right thing," Phoenix concluded. She ran a hand across her eyes, noticing as she pulled it away that it trembled with the weight of responsibility. The added stress revived the ache in her head from the earlier fall.

Voices came from the other side of the wood and Kirwan pressed his eye to the crack. Phoenix watched as he shook his head at the speaker. "It's okay," he promised. "She won't tell anyone." Kirwan withdrew his face and glared at Phoenix. His eyes held a frenzied glint in the dim light. "I won't let her."

She shook her head and backed away. Kirwan's fingers closed around her wrist, the pressure bruising the delicate skin. "I mean it," he growled. "I've been in the system long enough to know it doesn't give a shit about the people it's meant to help. The system will take these people and spit them back out because it doesn't care. I won't let that happen to them. Can't you hear them? They're terrified of going back. You're scaring them!"

"But it's against the rules." Phoenix shook her head. "They could speak to the government and ask for the right to stay. They shouldn't have to hide like this. Maybe my father could help by giving them work."

A fire rose into Kirwan's eyes and Phoenix jerked backwards to avoid the hatred filling his expression. "Your father," he sneered. "Yeah, he could really help. I bet he'd make this insignificant problem disappear in minutes. He'd make sure they ended up floating face down in a lake somewhere or in a mass grave on his precious mountain." The bile in his voice sounded genuine and Phoenix swallowed, afraid of him in a way which made her heart thud beneath her chest wall.

She sat back on her heels and remained silent while Kirwan spoke through the wood to the unknown man behind it. Phoenix wrung her hands together and listened to the disjointed snatches of conversation as the sense of misgiving grew to unmanageable proportions. Her delusions of heroism forgotten, the urge to follow the rules and do the right thing clamoured in her brain. Somehow, she would fix this. But how?

17

ROOM FOR ONE MORE

"They're all Syrian," Kirwan said. He kept his voice low and scanned the surrounding bush for danger. "Only one of them speaks English and he said his name was something that sounded like Elephant. They paid a fortune to come here. Their families sent them ahead to Australia."

"Australia?" Phoenix's brow furrowed. "Do they realise they're in New Zealand?"

"They do now." Kirwan waggled his eyebrows. "I told Elephant. He said the first boat broke down out to sea somewhere and the traffickers sent another to rescue them. But now there's a delay and they need to stay here. He suspects they want more money."

Phoenix stopped on the path and stared up at him. "For real? Why should they pay extra when they haven't even ended up at the right place?"

Kirwan shrugged. He seemed philosophical about the refugees' misfortune and his earlier rage had dissipated enough to make Phoenix walk next to him without fear. "Economics," he replied.

"If the traffickers lost a boat, they're looking for reimbursement and they don't care where they get it. Elephant thinks they'll kill them if they don't come up with the money."

Phoenix blinked in horror and resumed walking. She didn't mention her father again, not wanting to stoke Kirwan's anger until she'd had time to formulate different options. But her mind worked and she focused on the image of the telephone in the office, vowing to call home as soon as she got the opportunity. "Elephant? We can't call him that. It's rude."

Kirwan sighed. "It's an excellent code word. We need to be careful, Phoenix. If someone overhears us, it will sound better and we can pass it off as a private joke." He blinked and Phoenix saw a predatory expression flash across his dark irises. He took her elbow and his hand warmed the skin through her fleece. "Let's keep it between the two of us."

"But what about Grant? We could tell him."

Kirwan snorted. "What? Big Fish? He couldn't fight his way out of a paper bag. Can you imagine him against a group of traffickers?"

Phoenix nodded. "Okay, just us. For now." She pursed her lips and picked her way along the path.

They split up before the edge of the camp, Kirwan displaying an unusual reluctance to release her arm. He kept hold of her until the last minute, his fingers brushing across her olive wrist as he released it. "Tell no one, remember?" he insisted. "I have a nasty feeling about this."

Phoenix paused and watched him stride through the undergrowth. His long legs stepped over trailing supplejack vine and skirted the spiteful outstretched limbs of bush lawyer. When he disappeared from sight, she scurried into camp and began clearing the ash from the dead campfire. She needed to appear busy and justify her early activity if anyone peeked from a cabin window.

By the time the first camper emerged to use the bathroom, she'd shovelled the ash into a metal bucket and reset the fire using twigs foraged from the bush and logs from the spider filled wood store. Grant stumbled from his cabin and hauled his trousers higher. He glanced around him before noticing Phoenix's activity, ambling over with the kinetic energy of a tractor building speed from a standstill.

"You're a delightful girl!" he called, his face breaking into a wide grin. "You've saved me a job."

Phoenix stood back from her building task and returned his smile. "My father made sure we knew how to build campfires from a young age," she replied. "I went to the bathroom and it was already light. There seemed little point going back to bed just to get up again." The partial truth salved her aching conscience.

Grant stared up at the azure sky and beamed. "Looks like a cracking day again." He squinted against the strengthening glare of the sun. "You're an asset on this camp, young lady." He winked at her. "But I'd hop in the shower before the girls use all the water, if I was you."

Phoenix nodded and rubbed her palms together, spreading the sooty mess instead of containing it. The moment seemed more awkward than it should have and she strode towards her cabin with a sense of uncertainty. Grant's statement suggested something she'd already suspected. The leaders hadn't wanted her there. Any contribution she made would be better than expected.

The cabin door opened to reveal a group of the smaller girls gathered around Kylie's bunk. "What's going on?" Phoenix demanded.

Sharon rolled her eyes. She looked keener than ever to ditch the seven-year-old. Her hands settled over her hips and she pouted. "She does this at home all the time. It's only for attention."

"Does what?" Phoenix cut through the various bodies lined up next to Kylie's mattress. She stared down at the pale, childish face on the pillow. "What do you do, Kyles?"

Wide brown eyes blinked up at her in surprise at the tender nickname and the smallest smile lifted one side of her upper lip. "Bellyache," the girl replied. "It's sore."

Phoenix sat on the edge of the mattress and looked up at the other girls. "Hop into the shower before prayer time," she suggested. "Before the boys nick all the hot water."

Sharon gave an unladylike snort and lifted an expensive wash bag from her bunk. "Boys don't wash!" she scoffed. She left the cabin in a haze of strong floral scent and the gaggle of tiny females followed.

Phoenix frowned and turned her attention to Kylie. "I said hot water, but it's not much above body temperature, is it?" She wrinkled her nose and gave an involuntary shiver. "It makes me miss home."

Kylie nodded and pushed herself to a sitting position. The action appeared easy enough, but Phoenix watched for any tell-tale signs of pain to show she wasn't just looking for attention. "Sharon doesn't like me," she admitted. "She didn't want me to come."

Phoenix tilted her head. "Are you sisters?"

Kylie's eyes widened. "No!" Sadness turned down the edges of her lips and her jaw clenched. "My baby brother got took away by the people. Mum got sick and couldn't take care of us. I don't know where he is."

"Oh." Phoenix swallowed and imagined a world in which she got separated from her brother. Mac might not notice her absence for a while, but she'd feel his like a physical ache. And Wiri. She couldn't bear to think of a life without him. "Is Sharon your foster sister?"

"Yup." Kylie nodded. "But she doesn't want me."

Phoenix inhaled. "That's hard for you. My parents adopted my cousin, Wiremu, when he was younger than you. My other cousin, Tama, had nobody, so my mum took him on too. She already had me, but then she gave birth to my baby brother and not long afterwards, my uncle died. She took his daughter, Edin. They're my family. I can't imagine the house ever being empty." Phoenix frowned. "I hope they never feel unwanted. I don't believe they do."

"Are you horrid to them?" Kylie asked.

Phoenix shook her head. Her memory skipped to an image of Wiri lying in the long grass at the top of the forty-eighth paddock. Strong veins stood out against his biceps as he pulled her down on top of him. He'd stopped just shy of kissing her and the moment was heavy, laden with a storm neither of them wanted to face. Her father.

Phoenix cleared her throat and fought the flush creeping up her neck. "Not on purpose," she whispered. "But sometimes I'm unkind when I don't mean to be."

Kylie nodded. "Okay then," she conceded. "Does your Mum have room for just one more?"

A fragile thread snapped in the fine tuning of Phoenix's heart. It left her speechless along with the realisation she couldn't fix Kylie's problem. She held her breath. No suitable answer presented itself as hope faded from Kylie's open expression. The girl pushed her feet from her sleeping bag and Phoenix rose to give her space. "I'm better now," Kylie lied. She grabbed her towel and wash bag and stepped from the cabin, letting the wind catch the door and slam it.

18

FIXING IT

"There's nothing we can do!" Kirwan glared at Phoenix as though daring her to defy him. She'd washed in the remnants of tepid water left by the campers and dressed in clean clothes. Kylie's predicament had strengthened her restorative mentality. She'd somehow help Kylie and free the refugees. It seemed unthinkable to leave both situations broken. Kylie's plight would take thought, but the refugees needed food and water for an immediate easing of their circumstances. A bolt cutter would provide a permanent solution for the heavy padlock imprisoning them.

"We can't just leave them there," Phoenix argued. She glanced across at Tina as she set up a rope for a game of Tug of War. "It's baking hot outside, so it must be unbearable for Elephant and the others cooped up in the barn with no fresh air and nothing to drink."

"You don't know they have nothing to drink. You're just guessing." Kirwan shook his head and his brown hair rustled. His warm breath felt like a caress against Phoenix's cheek.

She gritted her jaw and exhibited her mother's familiar determination. "You heard what those men said. They're running out of water. I'm not leaving them," she declared. "I need to help."

Kirwan's lips curled back in a sneer. "What will you do, rich girl? Will you try to call Daddy again? Perhaps he can send in his men and rescue the refugees. Give them new lives and new identities and earn a lifetime's gratitude."

Phoenix's head reared back at the familiar, disparaging mantra. She glared at Kirwan. "You know nothing about my family," she snarled. "It's all myths and legends."

"I've heard enough," declared Kirwan. His eyes narrowed into an expression of victory at having pressed Phoenix's buttons. "Do you honestly think your father's reputation hasn't reached Auckland yet? I know enough about the criminal underworld to be familiar with the name Du Rose."

Phoenix lifted her hands and shoved Kirwan's shoulder. "Liar!" she shouted. "You know nothing!"

"Hey, hey, what's going on here?" Gus approached them with a frown and Phoenix gritted her teeth.

"Nothing," she replied. Gus looked from one to the other and his shoulders hunched. His tee shirt didn't quite tuck into his shorts, revealing a rounded hill of flesh covered in dark, hairy grass.

"You can cut the air between you with a knife," he said. "What's going on?" Gimlet eyes stared from Phoenix to Kirwan and back again.

Kirwan swallowed. "I said something about her family she didn't like," he admitted. He directed his next sentence to Phoenix. "I'll stay away from you." He shoved his hands into his pockets and strode away towards the bathrooms.

The flicker of irritation in Phoenix's brain grew to overwhelming levels. A voice in her head told her he should stay away from her permanently. Her heart cried something different. But she said nothing, offering Grant a smile of regret before retreating to the kitchen.

Phoenix didn't abandon her concern for the refugees or her decision to help them in their plight. Volunteering to clear up alone after dinner while the others played a card game around the fire, she put the food scraps into a plastic box. The discarded sandwiches had already wrinkled in the baking heat and she hid them in the shade beneath the building, pulling a tarpaulin over the box. She remembered the contents of Kirwan's pockets the night before and contemplated the mindset which prompted him to steal stores for his uncertain future. A readiness to flee hung around him like a shroud.

Setting out as dusk embraced the camp, Phoenix attempted to find the path back to the barn. She cursed herself for just following Kirwan and not logging her own landmarks. She wandered for an hour before hearing the leaders calling her name. Slipping back into the camp, she hid the plastic box back under the kitchen hut and appeared by the fire. She received a thorough and embarrassing scolding from Gus.

"You're meant to set an example," he said. Disappointment shrouded his face. "The younger kids might copy you."

"I'm sorry." Phoenix swallowed and stared at her boots. "The sound of the sea made me miss home. I thought I might sleep better if I visited the beach before bedtime."

Peering beneath her eyelashes, she saw the frown cross Kirwan's face and knew he'd guessed her mission. Gus cleared his throat and waited until she looked up at him. The younger children giggled from their cabins, but the older ones gathered around the campfire held their collective breath. The air buzzed with a peculiar pregnancy as they waited to see what might happen to Phoenix. She'd pushed a boundary and needed to suffer a consequence.

"See me in the morning," Gus snapped. "We'll talk about it then. I need to speak to the other leaders about your punishment. You broke a rule, Phoenix. No wandering off alone."

"Especially not after dark," Tina added. She frowned and Phoenix felt her confusion radiate across the metres between them. A flicker of satisfaction travelled up her spine as a tingle of pleasure. She'd burst Tina's bubble and proved they weren't alike at all.

The campers released their breaths with a whoosh of disappointment at their denial of the public flogging they craved. Phoenix went to bed early, listening to the giggles and chatter of the younger girls in her cabin as they settled down to sleep. She lay in silence, miserable at having made no difference to the refugees but having marked herself out as a troublemaker along the way. It hurt that she'd also alienated herself from Kirwan, although his attitude towards her father both perplexed and angered her.

Phoenix woke in the darkness, a sense of alarm unsettling her spirit. The waning moon provided a little light through a gap in the curtains, but not enough to illuminate the shapes in the room. She lay with her nose to the wall and froze as movement sounded nearby. Trying not to creak the mattress or rustle the blankets, she rolled over on the top bunk and strained her eyes against the darkness. A hand slid over her mouth and squeezed her lips closed. *Not again.*

"Don't scream," Kirwan hissed. "Come outside with me."

His hand disappeared and she heard the click of the cabin door closing.

Slipping from her bed, Phoenix pushed her feet into her boots, determined to go better prepared this time. She didn't stop to fasten the zips. As she snatched up her fleece, she reached under the bed and pulled out the plastic box filled with leftovers which she'd moved on her way back from the bathroom.

The plastic bottom swished against the floorboards and she froze, desperate for her second fumbled attempt at finding the refugees to succeed. Kirwan's clandestine visit and his urgency suggested he might help her and her heart gave a flutter of gladness. No one stirred within the cabin, the girls remaining sound asleep despite the disturbance. Lexi snored in the bunk across from her. She gave a grunt and turned to face the wall.

Phoenix slipped from the room, clutching her fleece and the plastic box. Kirwan met her on the deck and closed the door behind her with a soft click. Phoenix opened her mouth to greet him and he shook his head in the moonlight. Glossy highlights appeared in his hair with the movement. Placing a finger over his lips, he reinforced the command for silence. A jerk of his head indicated Phoenix should fasten her boots. She slipped off the deck and onto the dirt outside, not wanting to make sounds that might echo through the cabin.

Phoenix struggled with her boot zips, at the same time battling to keep the plastic box tucked under her left arm. Kirwan reached down and took it from her. He made no comment about her decision to risk following him into the darkness again. Phoenix hauled her fleece tighter around her shoulders and wriggled her arms into its warmth. Then she followed Kirwan towards the end of the camp site and the desperate people group hidden just beyond its reach.

<h1 style="text-align:center">19</h1>

PEOPLE ARE PEOPLE

Kirwan walked ahead with confidence, picking his way along a route familiar to him. He kept the plastic box under his left arm, showing no concern that the sandwiches and cake mingled because of the careless angle. Phoenix used her Du Rose wiliness this time, laying her own hidden tracks as she followed Kirwan. Her deft fingers left an unnoticeable trail of devastation which would have made her father frown in irritation. Picking bushes and trees at waist height, she bent and snapped small twigs and branches as she passed, knowing the die off would create a path of death for her to follow in the future. She doubted anyone else would notice unless they knew what to look for. The traffickers hadn't sounded like experienced bushmen as they'd crashed around the undergrowth.

Phoenix's continual pauses eventually grated on Kirwan's nerves and he turned to her with a frown. "What's your problem?" he hissed. "You're making enough noise to wake the dead!"

Phoenix narrowed her eyes and jutted her chin upwards in defiance. The moon slipped from behind a grey cumulus cloud and turned her eyes to glittering jewels. "My ngā mate sleep just fine!" she bit. "Worry about your own tangata whenua."

Kirwan rolled his eyes and took a step back towards her. He bent close, his warm breath coasted over her cheeks. Phoenix smelled toothpaste and cigarettes, blinking against the expected rebuke. Instead, he used his free hand to lift her chin. "You're beautiful when you're angry," he growled. His hard kiss left Phoenix breathless and gasping for air. An apple clanked against the inside of the box beneath Kirwan's arm as it tilted. He turned and continued his progress as though he hadn't detonated a bomb in her insides. Phoenix followed, her steps less sure and the gap growing between her trail of snapped twigs.

The timber barn loomed through the trees as Kirwan halted and Phoenix walked into the back of him. She grunted and released the bent frond she'd snapped with her fingers. Turning, he fixed his hand around the back of her neck and pushed her down to squat on the dusty ground. "Quiet," he whispered. "Let's listen for a minute." He laid the plastic box on the earth and slid it beneath the undergrowth, stopping the moon's glare off the white lid. When he settled onto his backside, he pulled Phoenix into him. "I'm sorry I upset you." His lips pressed a kiss against her temple. "I didn't mean it about the rich husband and the babies. Don't be mad at me or at what I said about your dad."

Phoenix swallowed and tension crept into her neck, emotional pain starting a dull headache which spread behind her ears. "I don't want to talk about it!" she hissed.

"It's okay." Kirwan tilted her chin with his index finger. "We won't. And I'll help you feed these people, but only if you promise to go out with me."

Phoenix frowned. She gazed around them at the thick undergrowth and the deep shadows emanating from the hard edges of the barn. "Go where?" she whispered. "We are out, aren't we?"

Kirwan grinned, his teeth bright against the darkness. "You crack me up, kid." He swallowed but his irises danced with amusement. "Yeah, we're out." The arm around Phoenix's shoulder slid lower and Kirwan's warm fingers found the hem of her pyjama shirt. They worked their way beneath it, coasting over the waistband of her shorts. His touch against her soft waist sent a tingle of sensation to her brain and she fought the urge to squirm beneath its power. Her stomach dropped as though she'd ventured too high on a swing. She held her breath and turned into Kirwan's caress. Every one of his soft kisses against her throat seemed to burn and she lifted her head to admit more. Heat fired every nerve ending until the sheer rawness set fire to her insides. Kirwan's knee dug into her hip as they sat in their awkward embrace, his shin forming a hard line against her thigh. As she turned further into him, craving more of the sensations created by his kisses, his right hand left a burning trail across her spine and his other hand replaced its spot over her hip. His arms enfolded her in a cage of pure lust and she allowed it, leaning in with a sigh as his lips finished searing a path across her jaw line and settled over her mouth. Her lips parted and Kirwan's tongue flicked like a hungry flame over hers. His left hand edged higher, cradling the soft flesh of her waist and coasting over her ribs until his thumb rested against the naked arc of her breast.

Kirwan's kiss changed, its tempo increasing with an urgency which replaced the open gateway of Phoenix's heart with a wall. In the space of a millisecond, sex with Kirwan went from something she wanted to a monster she needed to escape. Phoenix pulled back with a sharp inhale and Kirwan's grip tightened for long enough to instil fear into her. He regained control over his raging hormones and released her. His irises flickered beneath the weak moonlight and the frenzy faded. "Too fast?" he whispered.

Phoenix nodded, though her brain refused to clarify her muddy thoughts. She didn't know how to answer, a curious surge of adrenaline piping through her blood. Conflict wobbled her chin and her nerves and sinews twitched in a palsy of confusion.

Kirwan frowned and his arm slipped around her shoulder again. "It's fine," he said, though he attempted to turn the sentiment into a reality. He cleared his throat in a sound which conveyed discomfort. "My fault." His side hug seemed to throw Phoenix out of his inner circle and she swallowed and tried not to care. Kirwan pressed a kiss to her temple, but it felt somehow different to any of its predecessors. "Let's check out the barn and see if we can get the food to these people."

Phoenix scrabbled for a hold on his shirt. She pushed herself onto her knees. "We're not just feeding them!" she hissed. Blood still pumped through her veins at an unnatural speed, infusing her with an excess of energy. "We're rescuing them."

"Whoa, what?" Kirwan's head shook from side to side in instant denial. "No, we're not! I want no part of that, thanks. Whoever brought them here will come after us." His voice rose to a squeak still hindered by adolescence. "These people aren't buggering about, Phoenix." His head shook in the darkness, his hair highlighted with silver tips from the moon's light. "We'll give them food but right afterwards, I'm taking you back to camp."

Phoenix frowned while her mind performed flips. An inherited determination rose inside her to obscure all common sense. She was sick of being told what to do but feared if she made a fuss, Kirwan would take her straight back to camp. Phoenix intended to paddle her own canoe, but she'd do it with stealth and cunning. She focused on Kirwan's brawny forearms to give her time to prepare her facial expression and craft it into something suitably contrite. He moved and veins and sinews stood out against his olive skin.

"Ready?" He leaned sideways to whisper into her ear and Phoenix held her breath. A wave of regret washed over her. Wiri would have known she intended to disobey him. He would have read the stubborn tilt of her head and the sparkle in her eyes and just known. It left her hollow to see the lack of guile in Kirwan's expression and not have to negotiate a devious counter measure. Her lips turned down and she sighed, pausing as Kirwan rose and set off through the undergrowth.

"You're no fun," she whispered under her breath and he turned back towards her.

"What?"

"Nothing." She pursed her lips and used the ridged trunk of a tōtara tree to haul herself to a standing position. "Coming."

Kirwan took care approaching the barn. He navigated a wide circle to check all four faces of the rugged timber structure before concluding they could proceed with caution. They picked their way through the darkness to the hole they'd peeked through before, hearing no sound from inside and seeing no movement in the dim interior.

"I can't see anything. Maybe they left." Relief and disappointment mingled in Phoenix's voice as Kirwan nudged her aside to take a turn. Disappointment because she couldn't play the hero. Relief because she didn't need to get involved. He pressed his right eye to the hole and held his breath.

"That's good." Kirwan's voice rose as he ticked a task off a mental list. "One worry less. Maybe now I can stay in bed at night." He winked at her, one eye sparkling in the moonlight as he grinned. His left hand snaked out to cup the back of her neck. Phoenix sensed his affection returning in the gentle squeeze.

"Hello?" The voice hissed from the barn's interior, unexpected and too loud for the night-time hush of the bush canopy. "Hello?" It came again, heavily accented and male.

Phoenix flew backwards with a squeak of terror. Her arms flailed sideways like a tightrope walker as she pitched over and her backside hit the dusty earth. Kirwan grunted as her uncontrolled hand slapped him in the face, but he remained in a dignified squat without toppling. By the time Phoenix picked herself up and scrambled back to the barn's weathered side, Kirwan was already in conversation.

"What's happening?" she asked, her voice croaky with fear. "Who is it?"

Kirwan snorted. "Who do you think? Father Christmas? It's the bloody refugees."

Phoenix blew out a breath through pursed lips. She took a moment to rally her thoughts and absorb the insult. "They kept so quiet I thought they'd gone."

"Really?" Kirwan grinned. "I hadn't noticed."

Phoenix ignored his jibe. "Is there a bigger hole somewhere where we can fit the sandwiches through for them?" She leaned back and tried to inspect the bottom of the barn. Tattered boards hung from support beams along the side and she winced at the thought of fitting her fingers through the gaps. She'd lived on the mountain for long enough to know what creepy crawlies made their homes in crevices.

Kirwan repeated her question and the male voice answered. Phoenix missed the relevant words in the lilting cadence of the man's sentence and followed Kirwan without understanding. "There's a bigger hole near the front doors," Kirwan said, waiting for her before setting off around the second corner. "But don't get any ideas, Phoe. I'm not helping them escape."

"Okay." She followed like an obedient puppy walking to heel until his back turned. She made a rude gesture from her first two fingers and jabbed it into the air behind him. The realisation returned like a stab of pain. Wiri would have expected her to do that and turned at just the right moment to catch her. He would have acted insulted while his grey eyes danced with the thrill of the challenge. The ability to fool Kirwan made life easier, but Phoenix realised she didn't crave ease. "Who knew?" she breathed. "It seems I like a good fight."

Kirwan fed the sandwiches and cake through a letterbox sized hole at the same level as the padlock holding the wide roll doors closed. A decent lock, it hung from the clasp as an impenetrable barrier. Phoenix doubted the camp contained anything grunty enough to break either padlock or clasp, especially not when wielded by her. Her mind formulated and discarded plans on a loop which ran along the same well oiled tracks as her father's analytic brain. Short of finding a tractor and bulldozing the barn, it seemed she would have to admit defeat. Du Roses didn't admit defeat and Phoenix straightened her spine as she passed Kirwan the apple and watched him try to fit it through the narrow hole. It popped through the gap and left a chunk of skin clinging to the wood.

Kirwan chatted to the man in a low voice and others joined the conversation. When the plastic box was empty and all the food pushed through the slot, Phoenix stepped back and leaned against the timber. Her fingers coasted across the knots and ridges, her mind straying elsewhere as the voices dulled to a monotonous hum. Then Kirwan nudged her thigh with his elbow.

Phoenix jumped and searched his face. He hadn't involved her in his conversation. "You'll never guess what?" He stared up at her and Kirwan's voice held a breathless quality. "They're Christians."

"What?" Phoenix pushed away from the wall with a dull thud and squatted next to Kirwan. "Let me listen," she begged, a frantic note in her voice. "Are they, or do they think that's what you want to hear?"

Kirwan shrugged. "Does it matter?" His gaze searched her for any sign of double standards. "People are people, aren't they?" he demanded.

"Yes!" Irritation budded in Phoenix's chest at the veiled accusation. She'd assumed she cared about their plight whether they were Sikhs, Muslims or Buddhists. It bothered her that their claim of kindred Christianity seemed to have piqued her interest more. It revealed an inequality in her values, which she wasn't ready to acknowledge.

Phoenix squashed her biting retort, refusing to grant it airspace. "Do they have food and water?" she asked. "Are they okay?"

Kirwan put his face to the slot and relayed her questions. He paused as the rumbling voice gave the answer. He turned towards her with a nod. "Food and water gets brought to them every night. He says we should leave. The traffickers will arrive soon. He doesn't want them to catch us."

Phoenix gave a nod of acceptance and scrabbled away from the barn. She moved backwards on her knees before rising. "Tell them we'll come back," she insisted. But Kirwan shook his head and refused to comply.

"I'm not making promises I can't keep!" His voice rose, laced with antagonism. Phoenix swallowed, stilled by the vehemence in his eyes. She couldn't bring herself to disobey him so openly. His words were a rebuke which came almost word for word from her father's lips. Logan Du Rose knew pain, neglect and loss. It was the same principle he'd spent his life drilling into his children. He always followed through on his promises even if the result looked somewhat different from the original intention.

Kirwan muttered a goodbye through the gap and a hand appeared from inside the barn. Tears pricked behind Phoenix's eyelids as the fingers stretched outward, her keen eyes seeing dirt beneath the fingernails and knotted, scarred knuckles. Kirwan clasped the hand and gave it a squeeze. Then he turned away, his face a blank mask and his jaw set in determination.

Phoenix followed him, not able to look back at the pitiful sight of a prisoner seeking comfort and assistance while perhaps knowing it wouldn't come.

But it would come. She didn't know how or when, but she'd make sure it did.

20

RULE BREAKERS

Phoenix crawled into the bunk still wearing her boots. A little voice croaked from the darkness as she summited the rickety ladder. "Where did you go?"

"Bathroom," she whispered. "Go back to sleep."

Kylie gave a sigh and her bed creaked. "No, you didn't. I looked for you."

"I did," Phoenix said. Truth backed the certainty in her voice. "I went to the bathroom and checked on Mikaere."

"Oh." Kylie sounded deflated. "You were ages."

"I had to settle him." Phoenix groaned and unzipped her sleeping bag. She draped it over herself like a sheet. "He misses his family and he can't stay in the paddock with the other horses."

"Why?" Kylie raised her voice and Phoenix shushed her and flapped her hands in the darkness.

"He doesn't like strange horses," she hissed. "Please, go to sleep, Kylie."

"Aren't you worried about your punishment?"

"For checking on my horse?" Phoenix struggled to keep the fear from her voice. Kylie could cause her real difficulty with a word to the wrong person.

"No, for wandering off during the campfire. Gus got anxious about you."

"I'll be fine," Phoenix replied with a sigh of exhaustion. "Go to sleep."

She woke a short two hours later to the sound of whispering and her brain went on high alert. Sharon's infectious giggle cut the air like a siren and didn't bode well. Phoenix rolled onto her side and peered through the wooden slats of the top bunk. "What are you doing?" she growled.

"Giving Kylie a trim," Sharon replied. She wielded a pair of pink paper scissors above Kylie's bowed head and lopped off a decent chunk of hair.

"Ouch!" Kylie squeaked. "You tore that out."

"Girls! Stop!" Phoenix pushed her legs over the side of the ladder and slid to the cabin floor. Her boots thudded against the wood but the girls didn't notice. "You don't know what you're doing." She confiscated the scissors with the same dexterity which frustrated Mikaere's sharp teeth. Sharon gave a growl of irritation.

"Tina wants Lexi and Phoenix in the office." An older girl poked her head through the cabin door, a damp towel encasing her black curls. "The boys have used almost all the hot water, girls. I'd get there fast if you don't want a cold shower."

Phoenix thanked her with a nod and released the held breath. The girls piled from the room with squeals of protest, towels draped over their shoulders and wash bags dangling from their fingers. Only Kylie lingered in the doorway, her face drawn into a frown. "Are you worried about your punishment yet?" she asked, her tone loaded with foreboding.

"Nope." Phoenix bent and released the zippers of her boots. She kept her pyjama shorts on and hauled track pants over the top.

Kylie gave an upward tilt of her chin and left, seeming to suck the oxygen from the room with her. Lexi sank onto her mattress. "Shit!"

she exclaimed. She watched Phoenix put her boots back on, though her eyes appeared glazed and unseeing.

Phoenix turned in surprise at the expletive but she uttered no rebuke. Lexi's complexion had acquired a waxy hue. "What's wrong?" Phoenix demanded. "Are you okay?"

"Not sure." Lexi rose and straightened her spine. "Let's find out, shall we?"

Halting steps took the girls onto the porch in front of the office. Lexi lifted a shaking hand to knock on the door. Tina's voice called for them to enter and Lexi turned the handle.

Tina's nondescript features eyed them from above a slice of buttered toast which oozed yellow liquid onto the desk before her. "Good morning girls." Her tone sounded formal which heightened Phoenix's misgivings. "Thank you for coming," she said, not acknowledging their lack of choice in the matter. "I'll deal with Phoenix first." In an action which seemed deliberately timed to extend their agony, Tina shoved the remaining crust of toast into her mouth and forced the girls to wait until she finished chewing. Leaning across her desk, she lifted a mug of cooling tea and took a loud slurp. Phoenix watched the grease pool on Tina's pink lips, reminded of the slugs Wiri once unearthed in the compost heap at home. She gave an involuntary shudder and focused instead on the wonky ordinance survey map replaced on the wall behind Tina's head.

"Gus and I have spoken at length about your tendency to wander." She rested her elbows on the desk and steepled her fingers in front of her face. "It needs to stop. I realise you come from an extensive property and have a free rein there, but your mother signed responsibility for you over to us the moment you reached this camp. You can either abide by our rules for the rest of the week or we can send you home."

Phoenix kept her features schooled into an expressionless mask. She had learned the art from an early age; the Du Rose men providing her with a canvas of expertise. Tina was wrong on two counts. Logan's children never had a free rein on the mountain. And to send Phoenix home, Tina would need to contact her parents, which meant that Grant's contingency was a mobile phone.

Phoenix raised her gaze to meet Tina's stern expression and waited for her punishment to emerge from beneath the threats.

"As it's your first offence, Gus and I have awarded you leniency. And you found Kylie when no one else seemed able. In that case, we've decided that you will clear up after two extra meals. Lunch and dinner today should suffice as a warning to anyone else choosing to copy your behaviour.

Phoenix pursed her lips and attempted a decent expression of contrition, but inside, her stomach contained the rising ball of laughter. Tina's naïve punishment had provided Phoenix with two more opportunities to collect food for the refugees.

Lexi shifted next to her and her elbow brushed Phoenix's side. Sensing she should leave, Phoenix turned. Tina's hand lifted in her peripheral vision. "Stay," she commanded. "This involves you." She sat up straighter in her seat and her lips pursed into a smile of victory. "What are your views on sex before marriage, Lexi?" she demanded.

Phoenix blinked at the unexpectedness of the question and her gaze tracked to the heightened blush of Lexi's cheekbones. Guilt bubbled into her own throat at the memory of Kirwan's urgent kisses. As she jumped into the fray in Lexi's defence, it surprised her to realise she had strayed so far from her own moral code. "I think that's Lexi's business," Phoenix replied. "She's aware of the camp rules regarding fraternisation."

A look of satisfaction settled over Tina's narrow features. Her nose hung in her round face like a beak. She directed her next sentence to Phoenix. "I have it on good authority that Lexi left her bunk last night and has engaged in a relationship with a boy." Tina's gaze shifted to Lexi. "Someone reported it to me this morning and it's fortunate for you, young lady, that I don't have a more reliable witness. In all our years of running this camp, we have never yet sent a camper home pregnant. The rules exist for a reason. Let this be your first and only warning, Lexi. Flout the rules at your own risk."

A flap of Tina's hand indicated they should leave and the girls shuffled from the office in silence. Once outside on the deck, Lexi released a gigantic sigh of relief and opened her mouth to speak. Phoenix gave a frantic shake of her head and raised a finger to her lips. A jerk of her head silenced Lexi until they reach the safety of their empty cabin. Still not content, Phoenix checked under the beds before releasing her own sigh.

"I thought for a minute there you'd grassed me up," Lexi said. Her knees buckled and she sank onto the bed. Phoenix's eyes widened in horror.

"I didn't think you'd actually done it!" she gasped. Shock sent her spiralling backwards until she found Kylie's bed behind her knees. She sank onto the mattress and dropped her head into her hands. Lexi's revelation meant the sleeping girls had been alone for part of the night with both their leaders engaged in illicit activity. Sickness roiled in Phoenix's gut, dispelling any notion of breakfast.

"It's fine," Lexi protested. "I met Josh and we hung out at the beach." Her eyebrows narrowed into a manicured line. "I wonder how Tina found out."

Phoenix ran a shaking hand across her face. "She said someone told her. That means someone else saw you, but she said they weren't a reliable source, so it couldn't have been a leader. It must have been another camper."

Lexi grimaced. "Well, I hope they didn't see everything," she said. "We did it twice in the sand dunes and once in the surf." Her teeth grazed her full lower lip as she tried and failed to suppress a grin. "Someone had an in-depth lesson in the birds and bees."

"Just think yourself lucky they didn't have a mobile phone with them!" Phoenix bit.

Lexi winced. "Yeah. It would have made a brilliant porno movie, but given my father another reason to send me to live with my mum."

Phoenix closed her eyes and gave a slight shake of her head. Her night time jaunts with Kirwan made her unable to stand in judgement on Lexi's behaviour. It wasn't a familiar stance, having always viewed life from the balcony of the castle of Higher-Moral-Ground. Phoenix's change in status left her floundering and ill-equipped to deal with the glint in Lexi's eyes which told her she would do it again.

Phoenix rose on trembling legs and grabbed her wash bag. "Take the girls to breakfast," she ordered. "Then I'll come back and lead morning prayers while you take a shower." Phoenix headed for the door, stopped in her tracks by Lexi's last comment.

"We washed in the sea last night."

Phoenix heard the grin in her voice and stepped out onto the porch, closing the door behind her. Just a few short weeks ago, the chatter of her classmates as they detailed their sexual exploits had repulsed her. Phoenix Du Rose had set herself apart from their base human drives and stationed herself with the angels in pursuit of higher goals. But that was before Wiri's confession, before Kirwan's kiss and before the awakening of the terrifying and uncontrollable fire in her belly.

Phoenix gripped her wash bag to her stomach as though the external pressure might lessen the turmoil within her. The girls from her cabin clattered from the bathroom amid a hail of giggles as Phoenix arrived. She drowned out their efforts to communicate whatever stupid thing Sharon had done in the bathroom to bark orders at them. "Lexi's waiting for you in the cabin. It's breakfast time. Hurry."

To Phoenix's chagrin, Kylie hung back from the group. Her hair hung down her back in wet tresses, her ponytail wonky from Sharon's impromptu hairdressing. It created a damp stain on the back of her tee shirt. "What punishment did Tina give you?" she demanded. "Is it bad?" Despite the youthfulness of her features, her eyes revealed the psyche of a much older person. A devilment Phoenix hadn't noticed before sparked behind her irises.

Phoenix swallowed, uncertain of what she'd seen but governed by the sense of fear it created. She picked her answer with care. "It's sucky," she said. "They're making me clear up alone after two meals today."

Delight budded in Kylie's face. "You'll miss campfire time tonight then," she concluded. The machinations showed in her face as she made plans to sit next to Kirwan during the singing. She hadn't yet learned the art of hiding her motives, but Phoenix sensed that would come with age and experience.

She nodded. "I'm sure Kirwan will find someone else to sit next to," she concluded. "Maybe even you." Phoenix forced her lips into a smile while suspecting Kylie knew far too much about the previous night's activities. She'd noticed Phoenix's absence but might have told Tina about Lexi's. She fit the description of a less than reliable source and Phoenix sensed the walls closing in on her goal to liberate the refugees.

As Kylie wandered across the scrubby lawn towards the cabin, Tina approached from the office. She raised a hand to get Phoenix's attention, denying her the ability to escape while pretending she hadn't seen her. "There you are," Tina said. "I just wanted to compliment you on how you accepted your punishment this morning. I could see from your expression that you hadn't realised Lexi was missing during the night."

Phoenix nodded, relieved at how easy it was dealing with the truth instead of the litany of lies she'd built around herself. "No, but I would agree with your assessment of Kylie as an unreliable source." She studied Tina's expression, noting with satisfaction how the other woman's lips tightened.

"Quite," Tina agreed. Then her eyes narrowed, revealing the sharp featured slyness of a fox. "But Lexi won't get away with it again." She tapped the side of her nose, indicating she had a plan to thwart the junior leader's sex life.

To Phoenix's disappointment, she revealed nothing more, turning on her heel and striding towards the enticing scent of bacon coming from the dining room.

21

CHASE

Morning devotions left Phoenix wrung out and confused. The girls asked questions which caused her to delve into the deepest recesses of her memory to recall Pastor Sam's wise teaching. The more she agonised, the more she realised her knowledge of God was filtered through the lens of those around her. She wondered if she knew her own version of God at all.

"Does God wear pants?" Sharon bounced on her mattress with her bible balanced on her head. When challenged, she reasoned the good Lord wanted her to have better posture. "Jesus wore a dress."

"It's not a dress." Lexi frowned and looked to Phoenix for clarification. She shrugged and stared at a knot in the wooden floorboards, wondering if prayer would make it open up and swallow her. Then she thought of Kirwan and all hope of praying disappeared. She was a sinner and had classed herself with those she'd once thought of as bound for Hell. Like Lexi, who went to the beach to have sex with a junior leader. Her shoulders slumped further.

"I don't have Google," Phoenix concluded. "I can search for it when I get home and email you."

"Doesn't matter, anyway." The mattress creaked with Sharon's energetic bouncing. "I'd rather imagine him like a big, fluffy cloud."

"Why?" Carrie's question sent a wince careening across Phoenix's features. Sharon wasn't the best candidate to answer something deep and meaningful.

Sharon's eyes bugged and her lips turned downward in a fish-face. "Because then he can't get me, can he? The worst he can do is rain on me."

Kylie's jaw hung slack and she inhaled in a hiss. "He can!" she exclaimed. She reached out and touched Sharon's arm just as the girl descended to the mattress at the tail end of an uncontrolled bounce. "He can strike you with lightning. It happened to someone my mum knew."

Bounce. Wail. Blood.

The bible shot from Sharon's head and landed in her lap, hitting her on the nose and chin as she tilted her head to stop its fall. Obviously, she blamed Kylie, the mattress and everyone else in the room instead of taking responsibility. Lexi confiscated the bible while Phoenix found tissues for the blood. She squeezed Kylie's shoulder in sympathy.

Sharon silenced at someone's unhelpful suggestion that the Holy Trinity might wander around Heaven naked. It spawned a whole new conversational direction which the leaders still hadn't shut down by the time they reached the tack shed.

Phoenix gave an inward groan at the sight of Tina leaning against the gate to the main paddock. She held a hard hat and a riding crop and jerked her head towards Mikaere. "I thought I'd give your horse a try," she said, a veiled challenge in her eyes.

Phoenix sensed the prickle of Lexi's curious gaze burning into the side of her face and kept her expression bland. "Go right ahead," she heard herself say, although it wasn't the sentence she had planned. *That* sentence included significant warnings about Mikaere's dislike of humanity and his reluctant tolerance for people with the surname Du Rose. Namely, Phoenix and her father. One he put up with and the other he'd learned he couldn't defeat. Those Du Roses, to be specific.

"Give me your tack," Tina demanded. She fluffed her chest like a bantam and strung the chin strap of her riding hat over the gate post. Phoenix raised an eyebrow and stepped into the shed where she retrieved her expensive, embroidered leather saddle and the lunge rope she attached to Mikaere's head collar.

"Where's your bridle?" Tina's forehead crumpled into a series of lines. She cocked her head like a bird.

"I didn't bring one." Phoenix swallowed, sensing the atmosphere change.

"Of course, you brought a bridle!" Tina wiggled her fingers as though Phoenix could conjure one up from mid-air.

She shook her head, her curls bouncing against her spine. "I didn't," she replied. "I don't need a bridle or a saddle. We ride bare foot and bit-less at home."

"Barefoot and bit-less." Sharon sniggered. She leaned sideways to look at Phoenix's feet and her brow furrowed at the sight of her boots. It seemed pointless telling her it meant the horse remained unshod. Biting back her retort, Phoenix lifted the heavy Western saddle, taking its weight across both arms. It represented so much of who she'd become and where she'd originated. Her father had commissioned it for Mikaere's wilful mother, paying an exorbitant price for the handmade craftsmanship. Embroidery covered the skirt of the tan saddle, made darker over the years by constant polishing with saddle soap. He'd given it to Hana along with the horse and it had grown dusty in the tack shed after Sacha's exile. He'd had the inner tree altered to fit Mikaere and the legacy gift had both thrilled and terrified Phoenix. It pained her to heft it over Tina's unworthy forearms and she wished she hadn't brought it.

Lexi drew close enough to whisper in Phoenix's ear. "I thought no one else could ride your horse."

The campers turned to watch Phoenix's expression. Five pairs of eyes focussed on her reaction. She forced brightness into her tone and widened her eyes at Lexi. "There's a first time for everything," she said, her tone bright. It satisfied the younger girls but Lexi clamped her teeth down on her lower lip and disappeared into the tack shed to release the inappropriate snort.

Twenty minutes. Phoenix decided it had to be a world record. Many people had tried to catch Mikaere over the last couple of years and they all admitted defeat faster than the camp leader. As the sun beat down on Tina's red face, Lexi debated sending a girl back to camp for the first aid kit. "She looks like she's gonna blow," she whispered to Phoenix. Sweat created dark patches on the back of Tina's pink tee shirt and collected beneath her armpits.

Phoenix shrugged. "She's the first aider. I'm not sure she'd know what to do with a respirator even if we had one." Her deft fingers tightened the girth on Kylie's mount. She tapped the girl's skinny calf to ask her to lift her leg. "I need to shorten your stirrups," she said. Kylie nodded and moved her leg, allowing Phoenix to lift the skirt and release the stirrup buckle. Like the other girls, Kylie didn't remove her gaze from the sight of Tina trying to outwit the cunning gelding.

Mikaere knew all the tricks. Logan figured Sacha had given him a detailed rundown before she presented her foal to the family. He possessed every facet of his mother's devious nature plus whatever his mysterious sire had bestowed on him. He served as a constant challenge to Phoenix's restorative nature; Mikaere was the one thing that resisted all her efforts to fix him. He liked himself just the way he was.

Tina turned towards the gate, her blonde hair stuck to her head in a frizzy haze. Lexi snorted. "I hope that's not her profile picture on Christian Mingle." She giggled and Phoenix looked away to avoid revealing her growing hysteria to the campers. She'd spent most of the time trying to ignore Tina's antics, certain if she started laughing, she'd find it impossible to stop. Mikaere finished another circuit of his paddock, arrogance giving him perfect conformation. Phoenix hid her pride behind the brim of her cowboy hat as he shook his head in disgust and kept his unshod hooves moving in a fluid gait. His trot flowed with ease, diagonal pairs cutting through the grass like shears through butter. His stubby Appaloosa tail stuck upright in the air like a dog's and his lips drew back from his teeth as though he found the whole thing hilarious. Which he did.

Phoenix turned her attention to Lexi's horse, helping her to tack up and holding the offside stirrup while she mounted. Lexi jerked her head towards the girls. "We're all ready," she said. "What should we do?"

"I'm bored now." Sally sighed and lay back along her horse's spine. Her reins hung like washing lines and Phoenix winced as her horse took advantage of her lapse in control and dipped his head to eat grass.

"I'm not washing that bit when it's covered in pulp," Lexi commented. "Get up, Sally. If he bolts, you're toast."

"I'm not sure what to do." Phoenix pursed her lips and watched Tina creep up to a grazing Mikaere. The blue wall eye he'd inherited from Sacha rolled in his head and Phoenix held her breath. "He's getting fed up and that's when the real trouble starts."

"I don't think she's gonna catch him." Sharon shortened her reins and moved her horse to face the same direction as the others. Sally did a great impression of a beached turtle as she tried to haul herself upright again.

"You're not nice to Tina." Kylie's rebuke came as a surprise. "She just wants the best for everyone." Her voice held a hint of pique and Lexi frowned and got eye contact with Phoenix. Her lips tightened as she reached the same conclusion Phoenix had after her earlier conversation with Tina. When nobody answered, Kylie stuck her nose in the air. "Tina's got a surprise for everyone later." She looked from Phoenix to Lexi and a smile touched her lips. "Some of you aren't going to like it."

Tina dragged herself to the fence and clung to it with white-knuckled fingers. "That's a very disobedient horse," she panted. "I don't think he should be here."

Phoenix's eyes narrowed as she absorbed the insult on Mikaere's behalf. "Why is that?" she demanded.

"He's unpredictable. I gave up after the second time he tried to bite me. He's not safe around the campers." Tina raised an index finger and pointed it at the spare horse Phoenix had tacked and tied to the fence. "I'll take Georgia today." She relinquished her sweaty hold on the lunge rope, lifted her foot and placed her boot sole on the bottom rung of the fence. Her chest heaved with heat and exertion and she thought better of it, deciding instead to walk across Mikaere's paddock and through the adjoining gate.

Phoenix ground her teeth and hopped over the fence with little effort. She retrieved the saddle blanket from the ground where it blew during Tina's marathon and trapped it beneath the saddle. Then she raised two fingers to her lips and blew out a whistle. Mikaere's head lifted and he shook his mane as though considering the request. Then he turned his half ton body and strolled towards Phoenix.

The campers gave a collective inhale of awe and Phoenix tamped down her sense of elation. As Mikaere blew grass seed from his wide nostrils, he tossed his head and snorted. Phoenix fixed her teeth over her lower lip, letting the pleasure of success blossom outwards from her belly. She waited until the horse got close enough to run her hand over his forehead and slip her fingers through his head collar. Leaning close, so he could scent her mood from her breath, she praised him. "Good lad," she whispered. "Thanks for not embarrassing me." She pressed a kiss to the soft fur over his cheek and led him towards the fence.

"She's a horse whisperer!" Carrie gushed. "I knew it."

Tina humphed. The lunge rope showed imprints from the grip of Tina's sweaty fingers and Phoenix fixed it to the metal ring beneath Mikaere's chin. She laid the rope over his withers. His skin gave a mechanical twitch beneath the soft touch.

Tina stamped off to mount Georgia, hauling the saddle sideways on the unfortunate mare's back as she clambered into position. Deciding not to push her luck by riding bareback, Phoenix settled the blanket and saddle over Mikaere's withers and fastened the girth. She left it loose, but not swinging as her father preferred.

A last check of Mikaere's feet and legs set Tina tutting in exasperation. Phoenix regretted not running a curry comb over his stomach and flanks. "I'll do it when we get back," she promised, springing onto the top rung of the wooden fence. She swung her leg over the horse, grateful when he didn't play his favourite game and move forward or sideways to embarrass her. Settling into the saddle, she sensed the familiar oneness of horse and rider, each plugging into the other along an emotional connection. Phoenix leaned forward and patted Mikaere's neck, thankful she at least had one ally, even if it might prove temporary.

"Lexi, open the gate please?" Tina called over her shoulder.

"What?" Lexi's eyes widened in question. "Aren't we just riding in the arena?"

"No. We're hacking to the beach." Tina dug her heels into Georgia's side and Phoenix blew out a nervous breath. As Kylie's horse followed close behind Tina's, it demonstrated the child's complete lack of control by snatching at a nearby crop of grass. Kylie's body tilted forward and she clutched a handful of mane in white-knuckled fingers.

"Welcome to today's shit show," Lexi muttered beneath her breath. She jerked her head towards the gate on her side of the fence. "Meet you there," she said with emphasis.

Phoenix hustled Mikaere to his gate, opening and closing it without dismounting. She met the string of riders on the other side and opened their gate before Lexi arrived.

"Hope you've got experience with heart attacks, head injuries and broken bones," Lexi mouthed as she reached Phoenix. She turned at the last minute to avoid Tina's mare as Georgia stampeded through the opening. The riders passed and Phoenix edged Mikaere towards the metal gate, using his shoulders to nudge it closed. She leaned down and clasped the catch.

Phoenix sat up and dropped the rope onto Mikaere's neck. "I don't have any medical training." She winced. "Maybe Tina brought the first aid kit. It's in the health and safety regulations." She clicked her tongue and Mikaere set off at a smart walk.

Lexi snorted with laughter behind her. "Which part of this camp fulfils any legal requirements? Hey, staying mounted to open gates is a neat party trick."

"It's not a party trick." Phoenix turned in the saddle to smile at Lexi. "Our property has over a hundred gates spread across two hundred hectares. Papa would get pretty fed up at the waste of time if all the stock hands dismounted for every single one. Time is money."

"I guess." Lexi sighed. "Your place sounds amazing."

Mikaere chose that moment to snake his head around as a warning to Lexi's gelding to stay away from his rear. The horse jerked his head upward and backed off enough to avoid Mikaere's dinner plate hooves. Lexi heaved out a sigh as Tina picked up speed ahead, her troop of followers bouncing around in their saddles like rag dolls. "What is she playing at?" she huffed.

Phoenix shrugged. "No idea. It seems crazy to me." She frowned and tilted her cowboy hat, so the brim protected her eyes from the sun rays dappling through the canopy. "I wonder what Kylie meant about Tina having a surprise we wouldn't like."

Lexi released a groan which caused Phoenix to turn around in the saddle. "Do you know what she's planned?"

Lexi closed her eyes and gave a nod. "Maybe. I think I've guessed. You'll be fine but it will ruin my life for sure."

22

HACKS & HORSES

The hack was not only a health and safety nightmare, but a disaster of epic proportions. Tina moved too fast through the undergrowth and added a few ill-timed jumps for the girls to pop over on their hectic progression through the bush. It resulted in two falls after a clatter between Sharon's chin and a low-hanging branch and three separate cases of extreme hysterics.

Lexi and Phoenix brought up the rear like a pair of road sweepers minimising hurricane damage. "Someone should run a book and take bets on this," Lexi grunted. She shoved a reluctant Kylie back into the saddle and patted her knee. "Wipe your nose on your sleeve," she said, her sympathy extended beyond breaking point. Lexi grinned at Phoenix as she vaulted back onto her horse. Sharon clambered up alone amid grumbling and complaints. "I bet you ten bucks we have another three falls before we reach the beach." She cocked her head and held out her hand for Phoenix to shake.

"No." Phoenix frowned. "I don't gamble."

Lexi withdrew her hand and tossed her hair in an irritated tic. "You're boring. Anyone ever tell you that?"

"Lots of people," Phoenix replied, an air of resignation in her tone. "But rules are there for a reason. The alternative is anarchy."

Lexi wrinkled her nose and rolled her eyes. "You sound like a fifty-year-old man. I bet your dad is a rule follower, isn't he?"

Phoenix smiled and thought of her powerhouse of a father. She missed him in that moment with a tangible ache in her soul. Missed him and missed the whenua; the land they both loved so much. "No," she replied with honesty. "My father makes the rules. He doesn't always follow them."

"My stomach hurts." Kylie released an exaggerated moan and bent double in the saddle. "I want to go back to camp now."

"My head hurts worse." Sharon rubbed at a bruise beneath her chin. Her lips turned upward in pride though the action made her wince. "Does this look terrible? Will people feel sorry for me?"

"Definitely." Lexi pressed her heels to the rounded stomach of her horse and guided the gelding back towards the track. She left Phoenix to round up the stragglers.

"Let's get to the beach and see how you feel." Phoenix addressed Kylie and forced a smile onto her lips. "We'll tell Tina and maybe she'll let us ride back before the others."

"She won't," Lexi called over her shoulder. "You need a helper for every one and a half campers. That's the ratio. Gus said."

Kylie's eyes widened. "One and a half? I don't want to be a half."

Phoenix groaned. "It's just maths. Don't worry about it." She turned Mikaere in a circle behind Kylie's horse, a familiar satisfaction bubbling in her chest as her gelding's combative nature meant the mare didn't resist. She picked up her hooves and crashed through the undergrowth after Lexi. Sharon trotted her horse until she reached the front of the string and pushed onto the track ahead of them.

"Wait!" Lexi called. "We don't know where the others went."

After a fifteen-minute walk, interspersed with haphazard periods of light trotting, the little group emerged from the darkness of the canopy to a swathe of black sand. It glittered in the sunlight like a billion tiny diamonds hid among the iron ore. Lexi shielded her eyes and saw the other riders splashing in the sea. Mikaere lifted his head and snorted with excitement. His body tensed beneath Phoenix, the muscles bunching and storing energy ready for his lurch into the ocean.

Phoenix hated suppressing his enthusiasm, but she lifted the rope off his withers and used her seat to keep him under control. Rebelling, he arched his neck and jogged backwards. His wall eye flashed as he arced his body into a reversed circle to get to the water without open disobedience.

Kylie's eyes resembled light-coloured saucers as she watched Tina canter through the surf. "I'm not doing that," she stated.

"No one will force you." Phoenix gave her a reassuring smile. "We can just walk through the water. It's good for the horses' legs. Follow me." She clicked her tongue against her soft palate and Mikaere lurched forward, his front hooves dancing on the spot. Kylie's mare grew edgy at his naked excitement and steered away from him. Phoenix sensed Mikaere's frustration building and called out to Lexi. "Please can you stay with Kylie for a minute? I need to just let Mikaere splash for a second or he'll play up like this the whole time."

"Okay. We'll take turns." Lexi doubled back to stand with Kylie, her horse avoiding the reach of Mikaere's dangerous rear hooves.

The second Phoenix relaxed the rope onto the horse's neck, he lurched forward like a runner released from the blocks. He sped towards the water with a snort of glee and hit the surf with a series of excited bounces. Phoenix kept her seat as he gave three hearty bucks, but she almost lost it when he reared and pawed the air with his front hooves. "Enough!" she shouted. A white ear flicked towards her in response, but he shook his head in defiance and pawed the surf with his hooves. "Why do you always ruin things?" She turned him in a tight circle to prevent him bunching power into his back legs. Driving him round with her inside leg, she wasted some of his energy with a lesson in obedience. Water kicked up around them, soaking the legs of Phoenix's shorts and creating darker patches on the saddle. The flow of the tide expended Mikaere's enthusiasm and his pace slowed to a steady trot. Phoenix changed direction, pushing him into a lazy figure of eight until he shook his mane and released a sigh which demonstrated his acquiescence. "Why do you always make everything into a battle?" Phoenix grumbled. She slowed him to a walk and released the tension in her gut, forcing herself to send thoughts of relaxation and peace through their tenuous connection. "Perhaps one day you'll just follow the rules and stop fighting." She heard herself say the words out loud and recognised the futility of their sentiment. Mikaere would spend his life fighting as his mother did before him. Sacha had both loved and hated with passion. Mikaere would follow her lead.

"You took your time." Tina trotted her horse through the surf towards Phoenix and her voice carried on the breeze.

Phoenix remained stationary and let Mikaere paw the sand beneath his feet.

"Kylie fell off and Sharon lost a fight with a tree branch," she replied, keeping her voice free of condemnation. "Some of these girls aren't competent riders."

Tina frowned. Her horse refused to move any closer to Mikaere and she paused in the surf like someone stopping for a brief conversation on the stairs. "I forgot they're not all intermediate riders." Her eyes narrowed. "There should be repercussions. Their carers signed the forms."

Phoenix nodded and gave a nonchalant shrug. "If someone wants to do something badly enough, they'll exaggerate their abilities. Tourists do it all the time at home."

"What do you mean?" Tina's horse crunched on her bit and stretched her head lower to sniff the water.

"My father started a trekking company as part of the hotel business. It keeps the stables busy when it's not serving the stock horses. He uses a station-bred stallion to get good trekking horses and trains them himself during the winter when he has more time. We had few accidents when people lied about their capabilities."

Tina winced. "Did they sue your father for damages?" She sounded concerned, like someone who'd been on the end of a lawsuit.

"No." Phoenix shook her head. "Everyone signs a waiver and they ride at their own risk." Her lips curved upwards and her admiration for her father shone from her grey irises. "Papa's smart. He always says they must get up real early to catch him."

A smile cracked Tina's lips into an unfamiliar expression. "I think I'd like your father," she admitted.

Phoenix seized on her sudden good humour to make the request she'd been allowing to play at the back of her mind. Her voice sounded breathless and Mikaere fidgeted beneath her. "I have a favour to ask from you," she ventured. "Is it possible to borrow Grant's emergency phone for a few minutes when we get back?"

"Why?" Tina's expression soured. "This is a technology free camp. You know the rules." Her eyes widened as she realised her error in acknowledging the phone's existence. She cleared her throat to give her time to think. "Grant has a contingency for desperate measures. I never said it was a telephone. If we let you contact home, then we need to do it for anyone else who asks. It's not fair to have different rules for different people." She wagged her finger at Phoenix as though speaking to a toddler.

Phoenix nodded and avoided Tina's gaze as she told the lie. The words seemed to burn her lips. "My Poppa Alfie just celebrated his eighty-eighth birthday and he's had a few health problems. I'd like to ring my papa and just check he's okay." Phoenix kept the lie vague. Apart from the arthritis which had turned Poppa Alfie's body into a pretzel, his worse health issue was the constant earache from his opinionated wife's nagging.

Tina's expression softened. "You mentioned that once before and I let you use the office phone." She didn't acknowledge that it hadn't worked. "Grant keeps the location of the emergency device a secret, even from the leaders. He doesn't want anyone tempted. There is a short-range radio, but that won't help you. It doesn't reach beyond the beach. It's a pity the office phone is so unreliable. The telecom company think lightning hit the telegraph pole over the winter." She shrugged. "Sorry. I'm sure everything is fine back home. We'll put him on our prayer list. How's that?" Without waiting for an answer, she opened her reins and turned her horse into a wide circle. Georgia's front feet kicked up black sand in the foaming surf as she trotted back to the group.

Phoenix walked Mikaere to where Lexi waited with Kylie. With a whoop of pleasure which spooked Kylie's horse, Lexi cantered into the sea until the water touched her girth. Mikaere sighed and watched her antics with interest as the horse splashed along the foreshore. Phoenix turned to smile at Kylie. "I'm sorry you're not enjoying this," she said. "Would you like to walk along the beach for a little while? I'll stay with you."

"Okay." Kylie's expression brightened. "I'd like that."

They walked side by side, Kylie's horse leaving a healthy distance between herself and Mikaere. The sun beat down on the girls' backs and turned any exposed skin a mottled pink in the first warning of sunburn. Phoenix pushed her Jillaroo hat off her head and let the cord keep it safe against her shoulder blades. She ran her wrist over her sweating brow. Kylie watched her action and dipped forward as she spoke. "Why don't you wear a riding hat?"

Phoenix shrugged. "I used to when I was younger. But the stock men don't wear them and I hated being different." She tapped the cord at her throat. As though to rebuke her, the bruise behind her ear gave a dull throb. "My mother lent me this hat. It once belonged to my Kuia Miriam, so it's old."

"Kuia? Is that a grandmother or an aunty?"

"She was my grandmother." Phoenix blinked and thought about Logan's mother. The hat provided the only point of reference, Miriam's body charred in a fire which ended her life only hours before Phoenix's began.

Kylie nodded. "It's a nice hat." She offered the compliment along with a smile. And a confession. "I'm sorry I told Tina about Lexi. She's having sex with Josh. If she gets pregnant, she'll end up with a baby and not want it. That's what happened to my mum."

Phoenix nodded, but no ready answer presented itself. Kylie possessed a knack for pushing her into conversations which made her uncomfortable. Lack of experience always forced her to say things she hadn't processed. For once, Phoenix remained silent. Kylie took that as understanding. "I didn't tell Tina about you though," she said. She turned her wide-eyed gaze towards Phoenix. Hope blossomed behind her irises. "I think you'd love your baby. You wouldn't forget to feed it because you got high on drugs so the social worker took it away."

Phoenix ground her teeth in her jaw and her reply sounded stilted. "I'm not having babies," she said.

"Oh." Kylie nodded. "That's okay then. I guess Kirwan will dump you soon then. He wants lots. I heard him telling Gus."

"I'm not having sex with Kirwan." The tension returned to her gut and Phoenix's spine straightened. Mikaere sensed the change in energy and his walk became jerky and stiff. "So, it's not a problem."

"That's good." Kylie cheered as though given an unexpected gift. "Then Tina won't catch you leaving in the middle of the night when she sleeps in our cabin."

"When she what?" Phoenix's jaw dropped in surprise. "Tina's moving into our bunk?"

"Yep." Kylie nodded. "She already put her stuff in the spare bed above Lexi." Her lips twisted with mischief. "It's hilarious."

23

WORLD'S APART

The return journey proved less hazardous. With tired horses and riders, Tina kept a more sedate pace. She used the opportunity to deliver a lecture on keeping the rules and to issue a veiled warning about what happened to those who chose their own path.

About fifteen minutes away from the camp, Phoenix spotted a trail of dying leaves to her left. Less noticeable from the ground, her view from Mikaere's saddle offered a panoramic perspective. She clamped her teeth over her lower lip and smiled. The slower journey had given her an opportunity to search for the route to the refugees' barn and the path she'd laid. The brown colours looked faint amid the riotous greens of the bush, but a few more days of dieback would create a decent path for the authorities to follow. Her father must never learn of her trail of devastation through the bush. Phoenix shook her head and smirked behind a fake yawn. Kirwan had tried to fox her by taking her off the main track. They'd bashed through the undergrowth in a line perpendicular to it and Phoenix hadn't noticed in the darkness. "You need to get up early to beat a Du

Rose," she whispered to Mikaere. He snorted and shook his mane so that dust mites floated around them in the dappled light.

Back at the horses' paddock, Phoenix directed the girls to untack their mounts and stow the saddles and bridles in the tack shed. She supervised the operation with military precision. But Lexi released a groan of dismay when Tina collected the girls into a group and ordered them back to camp. "Phoenix and Lexi, you can groom the horses and settle them. Phoenix don't forget you're cleaning up after lunch and dinner. Alone."

"I hate this camp," Lexi breathed as she waited for Phoenix to run water from the rainwater tank into a bucket. A pipe ran from the guttering of the tack shed and fed into a hole in the top. "I'm not coming back next year."

The sound of a hand bell clanged in the distance to signify the forthcoming meal. "Go back to camp now," Phoenix offered. "I'm happy to stay and take care of the horses by myself."

Lexi snorted. "Can you imagine Tina's face if I swanned back into camp against her explicit orders?"

"Then stay out of her way." Phoenix slipped the next bucket under the stream of water and lifted Lexi's free. Experience meant she wasted almost nothing.

"Nah, I swear that woman has cloned herself. She'll find out because she gets everywhere." A frown crossed her pretty features. The piercings lining her ears glinted in the sunshine. "I can't believe she's moving to our cabin."

Phoenix's eyes widened. "You heard about that? Kylie told me on the beach."

"Yep." Lexi hefted the bucket and set off across the paddock to the waiting horses. "But she won't catch me, so don't worry about that."

The girls sponged and curry combed all eight horses between them. Phoenix got an extra bucket of cool water to tip over Mikaere's head. Lexi watched, laughing as he stretched his neck to its full extent and twisted his lips into a smirk. "I can't believe he likes that," she said, giggling. "That is one crazy horse."

"I know." Phoenix jerked her head towards the last horse. "Did you pick out her feet?"

"Yep." Lexi produced the hoof pick from her back pocket and Phoenix waved it away.

"I have my own. I already did his." She ran a hand over Mikaere's damp rump. The muscle twitched beneath her touch. Turning his giant head, he nuzzled her shoulder looking for attention. Phoenix sighed and stroked his bristly chin. A dark cloud seemed to settle over her head and Phoenix bent under the weight of it. Having Tina breathing down her neck promised to make the disastrous camp experience even worse than she ever imagined. She gave herself a mental shake and stroked Mikaere's soft muzzle, knowing as he lipped her fingers that he wouldn't actually bite her. "It doesn't matter," she whispered. "Just a few more days and we'll be at home on the mountain." His ear brushed her cheek as he dropped his head and his blue wall eye blinked in approval of her forced positivity. Phoenix wrinkled her nose and puffed out a breath. "It's over for me now," she muttered. "I can't get out at night or help the refugees with Tina in our cabin. I need Kirwan's help to get that phone, then I can give the problem to someone else."

Thoughts of Kirwan heightened her sense of failure and Phoenix returned to business. She removed Mikaere's head collar after putting him in his separate paddock, then carried her saddle to the tack shed and closed the hasp on the hefty padlock.

"Do you think there's enough water?" Lexi sat on the gate swinging her legs. She stared at the water tank next to the shed.

Phoenix nodded, her gaze registering the fluid level recorded by the height of the ball indicator. It stuck half out of the tank, its red bobble faded to a muted pink. "Yeah. We're only here for a couple more days. The gravity fed troughs are both full and the horses drink an average of thirty litres each every day. Exercise makes them thirstier and they're working hard with all the campers taking turns to ride them. But it's a big enough tank. I'm sure Grant is monitoring it."

Lexi pouted. "I hope so, otherwise you can lead a chain gang with buckets to fill this tank from the one at the camp."

Phoenix groaned and winced. "Thanks for that. I can't imagine anything worse. Think of all the spillage."

"And the complaining." Lexi rolled her eyes and slid off the gate. "We should get back before you-know-who sends a search party."

Phoenix nodded and turned her reluctant feet towards the track back to the camp. "Prepare to meet your new bunk mate," she said with a sigh. "Let's hope she doesn't snore louder than Sally."

"Or fart." Lexi closed the gate behind her. She fixed the clasp in place and then pressed her forefinger and thumb over the bridge of her nose. "You realise she's sleeping right above my head, don't you?" Phoenix wrinkled her nose and they walked back to camp in silence.

Phoenix arrived late at the campfire circle that night after fulfilling her last punishment duty with grace. She dragged it out to avoid a Tina-overload now that even the cabin provided no escape from her. Guilt assailed her for not collecting leftover food for the refugees. It seemed pointless. Tina's presence as Lexi's new bunk mate ensured no one could go anywhere during the night. Phoenix thought through a million unique ways of asking Kirwan to steal Grant's phone, but each one snagged on her super-sized conscience. He'd already said he didn't want to help her release the refugees. Making him steal seemed beyond her heightened sense of right and wrong. But short of acquiring a pair of bolt cutters and new biceps, she had nothing to offer the little band of captives.

Despite Kirwan's efforts to get her attention, Phoenix ignored him during the torturous campfire singing session that evening. He pursed his lips when she didn't join in with the laughter over one of his more respectable jokes. Kylie sat next to him, her arm linked through his elbow and a wide grin on her face.

Kirwan stared at her across the flames, his gaze coasting over her face like an itch she couldn't scratch. Gus gave a lengthy and confusing sermon about Saint Mark, achieving a round of applause but no new converts. Tina sang the final song with exaggerated gusto, beaming at Gus as he played the guitar. Her fluttering eyelashes betrayed her budding obsession. Gus wore a visible gold band on his wedding ring finger but seemed well aware of his newest groupie. He played to the crowd of one with enthusiasm.

But the hypocrisy rankled Phoenix as Tina put her hormones on show. She shook her head and recalled Tina's earlier rebuke about fairness and not changing the rules for her. Then the woman sat at a campfire and flirted with a married leader in front of groups of impressionable children. The kids weren't stupid. Covert smiles and sniggers showed they'd all noticed.

Phoenix ground her teeth and wondered why she hadn't recognised the double standards before that moment. It hit her like a physical blow that she was also no better than anyone else. She'd broken enough rules so far to find herself on God's hit list. *Lying. Kissing. Thinking about more kissing.*

"Phoenix!" She jumped as Sally dug her elbow into Phoenix's ribs. She blinked and discovered everyone looking at her.

"Come on, Phoenix," Grant repeated his request. "I'm sure you can teach us all a short Māori karakia." He turned to the assembled children. "That's a prayer in Te Reo."

Phoenix swallowed and an unexpected anger filled her breast. "It isn't, actually," she bit. Her voice lifted in irritation. "A karakia is more like a poem to celebrate the natural world. If you're looking for a prayer, then you want an inoi."

"Oh." Grant's brow furrowed. Phoenix sensed all eyes on her. If they wanted a token Māori, then she'd give them one. Her lips curved upward in a smile as temptation bit at her. She could say anything. She could curse the whole darn lot of them and they wouldn't realise. Instead, she reached inside herself and sent her mind to draw strength from her heritage. Her impenetrable fortress of right and wrong wouldn't permit her to dishonour her ancestors.

Phoenix pushed her shoulders back and began to speak, repeating the first line of her mihi which gave God glory. "Kororia ki te Atua," she said, her voice a gentle, lyrical tone. "Honore ki te kiingitanga, e ngā mate, moe moe moe mai ra." She closed her eyes after honouring the Māori king and moving onto her ancestors, her ngā mate.

She'd accidentally given the next two lines of her personal mihi, her greeting, dropping into the familiar rhythm without breaking her stride. 'Sleep, sleep, sleep in peace,' meant her words. As she said them, she imagined smiling at the gathered faces of those who had gone before her; Poppa Rueben and Kuia Miriam, their features memorised from photographs. They sat at the front of a crowd built from portraits and written accounts held in the family museum. They smiled in acknowledgement in her inner vision and Phoenix halted. Her eyes popped open and she saw herself as the freak show, the entertainment. She blew out a pursed breath and stopped playing the one-sided game, realising the terrible mistake she'd made.

"Amien," she said, finishing it with abruptness. A chorus of the same rippled around the group and she risked glancing across at Kirwan. A grin pulled his lips back from his white teeth and she knew then. She wasn't the only freak at the circus. The wily teenager understood Te Reo and he knew she hadn't delivered any kind of prayer. He also knew she'd broken tikanga by speaking it outside as a woman. Her father would go nuts if he found out what she'd done.

A sense of solidarity with Kirwan reached her like the tendrils of a stolen caress and she allowed herself to return his smile. Then she excused herself from the group under the pretence of using the bathroom.

24

SMALL ACTS OF REPENTANCE

Phoenix stared at herself in the speckled bathroom mirror, rust spots bleeding over her reflection in its antique, mottled patina. She released a breath which fogged up the surface and covered her image for a moment. A cricket bounced along the floor beneath the sink unit and she winced. Regarding creepy crawlies, she was not her father's daughter. "Rule breaker," she whispered to her reflection. The disciplinarian in her battled the rebel and won. She needed to restore order in her own heart and to do that meant going back to her proper task, offering hope and friendship to those on the fringes.

Phoenix washed her hands and waved them in the air as she left the bathroom. The towel looked too stained and dingy to risk a bout of diarrhoea for the sake of a few moments of discomfort. With her purpose resolved, she returned to the cabin and supervised the girls getting ready for bed. Tina appeared as she finished telling them a story about the time Sam caught Wiri and Mac skateboarding inside the church. He'd made Logan pay for the cost of the floor to be sanded and re-varnished.

"They sound like very naughty boys," Tina commented. She sat on Lexi's bunk with a thud and it creaked. Lexi rolled her eyes at Phoenix and stared at the soft toy suffocated beneath Tina's buttocks. One of its button eyes protruded from underneath, its stitched mouth pulled into a grimace. Lexi's lips tightened and her fingers twitched in the air as though desperate to yank the poor creature free.

Phoenix rose to her feet. "Lights out in an hour," she said to the girls. "I'll check on Mikaere and make sure he's still in his paddock."

"I bet he's not." Kylie grinned over the rail of her bunk. She rested her chin on her fingers and her eyes became almond shaped as she smiled at Phoenix. "I bet he's gone for a run on the beach by himself."

"Then I'll make him clean up after lunch tomorrow." Phoenix addressed her comment to Kylie and the little girl blossomed under the spotlight. "What do you think?"

Kylie giggled. "I think his hooves will break the plates when he tries to wash them."

"That's stupid!" Sharon commented. She stopped, seeing the subtle shake of Phoenix's head. Pushing her face into her pillow, she still grabbed the last word even though it sounded muffled. "I think it's stupid."

"Would you like to come with me?" Phoenix turned to face Tina in a show of camaraderie and the older woman jerked her head back in surprise.

"Oh. Okay," she said. Her left foot chased her boot around to get it back over her sock and she rose, appearing unsure of herself beneath the unexpected glow of friendship. Her standing released Lexi's cuddly toy from beneath her bottom. The girl grabbed for it and held it to her chest with fierce mother-love glazing her eyes.

The door clicked shut behind them and Phoenix pursed her lips at Lexi's sigh of relief. "Thank God for that!" she said, her voice over loud. Phoenix frowned as she pushed her feet into her boots and glanced at Tina. Clattering down the steps, she showed no sign of having heard the comment. A cacophony of protest issued from inside as the girls rebuked Lexi for taking the Lord's name in vain.

Phoenix steeled herself for the growing impossibility of redeeming her reputation. She set off for the path through the bush, Tina following close behind her.

Phoenix picked her way along the bush path as darkness closed around them. She wished she could pull her mobile phone from her pocket and activate the handy torch she used at home. Without it, she relied on her vision and keen sense of hearing. Having grown up on the mountain, she was perhaps more aware of the dangers than Tina. A juvenile expedition with Wiri had once resulted in a frightening tussle with a wild pig. But for Wiri's excellence with a slug gun, it would have gored them both. A lucky shot through the pig's left eye and into its brain had provided a freezer load of half decent pork, but the possibility of a different outcome had shaken Phoenix.

She halted at the sound of rustling overhead. Pausing on the narrow path, she gulped as Tina ran into the back of her.

"Oof!" Tina toppled sideways and grabbed Phoenix's arm to save herself. She almost sent them both cannoning into the undergrowth.

"Look up there." Phoenix pointed to a shadow overhead in the canopy. "We need to close off this part of the path."

Tina backed away, shaking her head. "We can't do that. This path runs to the paddock and the beach. It's too difficult to make a fresh one."

Phoenix turned to face her, her eyes narrowing in confusion. "That big clump of debris overhead is a widow maker. If that comes down on someone's head, it will kill them." She heard her father's urgency strung through her words, his bush knowledge imparted to her over more than a decade and a half of observation.

Tina's head shook from side to side with exaggerated vehemence. She flapped a hand in dismissal. "It's not going anywhere," she said, her tone becoming derisive. "Besides, you're making us stand here right underneath it."

Phoenix turned away with a blink of surprise. She shrugged. "I calculated its trajectory and if it falls, it will land there." She pointed to a spot on the path about five metres ahead of them. Her lips tightened into a grimace which Tina missed in the darkness. Phoenix's need to follow the rules reared its head. "It's basic health and safety." She tried not to speak through gritted teeth. "Now that I've seen it, it's my responsibility." She whirled around to face Tina. "And yours!"

"Fine!" Tina snapped. "I never met anyone who was even more of a stickler for the rules than me." She shoved past Phoenix and veered off the path, picking her way through supplejack vines and dense undergrowth. She muttered something under her breath and Phoenix tensed as the words hit their mark. "I didn't realise how annoying it was."

Phoenix plunged her hand into her fleece pocket and her fingers closed around a bunch of cut ribbons she'd forgotten to put back after card making with the girls that afternoon. She didn't intend to walk beneath the widow maker on her way back to the camp in the darkness. With deft movements as the light faded to an eerie grey, Phoenix used a nearby fallen tree to mark the start of the diversion. She looped a pastel pink ribbon around a thin branch, tying it tight but leaving the dangling ends to blow in the breeze and attract attention. Then she crashed through the bush in Tina's wake and tied the other piece where she exited.

Phoenix reached the paddock to find that Tina had already checked the camp horses. "I've turned off the hose pipe leading to your horse's trough," she stated. Her fingers coasted over Georgia's wide stomach as the mare nudged her shoulder. "We're getting low on water."

Phoenix glanced at the tank positioned next to the tack shed. The indicator's faded ball had moved down with the decreasing fluid, but not enough to worry her. Her gaze flicked to the hose pipe running from the tap to the concrete water trough near the fence. Sections of the pipe had become buried under mud and grass over the years. It worked on a ball valve, ensuring the trough remained full despite the horses' constant need to drink. A splitter valve divided the flow beneath the fence to Mikaere's trough. A wave of anger budded in her chest. "There's plenty for the rest of the week." She cocked her head. "Would you like help to check for a leak?"

Tina shook her head and her frown drew lines across her forehead. "Just leave it," she said. Her tone held an element of raw animosity. "I think your horse is the issue. We rarely need to run both paddocks."

"That's unfair!" Phoenix jumped to the defence of her horse. "He drinks thirty litres at most." She ground her teeth in her jaw. "I don't mind carrying buckets from camp to fill his trough if it helps, but I'd rather leave the trickle feed running."

Tina seemed reluctant to delve any more into the problem. She turned away and glared at her watch. The digital numbers flashed in the darkness. "I'll mention it to Grant," she said. Her tone made it clear she wanted no more discussion on the subject. She stamped to the tack shed and walked to the stack of hay beyond the hanging saddles and bridles. Reappearing huffing and puffing, she carried a bale which pulled her fleshy arms down to her knees.

Phoenix swallowed. "That's Mikaere's," she said, taking a step towards Tina. "We brought four bales in the horse box."

Tina ignored her, using a pen knife to cut the orange string. Phoenix smelled the sweet dried grass from her father's mountain paddocks. Its familiarity sent tears into her eyes and choked the back of her throat. Tina spread the quality mixture around her like flotsam and Phoenix balled her fists. Wooden movements took her into the tack shed and she seized the last of the bales. She hauled it outside with gargantuan strength. The sharpened side of her hoof pick slit the string and the bale burst open.

"Don't use all that!" Tina shrieked. "How selfish!"

"It's mine." Phoenix growled the words through her tightening throat. She recognised the budding of murder in her heart and hated Tina for waking it. "It's for my horse." With shaking fingers, she scooped up two slices and threw them over Mikaere's gate before Tina could object. Her horse buried his nose into it with enthusiasm.

"Ridiculous!" Tina huffed. She gathered the other slices into a haphazard bale shape and carted it back into the tack shed. "The Lord is unimpressed by selfish people."

Phoenix hopped the fence and stood next to Mikaere, her palm resting against the shallow dip of his spine. Warmth and familiarity grounded her and chased away the bite of her temper. She practiced breathing in through her nose and exhaling through her lips to calm her heart rate and reclaim control. In a rare moment of genuine affection, Mikaere abandoned his feast and rested his heavy chin on her shoulder. Phoenix stroked his muzzle and kissed the soft skin above his mouth. "Not long now, boy," she whispered. "Four more sleeps until we get back to sanity. Remind me never to complain about home again."

At thoughts of home, Phoenix sensed her heart settle and her fiery rage fade. A fly landed on the still surface of the trough and she closed her eyes against its desecration. She'd grown up valuing water above gold on the mountain. She'd seen her father's stress increase when the clear spring which fed their property became a trickle one year during a drought. He'd paid trucks to cart domestic water from the town and she remembered the scent of its chemicals in the shower and the way it left her hair feeling brittle and frizzy.

Mikaere snuffed out a warm breath which coasted over Phoenix's cheek. It provided a strange sense of longing for home and the sounds and scents associated with her father's mountain. She closed her eyes and tuned in to the surrounding bush, waiting for it to infuse her senses. It sounded different. Because it was.

Shouts and laughter issued from the camp less than half a kilometre away and Phoenix sighed. Responsibility settled on her shoulders like a lead weight. She wondered how she ever thought herself capable of leading a group of girls in their growing faith when hers lacked both depth and direction.

"Let's get back!" Tina sounded impatient. Phoenix fed Mikaere a secret handful of pony nuts from her fleece pocket and left him chewing. His smaller paddock contained a reasonable amount of wispy grass. It would last him until the weekend when Hana arrived with the truck to liberate both horse and rider.

Phoenix closed Mikaere's gate and ensured she'd latched it. He'd inherited Sacha's wiliness and proved himself capable of his own Houdini routine if boredom struck him.

Phoenix paused next to the splitter at the main trough. Her fingers hovered over the connection. Conflict attacked her and forced her to decide whether her love of Mikaere outweighed her fear of Tina. She bent as though fiddling with the zipper on her short riding boot. With a sleight of hand in the semi-darkness, she twisted the connector and heard the swish of water trickling back into the empty pipe.

"What are you doing?" Tina's frown cast shadows over her face, deep lines obscuring her eyes in the gloom. Her body stiffened and the action sent a frisson of alarm into Phoenix's chest. The teenager rose and stood on one leg, wiggling her foot as though she had something in her boot.

"Nothing," she lied, realising she'd lost count of the many untruths she'd told in the last few days.

With wooden footsteps, Phoenix followed the older woman towards the sound of children's voices. Tina stumped ahead with heavy footed steps like a hippopotamus crashing through the undergrowth. Their paths diverged at the first of Phoenix's markers and though Tina continued along the path, Phoenix skirted it to avoid the widow maker. She arrived back at the camp a good five minutes after Tina, her arms scratched by bush lawyer and her knees scraped from a fall over a supplejack vine in the darkness.

Washing her hands and knees in the bathroom, she fought the urge to cry more from Tina's treatment of her than the injuries sustained from doing the right thing.

Kirwan waited for her around the corner and hissed to her as she emerged. He smelled of cigarettes and kawakawa, evidence of his crafty smoke in the bush. "Lexi said you went with Tina to check on the horses," he said. The weak bulb outside the bathroom hut flickered, sending strobed highlights through his dark hair. "You're brave."

Phoenix nodded and leaned against the weatherboard. "Tell me about it," she grumbled. "I can't work the woman out. She got upset about how much water Mikaere is drinking. And she used his hay to feed the other horses and got snippy with me for giving some to him."

Kirwan winced and leaned against the wall next to her. His elbow brushed against hers, sending a ticklish sensation into her stomach. He tugged her wrist and led her around the rear of the bathroom building. "You know what's going on, don't you?" He leaned closer to whisper.

Phoenix's expression remained blank and she gave a slow shake of her head. Her boots ground against the gritty soil. Kirwan sighed and puffed out a nicotine laden breath. "It's about the refugees. The horses' paddock is the nearest source of water. The traffickers will use it for them."

Phoenix wrinkled her nose. "It's for the animals. There's no filtration system." She shrugged. "Besides, the water level is still fine."

Kirwan shrugged. "That's your first reaction? To worry about water filtration." He shook his head. "You don't think Tina might be part of the group trafficking Elephant and the other refugees?" Light from a half moon shrouded in cloud made his teeth gleam against the darker tones of his face.

Phoenix released an undignified snort. "Really?" Her voice shook with mirth. "No, I don't think she has the brains to think up a plan like that." She patted her chest with her hand. "But thank you for cheering me up with the thought of it."

"Don't be so sure," Kirwan replied. Pushing out his tongue, he used his finger and thumb to remove a stray piece of tobacco and wiped it on his jeans. "I've discovered that the most probable answer is usually the right one."

Phoenix tutted. "I'm trapped. The only way to help Elephant and the others is to get word to someone at home. Or wait until the camp ends on Saturday and hope the traffickers don't move them before we can tell someone what's happening. Now Tina's moved herself into the bunk above Lexi, it's curbed my night-time visits anywhere. I'll bet she even monitors trips to the bathroom." Phoenix pursed her lips. "I know Grant has an emergency phone. If I could find it, I'd be able to call my papa."

"No." Kirwan's head began shaking before Phoenix finished her sentence. "I'm not raiding Grant's cabin for you. One whiff of stealing and they'll send me back to social services. My foster family aren't home until Saturday, so they'll dump me somewhere else." He paused and Phoenix sensed him speaking from bitter experience.

"Okay. Sorry." She reached out and gripped his wrist. "For now, I need to concentrate on the girls in my cabin and help them grow their faith. I've been a rubbish bunk leader so far."

Kirwan wrinkled his nose. "The girls don't think so. Kylie loves you."

"Because I gave her a free pass to sit next to you at the campfire." Phoenix twisted her lips. Meant as a grin, it emerged as more of a grimace.

"Nice. I'm a commodity now, am I?" Kirwan used his free hand to tug one of Phoenix's curls. It had escaped from her ponytail and framed her face like a braided river before pitching onto her shoulder. The movement felt intimate.

"Maybe." Phoenix pursed her lips, reluctant to destroy the moment. "The only alternative is to talk with Grant and tell him about the refugees." She tipped her face up to look at Kirwan and he dropped the curl before shaking his head.

"Wouldn't recommend it," he said, his answer short but decisive. "Visitors arrived just after you left the camp. Check them out before you go making any rash decisions."

25

IDRIS

A happy yap sounded from the campfire as they walked towards it. Phoenix frowned. "A dog?" she demanded. Instinct made her drop back, so Kirwan walked enough in front of her to offer protection. Her father's intense distrust of them had communicated itself to his children without his intention.

"Oh, it gets better than that," Kirwan hissed. He spoke through the side of his mouth, turning his head so only Phoenix could see his lips moving.

A brindle and white boxer bounded across the camp until it reached them, its mouth open and tongue lolling. Phoenix held her breath, grateful when Kirwan reached down and grabbed its collar. Slobber dangled from its hanging jowls as it greeted them like old friends. Chocolate cake bearing friends. Phoenix recoiled from the hairy newcomer.

"Idris! Get back here!" A stocky man approached. His expression creased with apology. "I'm so sorry," he gushed. "He's just a pup. I'm still training him." His weathered fingers took hold of the collar and he yanked the dog against his thigh. Kind blue eyes stared from a rounded face, their edges tilted upwards in a genuine smile. "He must like you. I haven't seen him rush to someone he doesn't know like that." The man cocked his head. "Have we met somewhere before now?"

Phoenix swallowed and left Kirwan to answer. The teenager stuck his hand out and assumed a respectful tone. "No, sir. I'm Kirwan and this is Phoenix."

"Darrell." The man shook Kirwan's hand and nodded to Phoenix. "Nice to meet you. It's a marvellous thing that the church does here, isn't it? Getting all these young people back on track."

Still mute, Phoenix nodded. Sensing her confusion, Kirwan shifted so that his shoulder half blocked her. Gratitude flooded her like a palpable wave. He spoke, so she didn't have to engage with the man. "Yeah. I've been coming for years." His tone sounded chatty, but deferential. "I haven't seen you around the camp. Are you staying?"

"Yes." Darrell nodded. "Just bunking here for a few nights. We've been praying for the camp back at church, so I thought I'd drive up and make myself useful." He laughed, a lyrical sound which conveyed a man with a carefree nature. It seemed like such a stretch to see him as a trafficker of human beings.

Phoenix frowned and galvanised herself, shoving her mother's proverbial metal rod up her back for courage. She lifted a trembling finger and pointed at the dog. "Is he yours?" she demanded. The dog lurched sideways to lick her extended finger and she yanked her hand back and wiped it on her fleece.

Darrell cocked his head and the kindness radiating from his eyes confused Phoenix. "He is. I've had him for a year. I can tell you're not keen on dogs, but he won't bite you, I promise."

Phoenix nodded. Grit scrunched under her boot soles as she shifted closer to Kirwan. To her surprise, he stuck out an arm and wrapped it around her shoulders. "Yeah, Phoe doesn't like dogs," he stated. "Nice to meet you, Darrell." He eased Phoenix past the man and the pressure of his arm urged her across the scrubby grass towards the fire pit. "Steady," he warned. He withdrew his arm as they got within sight of the cabins and the kitchen. "Just keep quiet."

Phoenix closed her eyes as they marched across the camp. Her spine tingled as the man's eyes bored into the back of her head. "We're not allowed physical contact with the opposite sex," she groaned. "You just opened up another problem I don't need. He'll tell Tina and she'll put me on a total lock down for the rest of the week."

"Better than having you blurt out what you know." Kirwan nudged her upper arm with his elbow.

"I asked if he owned the dog!" Phoenix drew her lips into a pout. "I wasn't intending to ask if he'd taken it for walks near any barns in the middle of the night."

"Stop talking. Check in with your cabin and then I'll meet you behind the girls' bathroom in about ten minutes." Kirwan gave her a casual wave and dug his hands in his pockets, turning aside as the path divided in front of the buildings.

Phoenix sighed. "Yes sir, no sir," she grumbled. She stamped up the porch steps and into the cabin. "Where's Tina?" She directed her question Lexi before coughing spasmed her lungs. The haze of acetone hung like a heavy curtain across the room. She closed the door to the cabin behind her and surveyed the scene.

The girls lay on their beds in various states of undress. Sharon swatted a buzzing fly with a pair of knickers. Lexi had commandeered the only armchair and sat with her legs over the side. The heady scent emanated from the nail polish remover in her hand. She gave a dramatic sigh and raised her eyes to the ceiling. "Cruella is in the bathroom," she replied. "She's moved her stuff into my bunk and is making me take the top.

"Lexi has to remove all her colours." Kylie poked her head over the side of her bed. "Tina says it's an abomination."

Phoenix muted her ready groan. Tina's trip to the bathroom meant danger for her rendezvous behind it with Kirwan. Lexi gritted her teeth and Phoenix frowned at the sight of tears sparkling in her eyes. "It's just for a few more days," she murmured. Lexi gave her an answering smile, though it wavered on her lips.

"It's from Leviticus, apparently." Sharon missed the fly and swatted Kylie's face with the knickers. Deciding it was safer, Kylie lay back against her pillow. "Women shouldn't cover themselves with tattoos or shit like that." The knickers spun in an arc as Sharon pirouetted on the spot. The girls issued a collective gasp at Sharon's expletive and Lexi released a snort of laughter.

"Yeah. It also says we shouldn't eat anything with trotters and that woman scoffs bacon like it's going out of fashion."

Sharon stopped spinning and grinned. "She does, doesn't she?" The fly used the interlude to dive bomb her head and she resumed her flapping.

"I'm going for a shower," Phoenix stated. "I won't take long." She dug under her pillow for her pyjamas and pulled her damp towel from the rail surrounding her bunk. It smelled musty and had stiffened in place.

"The boys used all the hot water," Kylie stated. "But I don't know what for, because they still stink."

Phoenix smiled. "I'll manage," she replied. Tucking her wash bag under her arm, she stepped out onto the porch and closed the door behind her.

She saw no sign of Kirwan, but Idris made a beeline for her as she crossed the camp. She forced herself to stand still and let the enormous dog sniff her. It seemed clear he remembered her from their former meeting in the bush. Phoenix gritted her teeth and turned aside as the dog stood up on his hind legs to lick her face.

"Idris! Stop!" Darrell rushed across from the campfire and dragged the dog away by its collar. "I'm so sorry. I don't know why he's doing this."

"It's fine." Shaken, Phoenix eyed the lolling tongue and took a step backwards as the dog struggled. His almond-shaped eyes made him look like he wanted to smile her to death. "I grew up with horses. Papa won't have dogs on the farm. I'm just not used to them." She forced an inane grin onto her lips.

"Idris, come here!" Grant called from beside the campfire. Darrell released him and Idris gambolled across towards Grant. Phoenix stiffened as Tina strolled from the bathroom to join the other leaders in their evening prayers. She squeezed her round bottom between Gus and Grant, forcing the latter to move across the bench. Her wiry hair stuck up like a series of antennae and the dog slobbered a line of spit up her wrist as they arrived at the same time. Phoenix released a breath filled with relief at the near miss. She imagined Kirwan already behind the bathroom with a cigarette poised in his long fingers.

Darrell turned to Phoenix with a smile. "Are you joining us?" he asked, cocking his head on one side like a bird.

Phoenix shook her head. "I'm just a junior leader," she replied. "Although probably not anymore now that Tina's moved into our cabin."

"Oh." Darrell frowned. "That's a shame." Everything about him jarred with her image of the hardened human trafficker she'd conjured up after her observations in the bush. "You're very welcome if you'd like to join us," he said. "The others won't mind."

Phoenix gave a smile and nodded. After a glance at Tina's bowed head, she changed it to a reluctant shake. "Thank you, but I need to take a shower. Apparently, the boys used all the hot water." She jerked her head towards the bathroom. "Thanks again for the offer." Her heart yearned for acceptance. She wanted to find inclusion in their holy huddle, but too many factors made her an outlier.

Darrell smiled, the action instant. Laughter lines at the corners of his eyes betrayed a man with a sense of humour and an affable grin. It sent Phoenix into even more confusion. "See ya then," he said. Waving a hand over his shoulder, he strolled across to the gathered group and took his place between Grant and Tina. His head bowed in prayer.

"What the heck?" Phoenix breathed.

She found Kirwan waiting for her behind the girls' bathroom. He jumped as she walked around the corner. Deft fingers stubbed out a rolled cigarette on the line of exposed brick edging one side of the structure. "You took your time," he commented in a lowered voice. "I just had to endure Tina's singing of the *Hallelujah Chorus* for the last twenty minutes."

"Liar!" Phoenix snuffed out a laugh. "You're such an idiot."

Kirwan grinned and pushed the cigarette into the front left pocket of his jeans. "It's true. The water is freezing. What song will you sing to get you through the experience?" He reached for Phoenix and dragged her into his arms. His lips brushed her forehead. She swallowed and kept her bundled towel and wash bag between them.

"We shouldn't do this," she whispered. Her tone sounded harsher than she intended. "It's too risky."

Kirwan lifted her chin with a long index finger and smiled into her face. His eyes sparkled like glittering stars. "Risky can be fun," he whispered. His lips warmed hers with a tingling heat. Phoenix let her lips part enough for Kirwan to slip his tongue between them. His arms encased her in a cage of desire and Phoenix relaxed against the excitement of his heart thudding against her chest wall. He was an experienced kisser, teasing and coaxing until she forgot her need to breathe. She forgot everything.

The dog's sharp bark brought Phoenix back to her senses and she turned her face aside. Jerky movements took her out of Kirwan's arms and put distance between them. He didn't stop her, but the wrinkling of his nose conveyed his disappointment. He dug his hands back into his pockets and cleared his throat. "I don't suppose you can get out tonight, can you?" he asked. Fading hope laced his tone.

Phoenix shook her head. "No." She wondered what madness might swallow them if she tried and succeeded. She knew what Kirwan wanted and it both frightened and exhilarated her. Thoughts of her father intruded and she frowned. Logan Du Rose would kill Kirwan without a second thought. Not only for the liberties he'd already taken, but for the ones he wanted still. She blew out a breath and tried to change the subject. "Darrel is a trafficker, isn't he?" she said, her tone guarded. "You're sure?"

Kirwan nodded. "Yeah."

Phoenix took a step closer to him. "How can that be right?" Distress laced her question and her eyes widened in a plea. "He seems so nice. Why would he do something like this?"

"Dunno." Kirwan shrugged and half turned away from her. "Money, maybe. Christians are no different to anyone else, are they? Nobody is perfect. And they still need to eat."

Phoenix shook her head. The concept seemed beyond her understanding. Everywhere she turned she saw adults breaking the rules. Her heart ached with anxiety as her safe world tipped on its axis. "I'll see you tomorrow," she whispered. Sadness pushed icy fingers into her soul. Kirwan nodded and turned away, retrieving his cigarette from his pocket and flicking a lighter. He halted and turned back to face her.

"Oh. I've moved bunks. The new guy took my spot. I'm now with Josh and his crowd of stinky boys."

Phoenix allowed herself the smallest of smiles in response. There seemed little point suggesting he didn't spend the night roaming for fear of getting caught. The tilt of Kirwan's head told her he'd relish the challenge. Instead, she gave him the gift of a different warning. "Hey, I discovered a massive widow maker over the path." She swallowed and frowned at the look of confusion in Kirwan's eyes. "It's debris in the canopy. Dead branches, leaves, bird's nests and stuff that gets collected up there. It forms into a ball above ground. One strong breeze and it will crash down onto anyone walking on the path. Don't let it be you."

Kirwan grinned. "Are you saying you care about me, Phoenix Du Rose?"

Phoenix narrowed her eyes and shook her head in mock indignation. "Whatever!" she replied. She whirled around and the bathroom door closed behind her.

26

GOODBYES

Tina's presence in the cabin acted like a fire damper, crushing all joviality from the girls. It introduced an atmosphere of heaviness and Phoenix struggled beneath its weight. Deep sighs of sadness issued from around the room as its occupants settled down for the night without their usual chatter.

"Lights out!" Tina barked as her stubby finger flicked the switch. She cursed as she fell over discarded footwear on her way back to her bunk. Phoenix heard a muted snigger which sounded like it came from Lexi. Grinning to herself in the darkness, she rolled onto her side to face the wall. She imagined the other girl setting more elaborate traps for Tina as the week progressed.

Sleep refused to come as Phoenix's mind made unhelpful forays into her memory. Kirwan's kiss had brought more confusion to her door. Instead of distracting her thoughts from Wiri, it had intensified them. He'd loved her forever and she'd betrayed him. Guilt prickled at the edges of her psyche, overwriting any sense of pleasure in Kirwan's interest in her. Conflict formed a hard knot in her chest and reason told her that her father would no more accept Kirwan than he would Wiremu. She doubted any man would surpass Logan's lofty standards.

As much as Logan loved Wiremu, the unspoken rule had existed since before Phoenix had known enough to understand it. Du Roses didn't marry Du Roses. She knew the stories of how their whakapapa became polluted by intermarriage. Mental illness and haemophilia had decimated their family's genetics. Including Logan's. And hers. Phoenix rubbed a hand across her stomach in the darkness and grieved the children she'd never have. A lone tear plopped onto her pillow and another followed it. She released a faint sniff.

Something touched her hair and she jumped. The bunk bed creaked as she turned over with a gasp. Reaching sideways, her fingers contacted something warm and fleshy pushed through the side rail. Phoenix recoiled.

"Sorry." The voice sounded squeaky as a whisper. "Are you sad?"

"Kylie." Phoenix shifted nearer the wall as the ladder clicked and creaked with the child's steady climb. "What's the matter?"

"Don't cry." Kylie pushed her way into the narrow space and flopped down next to Phoenix with a grunt. The coolness of the wall seeped through the older girl's pyjama shirt and chilled her spine as she made room. A small hand snaked through the darkness and touched Phoenix's cheek. "Is it because of Tina?"

"No." Phoenix found Kylie's mouth in the darkness and pressed a finger over it. "Shush, or she'll give you a punishment."

"She won't." The voice sounded louder than a whisper and another ladder creaked as someone descended it.

"Who's that?" Phoenix pushed herself up onto her elbows and peered through the darkness.

"It's Lexi." Kylie gave an exaggerated sigh.

"Lexi, what are you doing?" Phoenix hissed. "Get back into bed."

Kylie grunted and sat up at speed. "Are you going out to have sex?"

"No. I'm not." Lexi sighed. Phoenix recognised the swish of her pulling on outdoor clothing. "We don't always have sex, Kylie. There's more to a relationship than just the physical stuff."

"What about Tina?" Kylie's pitch rose to indicate growing hysteria.

Bomb proof, the other girls snored or turned over in their sleep. Lexi grunted as she tied her laces. "Tina won't wake until tomorrow," she whispered. "She'll have a headache from that last cup of tea, so stay out of her way."

"You drugged her?" Disbelief echoed through Phoenix's words. "You can't do that!"

"Too late." A zipper made a metallic sound, followed by the rustle of a rucksack. "I've had enough. Tell her I'm gone when she wakes."

"Don't break the rules," Phoenix groaned. She moved next to Kylie and both girls peered over the side of the bunk. "It's not worth it. We only have a few days left here."

The door opened a crack and Lexi's silhouette stood in the gap. A faint moonlight cast an eerie silver pall over the camp. "There are rules and rule enforcers," Lexi said. "One differs greatly from the other. I can follow rules, Phoe. It's her hypocrisy I can't stand." She paused and Phoenix saw her silhouette turn. Lexi sighed. "You're a principled person, Phoenix, but if you're not careful, you'll end up just like her."

Kylie gave a whimper of pure terror and then Lexi left. The door clicked shut behind her and plunged the room into darkness. Her words cut Phoenix like a blade through her heart. She reeled as though Lexi had levelled a physical blow.

"Go after her, Phoenix!" Kylie pleaded. "Quick!"

Phoenix released a ragged breath and crawled towards her ladder. Unable to think straight, she descended so fast that she stubbed her toe on the bottom rung. Righting herself, she almost toppled forwards onto Tina's bunk in her haste. Barefoot and clad in her pyjamas, she ran into the night and halted. The promised rain had come, dousing the camp in heavy, wet pellets which smashed against the baked ground. A grumble of thunder sounded in the distance.

Phoenix knew she could track Lexi if she had to, but it shocked her to realise she didn't want to do it. She reasoned it was because Lexi had hurt her and she didn't want to hear more of the same.

But for the first time in her life she recognised the green tendrils of envy snaking up her spine. She regretted not having the courage to leave. The camp had proved a colossal mistake, but a heightened sense of obedience would keep her there until her mother came for her. Obedience, or cowardice. Phoenix wondered if one was just a convenient screen for the other.

"She's gone. And it's raining hard." Phoenix clambered back into her bunk and delivered the news to Kylie. To her surprise, the younger child nestled closer, seeking comfort she wasn't capable of giving. Kylie showed no intention of moving back to her own bed despite the dampness of Phoenix's rain speckled pyjamas. With great reluctance, Phoenix unzipped her sleeping bag and laid it over them both. She pulled her pillow into the middle, so they could share it. Settling down, she figured she wouldn't sleep much as Kylie wiggled around before stilling. The child's slender body seemed so frail and bony, her knees and elbows sharp against Phoenix's softness.

Kylie oozed emotional hunger like a dull scent and Phoenix knew her mother would love her. Hana Du Rose would take her broken little soul and fill it with confidence and comfort. Phoenix smiled to herself in the darkness and thought of all the people who'd passed through her family over the years. Tama, Ryan, Edin. And Wiremu. Hana served as a beacon for those treading an emotional wasteland. Mountain gossip hinted that her father had once been one of her mother's projects. Phoenix couldn't imagine anyone daring to hurt her powerful father enough for him to need Hana's tender restoration.

Kylie pressed her cheek against Phoenix's chest and something in the older girl snapped deep in her psyche. She laid an arm over Kylie's slender frame and patted her back until the child's breathing changed. Her personal mantra of fixing everything while remaining inside the boundaries of truth silenced its chatter in her mind. Perfection was unattainable.

Then she closed her eyes and slept as a sense of peace shrouded her like a warm blanket.

27

SUSPICION

The next morning brought rolling black clouds and more heavy downpours. The rain turned the dust of the camp to a sticky grease, which stained everything it touched to a dirty orange.

Phoenix woke to find Kylie back in her own bed. The child seemed less needy as the girls dressed. She whined less and didn't draw attention to herself as she had on other mornings. Her covert smiles for Phoenix appeared genuine and she sought the older girl out before leaving the cabin for breakfast duty. Slipping her small hand into Phoenix's, she smiled up at her and gave her fingers a squeeze. "It'll be okay," she whispered. "Tina hasn't noticed yet."

Phoenix nodded and frowned. The smell of yesterday's clothes wafted around her and she hated the sense of being permanently dirty. Tina stomped around the cabin like she'd got a wasp stuck up her voluminous nightdress. Listing from side to side, she eventually grabbed her boots and disappeared into the bathroom without speaking.

Sharon wrinkled her nose as the girls set up the dining room for breakfast. The rafters of the old barn creaked beneath the barrage of water as the heavens doused the parched earth with the enthusiasm of Noah's flood. "Where's Lexi?" she demanded. She spun in a tight circle and a ripple of confusion electrified the other girls.

Phoenix held her breath, trying to formulate a suitable answer in her head. Part of her prayed that Lexi would return, dripping wet but safe. Another part of her wished she'd taken Mikaere and gone with her.

"She can't be far." Kylie offered the explanation, sounding rational and calm. "She wasn't in the cabin when I woke. Maybe she went for a walk." She glanced across at Phoenix, seeking approval for having stayed as close to the truth as possible. Phoenix gave her a nod of recognition, the action appearing slight enough to communicate only with her. It was a solid answer and better than anything Phoenix's rattled brain had conceived.

"How would you like to ring the bell?" she offered Kylie. "It must be your turn by now."

The other girls grumbled and complained. The coveted reward for their hard work was ringing the hand bell to summon the hungry campers. Sharon had dived on the bell last time and they had forgotten Kylie in the ensuing scrum. She beamed and lifted the old brass bell from its position on the leaders' table. The brass clapper lolled like a tongue and gave a few feckless tinkles as Kylie hoisted it with her delicate fingers. Her wrist bent painfully backwards with its weight.

"Use two hands," Phoenix suggested. "Don't worry about walking around the camp today. You'll get soaked. Just stand at the door and ring it." She left Kylie trying to muster up a decent swing and jogged to the kitchen to push more toast under the grill.

Phoenix kept a steady stream of toast running for over half an hour before panicking. The camp's cook had arrived much earlier last time, making porridge and frying bacon as the girls lined up cartons of cereal. With no sign of her still, Phoenix attempted to start a saucepan of porridge. It resulted in a vat of grey sludge with the texture of wet cement. Grant appeared after the first delivery of unappetising bowls got rejected by the campers.

"Where's Cook?" he asked. He peered into the porridge pan and scowled.

"Not here yet." Phoenix stopped plopping mixture into bowls like a grumpy school dinner lady and jogged across the kitchen to the grill. She hauled out a batch of charred bread and lowered the setting before dumping more onto the tray and shoving it back under the flame.

"Have you seen her at all?" Grant enquired. His brow creased with concern. He didn't pick up the spoon to keep the porridge moving or offer to help Phoenix.

"No!" Phoenix cringed at her snippy tone as she dodged his stationary body on her way back to the porridge pan. "This is a nightmare!"

"Okay." Grant turned and strode from the room with no other comment.

"Bye then," Phoenix grumbled under her breath. She stirred the bubbling porridge, groaning as it gripped the spoon like a set of jaws. "Damn stuff!" she huffed. "Let go of the spoon!"

"Are we building a wall?" Kirwan's uninhibited laughter punctuated his question.

"It's all gone wrong!" Phoenix wailed. "Cook didn't show up and everything is burning!"

Kirwan's eyes sparkled with humour. "Yeah. We figured something was wrong when the girls started bringing out building supplies."

"What?" Phoenix wrestled the spoon free of the mixture and turned to face him. A glob of lumpy goop dangled from the spoon and struggled to release itself.

"Toasted bricks and porridge mortar." Kirwan's lip quirked upwards and laughter lines appeared at the corners of his eyes. "Don't suppose there's any bacon yet?"

"No!" Phoenix leaned her head back and gazed at the ceiling. "I forgot about that."

"Where are the beans and tomatoes?"

"I don't know!" Phoenix stamped her foot and the blob made a valiant dive for the floorboards and hit with a splat. It stayed as a lump where it fell. "Help me?" she implored, her grey eyes wide and pleading. "The girls haven't come back yet."

"I think they're in hiding." Kirwan stepped over to the sink and rolled up the sleeves of his sweatshirt. Fisting the soap, he turned on the tap and washed his hands. "Where's Lexi?"

Phoenix sighed and her shoulders slumped. "Long story," she replied. "I'll tell you later." A fine tendril of blue smoke sent her running back to the grill to rescue the next batch of charcoaled toast.

Kirwan prepared a large saucepan of baked beans and another of tinned tomatoes. He stopped Phoenix cremating any more bread and directed her to arrange rashers of pink bacon over the grill instead. Grant sent two of the other leaders to help and a sense of order returned to the frantic meal service. As a more edible version of breakfast passed into the dining room, the heckling stopped and Phoenix's girls came out of hiding in time to serve.

"We're not doing clean-up," Phoenix told Tina as she appeared in the doorway fifteen minutes later. With wet hair stuck to her forehead and a scowl on her face, she epitomised all withdrawal hangovers. She'd buttoned her blouse without looking and it gaped in several places. Phoenix rested her hands over her hips and faced Tina with determination.

"It's the rules," Tina growled. She stared around her at the devastation as though surprised by the kitchen's level of chaos.

Phoenix shook her head. Her heart thudded behind her chest wall and she channelled her father's authority into her voice. "No, the rules are for set up and set down," she asserted. A toss of her mahogany curls completed the image of haughty defiance. The girls gathered behind Tina in the doorway, their eyes wide at this uncharacteristic showdown. Kirwan stopped stacking dirty plates and turned to watch. "We also cooked." Phoenix peeled off the bright yellow rubber gloves encasing her fingers and laid them over the side of the sink. "The girls need to eat and I'm going for a shower."

Panic surged inside her and adrenaline pushed its way through her bloodstream as Phoenix acknowledged the actual issue at stake. She needed to escape before Tina discovered Lexi's absence. Sheer determination carried her past Tina and onto the narrow porch outside the kitchen. She jerked her head at the knot of girls blocking her exit. "There's bacon left and Kirwan saved beans and tomatoes for you. Eat your breakfast and we'll say our prayers in the cabin when I get back from the shower." She lowered her voice. "Get it quick and take it back to the bunk."

Her knees trembled as she stepped off the porch and strode towards the cabin. The lingering scent of Lexi's nail polish no longer hit her like a wall as she opened the door. Phoenix knew she'd gone for good. Standing up to Tina left a rawness in her soul and she stood for a moment to catch her breath. Lexi's empty bunk faced her. She'd taken everything.

Phoenix snatched up her damp towel and a fresh set of clothes. Braving the rain, she endured yet another cold shower and struggled to get the shampoo out of her hair. Her clean clothes stuck to her as she dressed on the slippery, tiled floor. A cloud of cigarette smoke drifted through an open window and she smiled to herself. Kirwan waited outside under the rickety overhang of the roof. Phoenix gathered up her wash bag and rolled her towel around it. Then she met him behind the girls' bathroom.

"Hey." She stood beside him and leaned her back against the building.

"Hey yourself," he replied. He pinched his cigarette between thumb and forefinger, keeping it hidden in the curve of his palm without burning himself. The action betrayed his ability to hide his vice at a moment's notice. "At least now I know you can't cook," he joked. His lips curved upwards and he took another drag of his cigarette.

Phoenix sighed and wrinkled her nose. "I didn't realise I'd need to," she admitted.

"Cook turned up a few minutes ago." Kirwan raised an eyebrow. "But did you notice that Darrell and the dog were also missing during breakfast?"

"I didn't notice much." Phoenix turned to face him. Her sweatshirt dragged against the rough surface of the untreated wooden planks. "Bit busy."

Kirwan smirked. "Yeah. Burning breakfast." He released a deep breath before pressing his fragile cigarette against the brick support at the end of the building. He performed the action with extreme care, ensuring he could relight the fragile paper at another opportunity. The orange glow extinguished under the pressure and he tucked the cigarette into his front pocket. Phoenix didn't get a chance to react before he stepped close and wrapped his arms around her. "Where's Lexi?" he demanded, at the same time as pressing a kiss next to her ear.

The swift changes in direction left Phoenix reeling and she gaped for a moment. As her lips parted to answer, Kirwan kissed her. The tang of cigarettes mingled with her toothpaste. His urgency left her gasping for air. Kirwan nipped at her full lower lip and groaned. His warm fingers worked their way underneath her sweatshirt and coasted along the underside of her bra. A warning fear ticked along the fringes of her reason and Phoenix tried to ignore it as Kirwan intensified the kiss and demanded more of her.

The towel unravelled beneath Phoenix's arm and her wash bag hit the floor with a clunk. A corner stuck out from under the cover of the wide roof and rain splattered over its red fabric. Phoenix squeaked and bent to retrieve it. She used the moment to let the warring parts of her mind stop fighting each other and give her room to think. Kirwan's fingers trailed over her spine as he released her with reluctance. Phoenix tried not to look at him as she rose, her fingers patting at the darkened patch on her wash bag. The scarlet had deepened to the colour of blood.

Kirwan pushed an index finger beneath her chin and lifted her face. His action forced her to meet his gaze. He smiled and she saw the doubt in his eyes. She forced herself to grin, imagining she looked like a maniac as she fought her own demons. Kirwan pressed another kiss over her lips but this time, he didn't linger. As he pulled away, Phoenix leaned forward and copied his action, seeing the pleasure bloom in his face as her lips touched his. "I should get back now," she whispered. "The girls will miss me."

"Okay." He smiled. "But tell me about Lexi before you go."

Phoenix groaned. "She drugged Tina's drink and left in the night. I don't know where she headed, but she took all her gear."

"Right." Kirwan frowned. "You know she had a thing with Josh, don't you?"

Phoenix nodded. "Did he go too? She didn't want anyone to stop her but now she's been out all night. What if something happened to her? I'm not sure what to do."

One side of Kirwan's nose lifted as he considered the issue. Then he shook his head. "Na. She's street wise. I bet she's home by now. Josh is still here."

"Oh." Phoenix frowned. "Damn! I assumed they left together." She tried not to fixate on the many terrible possibilities for Lexi. Walking through the bush alone at night and navigating isolated rural roads filled with lurking, faceless murderers, spelled disaster. Kirwan gripped her shoulders and gave her a gentle shake.

His brow furrowed. "I heard them arguing last night. She wanted him to do something and he refused. Maybe they broke up and that's why she left." He cocked his head. "She'll be fine."

Phoenix nodded and sent up a belated arrow prayer to guarantee it. "She's left me alone with Tina," she grumbled. "I'm not sure I can cope."

Kirwan froze at the sharp bark of a dog. "Darrell's back," he whispered. "I bet he and the cook waited until the rain eased to feed the refugees. That's what delayed them. It's not exactly a short walk and this weather is miserable."

Phoenix swallowed. The refugees' plight lurked like a black cloud above her head. She floundered under the weight of it as Darrell's voice raised above the barking. "Stop it, Idris," he said, his tone ragged. "Fetch the ball, there's a clever boy." A happy yap followed and then the squeak of a ball being put under pressure by canine teeth.

"Darrell seems so nice," Phoenix breathed.

Kirwan nodded. "He is." His eyes crinkled at the corners, but his lips didn't form a smile. "But he's still breaking the law. Elephant told us they got food and water at night, so it's bad they had to wait until this morning." He cocked his head and stared at a point in the distance until his eyes glazed. "Maybe they're getting ready to move them." He winced. "I hate to say it but I think you're right. We need to do something. And soon."

Phoenix gaped. A hidden sense of fury rose from within her and she gripped her wash bag with enough force to pop the lid off her shampoo bottle. "But you didn't want to get involved!" Her voice rose and Kirwan clapped a hand over her mouth.

"And you changed my mind," he whispered. "I walked back to see Elephant and the others last night. The storm terrified them, Phoe. You convinced me I should get involved. I couldn't get the padlock off the door, but I searched Darrell's gear for a key when he took a shower last night." His nose wrinkled. "I couldn't find it, but I've stolen a chisel from Grant's toolbox. Remember the slot we put the food through the other night? If I can make that big enough, we can get the people out. Come with me now and we'll do it."

Phoenix backed away, her head shaking. "But then where will they go? They can't just roam around like vagrants. The police will arrest them and send them back to Syria."

Kirwan cocked his head to one side. "Wait, what? But you wanted to get them out remember?" He paused for thought and his irises flared with earnestness. "I've just remembered something. Pastor Mike is coming to lead the worship service this morning. He seemed genuine when he came last year. We could tell him what's happening and let him figure out the rest. He'd make Darrell give him the key, wouldn't he?"

Phoenix struggled to formulate her sentences. Confusion settled over her like a heavy and unwelcome blanket, dulling her thoughts and muting her words. "I wanted to help but now I'm confused.

Darrell and the cook are likeable people. They're Christians and so are the refugees. What if they're trying to help them and we make a mess of everything? They might have new lives prepared for them with jobs and everything."

Kirwan blinked and shook his head. "You hypocrite!" His words stung more than any slap. He released Phoenix and gave her a rough push. "You bloody hypocrite. So, it's okay to do something illegal as long as you're a Christian?" His question forced itself like a knife through Phoenix's heart.

"No," she replied. But she sounded so unsure, it fuelled Kirwan's obvious disgust.

"Geez!" he spat. "You're not who I thought you were." He gave her one last agonised glare and spun on his heels. His boots kicked up damp earth and grit in the turn and Phoenix closed her eyes against the disdain in his expression.

She had no answer. Because she no longer recognised the girl she saw in the mirror.

28

TRUTH

"So Jesus said to the Jews who had believed him, 'If you abide in my word, you are truly my disciples and you will know the truth, and the truth will set you free.' That's what he said." Phoenix cleared her throat and paused. The thin pages of Bibles rustled as the girls followed her reading, their fingers tracing the sentences. Phoenix looked at their bowed heads and sickness roiled in her stomach.

Kylie nudged her with her elbow and tipped her delicate face up like a blossoming flower. "John 8:31-32," she confirmed. She sat on the bottom bunk with Phoenix, their thighs touching and no room between them. A sense of suffocation swallowed Phoenix. She forced her head to give a tight nod.

"That's right," she agreed. "Thanks Kyles. What truth does Jesus mean?"

Carrie's legs dangled over the rail of her top bunk and her voice sounded disjointed. "The big truth. That Jesus forgives everything we do when we ask. Even the naughty stuff." She sat up and pointed at Sharon. "Like when she took an extra helping of bacon at breakfast. She nicked it right off Grant's plate before she reached him." Carrie's blue eyes widened and she waggled her fingers. "She did it with no hands."

Sharon snorted and not an ounce of guilt showed in her face. She licked her lips as though tasting the spoils of her theft. "Jesus thought it was genius," she commented. "He's still laughing."

Phoenix remained silent. Her mind buzzed with a painful question. How could she lead these girls anywhere when she couldn't even follow her own straight path?

"Where's Lexi?" Carrie demanded. "Where's all her gear?"

Kylie stiffened and pressed herself against Phoenix's side. Her fingers leafed through Bible pages as though seeking the answer there.

"Perhaps with Tina," Carrie ventured.

"No. Because Tina's on the toilet," Sharon replied. Her nose wrinkled. "She's stinking out the girls' bathroom. Cook asked her if she was okay and she shouted back that she'd blocked the pipe."

A collective groan of disgust rippled around the cabin and Phoenix gulped. Whatever choice drug Lexi had administered to their leader had done more than incapacitate her for a few hours. Phoenix pushed away her fear of consequences as Sharon embellished the story. "Do you think she's turned inside out? Like a sock?" She shifted on her mattress and set her Bible on her knee. "I heard about this person on an aeroplane who got their guts sucked out of their bum hole. It was dangling from the bathroom bit of the plane until they reached Auckland."

Shrieks and giggles punctuated her tale of woe and Sharon basked in the glory of the attention. Kylie tipped her face up to meet Phoenix's gaze and her rosebud lips pursed into a straight line.

Truth and lies collided in Phoenix's brain like a train smash. A warning alarm sounded in her head like a claxon, telling her she couldn't continue to pursue a life of double standards. *Hypocrite.* The truth would set her free. She rose and her Bible dropped to the floor. "Finish the study," she said, her voice raspy and her tone sharp. "I'm just nipping out for a second." Her body moved like a plank of wood as she stalked across the cabin and hauled open the door. Frigid air surged around her ankles and the click of the handle sounded like a drum beat in her head. She pushed her feet into her boots under the porch and faced the inclement weather wearing only a sweatshirt and jeans. Her jacket hung from the end of her bunk along with her hat. "You're not going back," she hissed to herself. "It's now or never."

Gus called her name as she strode across the campground. Phoenix ignored him and focused on making it to the path which led through the bush to the horses. Idris bounced up to her and jogged alongside. His wide boxer mouth opened in a doggy grin. Greasy earth coated his white front feet where he'd busied himself digging a hole somewhere. He jumped up and tried to put his paws on her forearm, but she moved too fast and he missed.

"Idris!" Darrell's voice called out to his dog, reminding Phoenix of the night in the bush with Kirwan. The memory of his kisses burned her flesh in the present and tears welled up behind her eyelids. Phoenix hit the path and started running. He'd called her a hypocrite. Like Tina.

The dog kept pace with her until Darrell's shouts grew quieter. Phoenix halted at the sight of her carefully placed thread blowing against a tree trunk. Looking up, she saw the darkened shape of the widow maker as it hung there, growing heavier with rainwater and more exposed. A pure fluke had allowed her to spot it at all the previous evening. Just the angle of the fading light or a chance shadow had revealed its threat.

As she paused on the track, the dog jumped up and touched his front paws to her ribs. Phoenix jerked sideways, revulsed by his fetid breath. "Go back!" she ordered. "You'll make Darrell come after you and they'll stop me." She raised her voice and balled her fists. "I'm not a hypocrite! I'm proving I'm not like Tina!"

Idris ignored her, snuffing around in the undergrowth and busying himself with rogue scents. His body stiffened as he pushed his blunt nose into a tangle of supplejack. Then he gave an excited yap and tore off after something small and grey. Phoenix blew out a breath of exasperation. The dog wouldn't catch the mouse, but at least it drew his owner away from her. The quest lay itself out before her like a blueprint. Only one person could help her. She ploughed through ferns and bush lawyer to avoid the widow maker and prayed he'd cooperate.

Mikaere neighed as she climbed over the first gate. He sheltered in his own paddock under a wide pohutakawa tree bordering the fence. The camp horses huddled on the other side. His mane and tail glistened with rainwater and matched Phoenix's fringe, which stuck to her wet forehead and cheeks. Water ran down her spine and though the canopy had sheltered her from the worst of the rain, the paddock let it douse her with fat drops which stung her skin.

Phoenix used the numbered code to open the padlock on the tack shed and hauled out Mikaere's head collar and lunge rope. She lifted a man's dusty Jackaroo hat from the top shelf and inspected it before pressing it over her soaked hair. It smelled as though generations of mice had lived under its brim and she held her breath for a moment to avoid losing her nerve. A tattered wax coat offered covering for her torso and thighs. She fumbled with the zipper before realising it had broken long ago, the rungs of the mechanism rusted into place. A wide hole exposed her left armpit and explained the reason someone abandoned it on an earlier camp, perhaps even before she was born.

The door clanged behind her as Phoenix stepped out into the rain. The stink of her borrowed clothing dissipated on the wind whipping up from the south as it carried the unexpected bite of Antarctica. Phoenix's hand slipped as she forced the padlock closed and it nipped her index finger. Blood ran into the tattered cuff of the coat's sleeve as she raised her hand. "Shit!" she hissed, the word both unusual and satisfying on her lips.

Tamping down the sense of unreality, Phoenix climbed the second gate and strode across Mikaere's paddock towards him, the long coat flapping against her thighs and hindering her progress. Spooked by her unfamiliar outline, the camp horses scattered like petals on the breeze. Mikaere snorted and turned on his heel, heading in the opposite direction to Phoenix. She cursed her error as he lifted his tail into the characteristic Appaloosa sail and lengthened his trot. His ears flicked back and forward and Phoenix buried her face in her hands. "Idiot!" she shouted to herself. Her father's words echoed in her head. *'Catch the horse and then mess around with your gear. Even a hat can make you look different to them.'*

"I know Papa!" Phoenix wailed. "I know all that! But where are you when I need you?"

Ignoring the nervous horse, Phoenix walked to the fence and hung the head collar over the top rail. Then she stripped off the coat and hat and left them there. Rain spattered the grey of her sweatshirt and darkened its colour to a shade nearer its original newness. Blood peppered the left cuff with a faded pink and Phoenix closed her eyes. Wiri's scent still hung around the collar where he'd worn it last and Phoenix blew out through her nose. She shouldn't have taken it and still didn't know why she did. But the floral haze of her mother's washing powder filled her with comfort and reminded her of home. Phoenix wiped her bleeding finger on the thigh of her jeans and took a fortifying breath. Then she turned to her wayward horse and lifted her voice against the wind. "Mikaere Du Rose! Get your ass over here or you're pet food!"

She didn't expect him to come to her. She closed her eyes against inevitable failure and jumped as a wide muzzle nudged her elbow. Mikaere rubbed his poll against her shoulder, spreading dirt in a line over the fabric as he scratched the one unreachable part of his body. Phoenix turned to face him and his presence infused her with strength. "I need your help," she told him. "I need you to behave."

Mikaere snorted and lipped at her jeans pocket. Finding no treats for him, he shook his head and showered Phoenix with dirty rainwater. She ignored his pique, lifting the damp head collar over his face and knotting it at his cheek. Tucking the ends behind the rope and tying it again with practised fingers, she grounded herself in the safe perfume which rose from his damp coat. The lunge rope clipped beneath Mikaere's chin with a click and Phoenix held onto it while clambering up the fence. Mikaere's giant hooves shifted in the muck as the dust turned to slick grease beneath him. The coat slipped from the fence as Phoenix climbed onto his back and the

Jackaroo followed it with a thud into a growing puddle. The horse launched into a sideways jerk of fear and Phoenix gave a sharp inhale as her foot slipped on the top of the fence. Mikaere took a few halting steps away from her. Left with no other choice, Phoenix dived across his back and landed on her stomach over the sharp knots of his spine. She righted herself, the breath knocked from her lungs and her chest tight as she swung her leg over his back and sat. The rain plastered Mikaere's sleek coat to his skin and Phoenix gripped with her thighs to avoid falling. Still struggling to catch her breath, she flicked the rope against the horse's neck and urged him towards the gate.

A high-pitched bark halted their progress. Panic surged in Phoenix's breast and Mikaere's ears flicked back and forth as he read her fear. His front legs danced, churning up the scrubby, waterlogged grass as he arched his spine and stored energy in his powerful hindquarters. "No, no, no!" Phoenix hissed. "They're coming!" She spun Mikaere in a circle and weighed her options.

He'd jumped the fence with ease once before when the world seemed brighter and she'd wanted so much to impress Kirwan. Heavy rain had changed the landscape, pooling water and creating slick mud from the baked earth. She imagined her mother's frightened expression and overwrote it with her father's smirk of pride.

Phoenix made her choice. Confidence surged through her with the reminder she was the daughter of Logan Du Rose and the great granddaughter of the bravest horsewoman to ride the mountains of the north island. Kuia Phoenix Du Rose had been the daughter of a beloved Northland chief and Logan had named Phoenix after her. Touching her rope to Mikaere's neck and tilting her body forward, she used her heels to urge him into a standing start and sent her gaze beyond the corner of the fence. *'Look the way you want to go,'* Logan urged her in her memory.

So, she did. Phoenix Du Rose looked beyond the immediate obstacle towards hope and truth. She would break the rules to uphold them. And Kirwan would never again call her a hypocrite.

29

THERE IS FREEDOM

Mikaere loved a challenge and he cleared the fence with minor effort. But landing proved another matter. He skidded in the slimy mud which greeted his hooves, his legs splaying under him. Phoenix held her breath, using every muscle in her thighs and stomach to remain seated as he battled for purchase. Her mind emptied, leaving numbness in place of fear. She'd grabbed a handful of mane before they rose into the air and she clung to it as a lifeline as her horse slipped and slid as though on roller skates. The brave gelding gave a snort of temper and dug his hooves into the muck. At that moment, Phoenix knew they'd be okay. Mikaere grunted and his frustration with the poor landing restarted her brain.

Mikaere's dinner plate hooves found supplejack vine and then ferns. His ears pricked forward as he set out with surer footing, his head low and his keen eyes picking a way through the undergrowth. Phoenix released the hank of mane, pushing shaking fingers forward to slap his muscular neck. "Magnificent boy!" Her praise sounded overdone in the eerie grey of the bush.

Rain pattered on the upper leaves of the canopy and cascaded down as millions of tiny waterfalls. She let Mikaere walk until they found the path leading to the beach. With every plod of his giant hooves, her experienced mind waited for a misstep or a dip of his head betraying an injury. Her body remained connected with his and his stride seemed the same as always. Phoenix leaned forward and ran her right hand along his shoulder. His ear flicked backwards in response. Another bark from Idris preceded the sound of male voices and she stiffened. "We need to go my friend," she breathed. "It's time you and I found out what we're made of."

Mikaere snorted as Phoenix twitched the rope to the right and lifted it off his muscular neck. His feet danced on the spot as he jogged a few paces and then took off, moving through the gaits with ease until they reached a smooth canter. His hooves pounded in a loud three-beat against the rough path and she knew the approaching men would hear them. But they covered the ground too fast for human feet and Phoenix relaxed as the distance grew. She spotted a line of brown leaves scarring the bush off to the right and recognised the evidence left by her fingers. A moment of consternation ensued as she contemplated veering off towards the barn. Reason interjected. The refugees deserved better than a fifteen-year-old girl with no rescue plan.

Mikaere swerved around tall punga trees and navigated the familiar path, tuned in to his rider's movements and balance. For the first time in their tenuous relationship, Phoenix felt safe on his back despite the rain which made his coat slick and her seat precarious. Until they burst from the bush onto the beach and then his unpredictable nature forced itself free for a moment.

Mikaere's buck of glee at the sight of the ocean almost unseated her and Phoenix cursed as he put his head down for a repeat. "So much for Mr Sensible," she spat, turning him south and pushing him into a steady canter. Rain ran either side of her nose in rivulets and dropped from her chin. Her loose curls tugged at her scalp with an uncharacteristic heaviness as the wind whipped them behind her.

Phoenix lifted her left hand and used her sleeve to wipe her eyes. She registered the joyful bark too late as Idris flew over a dune and landed on the beach next to them. Mikaere gave an angry snort and bucked, sending his nearside rear hoof straight at the foolish animal. Phoenix gripped mane and horseflesh as his body twisted beneath her and her backside hovered in mid-air. Her tail bone took the impact as Mikaere's sharp spine met her on the way down and she forced herself to relax to regain her seat. The dog yelped in fright even though the kick missed. Deciding he disliked the risky game, Idris slowed to a walk and turned his body back the way he came.

Phoenix blew out a breath and waited for Mikaere to settle back into his stride. Then she screwed her body round to look behind her. Darrell emerged from the bush, a black umbrella covering his head. A tall man stood next to him, a black shirt and a dog collar peeking over the zipper of a rain jacket. "Phoenix!" Darrell shouted. "The boss is here to take the service. Tina said you need to come back for it."

The boss. She closed her eyes against the realisation that her own stupidity had blinded her. They were all in it together, the whole damn congregation. Such a scheme thrived with a band of willing volunteers hiding behind the cloak of righteousness. A united, devoted army. Kirwan was about to make a terrible mistake in trusting the visiting pastor.

Phoenix dipped forward over Mikaere's neck and he needed no other command. His ears flattened against his head and his stride lengthened. Black sand kicked up around them as his hooves beat the ground in a rhythm of four instead of three. Energy bunched in his shoulders and haunches and the gallop thrilled every muscle in his powerful body. Phoenix imagined the determination on his majestic face as he carried her over the distance. His speed exhilarated her senses. Wind and rain filled her mouth and his drumming hooves drowned out any other distractions.

In all her hours spent training Mikaere and fighting with him for dominance, Phoenix had never galloped with him. She hadn't trusted him enough to stop when she asked, half expecting him to dump her at the first opportunity and escape back to his mysterious origins. As the wet sand disappeared beneath them in a blur, she realised the treat she'd denied herself. It felt like flying. Her mind fused to Mikaere's and freedom swirled around them in the rain, lethal and addictive. Phoenix Du Rose would never be the same.

30

NATURAL OBSTACLES

The west coast beach ran for a few kilometres before ending in a cove backed by a sheer cliff. The tide which lapped at the shore had already visited the foot of the mountain where her parents lived. It gave Phoenix a sense of connection with them. She imagined her mother standing on the deck outside the back of their house and watching the surf moving north, not realising it would eventually pass her fleeing daughter. Phoenix put her head down against the battering wind and relaxed her stomach. Mikaere flowed like treacle beneath her.

She'd spent her life idolising her father and playing his advice on a loop in her head. He would always do whatever it took to achieve his goals, but Phoenix's mother always did what was right. Reaching for Hana's ingrained sense of fairness and justice, Phoenix determined to do the right thing for once. She would tell the sad tale of the refugees trapped in a rusty barn in the New Zealand bush. She couldn't control the consequences, but she could at least look at herself in the mirror and respect who she saw.

Mikaere had slowed to a canter of his own volition as the thrill of galloping lost its edge and sapped his energy. They'd left the camp a long way behind them and as his breathing grew more laboured, Phoenix sat heavy in her seat to urge him into a lazy trot. The rain eased enough for the birds to begin their cacophony in the bush which ran parallel to the beach. Cicadas resumed their noisy, high-pitched trill. Mikaere halted before the rough rock face of the cliff. He blew out a tired breath.

"Good boy," Phoenix said. "I'm proud of you." She ran her hand over his damp shoulder and enjoyed the slickness of his coat under her palm. He turned his wide head and lipped at her boot in response. Another gigantic sigh came from his deep chest.

Phoenix dismounted and fondled his left ear between her fingers. "I'll give you a breather," she said. "The tide is too high to go around this piece of headland to the next beach. But I'm sure that map in the office showed a stream we can follow. It should take us along the foot of the ridge to the nearest town." Phoenix stroked Mikaere's damp mane away from his eyes and steeled herself for the journey. New Zealand streams tended towards narrow, muddy fissures amid dense bush. Supplejack vine and dense undergrowth followed their natural terraces to make them one of the worst landmarks to follow anywhere. Kissing Mikaere's broad wet cheek, she made a silent apology and led him towards a break in the dark green of the bush line.

It wasn't as terrible as Phoenix imagined. Animal tracks had created a natural path allowing them to walk one behind the other for the next half an hour. When the rain stopped, she used a fallen tree to clamber onto Mikaere's damp back and resume their journey at a faster pace. Signs of humanity increased as they progressed. Discarded food wrappers fluttered in the undergrowth and they passed two defunct campfires surrounded by makeshift benches created from remnants of a felled tōtara tree. The noise of the cicadas rose to a deafening pitch in the canopy. Phoenix's ears seemed to buzz with the constant vibration.

They walked for another hour as the ground banked upwards at a sharp gradient. It grew more tiring to trot though Mikaere's steady plod seemed enough to cover the distance. The narrow track wound around rocky outcrops and forded two streams, becoming more defined with every kilometre. When Phoenix spotted a shiny, plastic triangle pinned to a kauri tree, she gave a loud whoop of elation. The Department of Conservation marker promised civilisation and the hope of assistance along the narrow track it indicated with its orange arrow.

The third stream proved harder to cross. Carrying the rainfall from the mountains, it ran with a bouncing current, flinging spray from treacherous dips and neck breaking underwater rocks. Steep sides kept the flow contained to a little over three metres in breadth. The powerful undercurrent had eroded the lower sections of the bank to leave slippery, mud encrusted overhangs.

Phoenix tried dismounting and leading Mikaere into the water. It required him to follow her down the steep bank and into the flow without being able to plan his footing. He baulked and tugged on the rope at the first attempt. Phoenix bolstered fake confidence and ignored his posturing. She slid down the bank and plopped onto the nearest protruding rock. The stream snatched at her ankles. "It's not deep," she called back to Mikaere. "Come on, boy. Let's go."

Mikaere refused. He shied backwards with a snort, almost overbalancing Phoenix. She clung to the lunge rope and it stretched taut between them. Mikaere blinked and Phoenix sensed him thinking. She knew he could tug the rope hard enough to force her to release it. Then what? She'd fall.

"Bloody hell, Mikaere!" she grumbled. She cast around her, peering through the bouncing current to find stepping stones or solid ground. A section of the bank crumbled into the water a few metres away and her gaze shot to the soft earth beneath Mikaere's hooves. "Damn you, horse!" Phoenix hissed. She held her breath and plunged her right leg into the flow. The bubbling energy snatched at her jeans, inviting her down to the shore on its chaotic, hazardous dance to freedom.

Clinging to the lunge rope, Phoenix dug her boot sole around beneath the surface and found solidity. Water splashed against her thighs as she placed her other foot in the current and turned, edging her way back to the bank. "Thanks for leaving me hanging!" she complained. Her breathing rasped as she scrambled up the rise with difficulty, dirt and leaves clinging to her clothes and fingers. Her jeans stuck to her like a cold second skin and the lunge rope dripped. Phoenix ran a hand along it to ring out the excess water. Her body convulsed in a paroxysm of shivering. "Thank goodness I listened to Papa," she sighed through chattering teeth. "Lunge rope before lead rope because there's more you can do with it. The current could have swept me away right then. Would you even care?"

Mikaere blinked and mischief flared in his wall eye. He gave a shake which began at his shoulders and rippled through his entire body to end with his scrubby tail. Rainwater and muck flew off him in wide arcs. Phoenix used her sleeve to cover her face and tamped down the bubble of exasperation rising in her chest.

They heard it at the same time. The strange mechanical noise sounded incongruous in the bush, overloud and raspy. Phoenix cocked her head to listen, her brow furrowed and her fringe covering one eye. Mikaere's ears flicked back and forth as though independent of their owner. He jerked his head upwards in alarm at the same moment Phoenix recognised the sound. "Dirt bike!" she gasped. "They're looking for us."

A spasm contracted her chest as fear vied with the discomfort of her heavy, soaked clothes. Phoenix stared at the rushing water and panic temporarily froze all sensible thought. "We have to run!" she panted. A frantic glance at the ground behind Mikaere showed his heavy hoof prints scoring the mud in a long trail behind him. It hadn't taken an expert tracker to follow the beginner's map they'd laid out for them. Phoenix cursed her stupidity in not using the cover of the surf to hide their escape. The thought served as a distraction and she flapped her hands to send it away from her. Darrell and the other man had watched them leave. Hiding their tracks would have made no difference. "Think! Think!" She slapped the side of her head with her palm, the action futile but rooted in terror.

A buzz rose as the bike moved closer with every passing second of delay. The breeze from the shoreline brought with it the sweet smell of low octane fuel mixed with butane. The rope shook in Phoenix's fingers. Her gaze met Mikaere's and she resorted to begging. "Help me, please?" she hissed. "We need to cross this stream, or we're finished. Please, Mikaere, please?" she pleaded.

It took a massive effort to tamp down the blind panic rising in her chest though Mikaere read her emotions, anyway. His movements became jerky and the whites of his eyes showed as Phoenix led him to a raised rock and positioned him next to it. "Just stand still for once, please?" she begged, certain he'd move as soon as she got one leg over his broad back. She vaulted on just in case, laying her stomach across his back before swinging her right leg over his hind quarters. Her heart sounded overloud in her eardrums as she settled in the gentle sway of his spine. Reaching around his neck, she looped the long rope underneath and bent it into a loose knot over his withers. "We can't go through it, so we're going over it," she announced, squaring her shoulders and facing the intrepid, bouncing current. The water flew across rocks and fallen trees with glee like a crowd of school children let out early from their lessons. "You've never refused a jump. This will not be the first time you do."

"Phoenix!" A woman's voice called over the bike's guttural growl. "Lexi! Where are you?"

Phoenix swallowed. The morning's drama had obliterated her worry over her missing deputy and guilt pricked her heart as she remembered. "Not now," she breathed, pushing away the horror scenarios of what might have happened to Lexi in the night. Instead, she imagined Tina sitting astride the bike and allowed levity into her mental chaos. It lessened her fear and she licked her lips and faced the stream. "It's the water or Prayer Warrior," she said to Mikaere. She sent him a mental image of the woman's buttocks spilling over the seat like overcooked muffins. "Choose!"

A metallic flash glinted through the trees. The bike coughed and the sound changed as it bumped over supplejack, digging its wheels into the mud to shake itself free of the infuriating vine.

"Phoenix! Lexi!" Tina called again, her voice sounding strained. It cut across the patter of rain against the leaves in the bush canopy. "You need to come back to camp with me. We can sort out whatever's happened."

Phoenix shook her head. "No. No, you can't," she hissed. The realisation crashed down over her. No amount of explaining could justify the hypocrisy.

The dirt bike roared from behind a stand of majestic kauri trees and Phoenix twisted her spine to look. Dressed in waterproof jacket and trousers, Tina sat astride the bike as though riding a racehorse. Her body bent in the middle to make her more aerodynamic. Filth and leaves covered the riding hat protecting her head. Phoenix saw fear in Tina's expression, but recognised an unhealthy dose of anger underpinning it.

"Phoenix!" Tina halted the bike at a safe distance, but its engine continued a low rumble. Mikaere whirled around to face the new threat and Phoenix almost lost her seat in the sudden spin of his hooves.

"You need to come back with me." Tina let go of the bike handlebars and adjusted the wonky riding hat on her head. She rubbed the back of her hand over her eyes and then peered at Mikaere. The bike leaned as she twisted to peer either side of him. "Where's Lexi? Isn't she with you?"

"What do you think?" The uncharacteristic sarcasm came with surprising ease, shocking Phoenix at how it lurked so near the surface. "Obviously not!"

"Where is she?" Tina's confusion appeared genuine. She frowned and cocked her head.

A knot formed in Phoenix's chest at her inability to provide an answer. She'd failed. The younger girl had walked out into the night and she'd done little to stop her. "Lexi left last night." Her voice wobbled. "I don't know where she went."

"Oh." Tina frowned. "But that's not why you're running, is it?" Her eyes narrowed. The bike edged forward as she twisted the throttle and Mikaere let out a snort of alarm. His rear hooves danced towards the edge of the bank and Phoenix looked down and held her breath. Her mind ran through scenarios of what might happen if they fell onto the rocks backwards, but she couldn't finish processing them. Each one ended the same way. She or the horse would break bones. Phoenix prayed it would be her, knowing Mikaere's wouldn't heal. A bullet would put him out of his misery. If he was lucky.

"Don't come any closer!" Phoenix warned. She raised a hand in the universal stop signal and Tina halted her steady creep forward. "Mikaere hates bikes," she lied. "I'll talk to you from here. I don't know where Lexi is."

Tina nodded. She kicked out the bike stand and dismounted, turning off the engine with a frown. Bush noise occupied the sudden silence as the growl ceased. "Okay." Tina took a step forward at the same time as unclasping her riding helmet. "Let's talk about you."

31

FEARLESS

"We're alike, you and me. We follow the rules but make exceptions. Like now. You think you have just cause in breaking the camp rules by leaving. I understand. Sometimes rules need breaking for the good of others. But not now. Come back and we'll chat." Tina morphed into the role of camp counsellor. She curved her lips into a smile and tried to appear amenable.

Phoenix shook her head. Tina's words struck at the heart of her self image and she squirmed beneath the comparison. This damn camp had broken her. Lexi, Kirwan and the refugees had exerted their influence over her carefully crafted discipline and wrecked everything. Phoenix ground her teeth so hard in her jaw it caused her temples to ache. She shook her head again and her fingers gripped the lunge rope.

"We're nothing like each other!" She lifted her voice to a shout and Mikaere jerked beneath her. His hind feet reversed towards the edge of the stream's terrace. Not wanting him to back over it, Phoenix relaxed her legs against his side and lowered the rope to touch his neck. His ears flicked back as he listened to her but the bunching of his muscles signalled his dislike of the showdown. "We're nothing like each other," Phoenix repeated. "Lexi ran away because of the way you made her feel. I hope no one ever dreads my company like they do yours, Tina. You enforce the rules but never apply them to your own behaviour." Phoenix lifted her right hand and pointed it at Tina. A sob caught in the back of her throat as the events of the last few disastrous days rubbed against her tender heart. "You're the hypocrite, not me. You!"

Tina's eyes narrowed and her shoulders squared. She fitted the riding hat back onto her head and cocked her leg over the bike. Her waterproof clothing rustled as she kicked away the stand. Mikaere's neck jerked as the bike's motor guttered to life and he turned his head to observe it through his better sighted brown eye. Phoenix felt the vibration as his teeth crunched together in his mouth. Tina yanked on the accelerator and shouted over the noise. "You need to come back with me! Now!" She edged the bike forward and Phoenix saw the pedals catch against the twisting supplejack vine.

"No!" Phoenix hissed. Mikaere's ears flicked forward as the bike picked up speed and his body tensed. Phoenix grabbed a hunk of mane and settled herself deep in the shallow curve of the horse's spine. Tina continued forward, the bike careening through the undergrowth like a missile. Phoenix realised too late that she intended to drive them over the edge backwards and into the stream. Anger flared in her breast in defence of Mikaere who would land heavily against the jagged rocks at the bottom.

"No!" she shouted. It sounded primal, a scream from somewhere deep in her soul which reverberated around the bush canopy and sent birds scattering overhead. Slapping Mikaere's neck with the rope, she dug her heels into his sides and drove him forward on the track. He obeyed, exhilarated by the unexpected game. His hooves thundered through ferns and over supplejack vine, tearing up the ground with the impact of his weight. Mud and damp fronds spattered either side of them as Phoenix steeled her nerve and leaned over his neck. Mikaere's shoulders moved beneath her and she fixed her gaze on Tina's frightened face.

The woman realised her mistake too late. She yanked on the brake as the horse thundered towards her like a steam train. Inheriting his dam's bloody-minded nature, Mikaere thrived on challenge. During his tenuous relationship with Phoenix, he'd never backed out of a jump, a turn or a death-defying race down the mountain. It had been Phoenix who pulled up at the last minute with a list of excuses to hide her own disappointment with her fear of risk. For the first time in her life, she trusted him not to baulk or lose his nerve and prayed she didn't either. It hit her like a divine epiphany that she had used her dogged discipline to mask a crippling fear of failure.

Phoenix closed her eyes at the last minute to stop her correcting Mikaere's course. She heard the clang of metal followed by the unnatural roar of the bike but felt no impact or deviation in Mikaere's direction. He gave a snort of glee and kicked his rear legs up behind him in victory. Phoenix sat up and raised her hands on the rope, slowing Mikaere's pace to a trot and then a walk. Spinning around, she surveyed the damage.

The bike grumbled in the undergrowth, its low vibration both eerie and ominous. Phoenix held her breath as fear of the consequences flooded back into her rational mind. Turning Mikaere's sweating body to face the bike, she edged him back the way they'd run. Tina lay still in a clump of bush lawyer. For a moment she appeared dead, her complexion pale and her riding hat dented and lying at a jaunty angle over her right eye. Then she sat up, crying out in pain as the bush lawyer snagged her hands and face with its clawed thorns. "Help me!" she demanded, her voice high and petulant.

Phoenix swallowed, edging Mikaere nearer to the tangle of bike wheels, arms and legs. Losing her nerve at the last second, Tina had jerked the bike left, riding through the undergrowth until she hit a punga tree. The fibrous trunk had absorbed the impact, scattering fragments of brown bark over the scene. The bike's front wheel twisted at an angle from its mid-circumference, a few of the spokes detached from the rim and pointing up into the canopy. Trapped beneath the chassis, Tina struggled to extract herself. "I can't move!" she wailed. "You need to help me."

Phoenix wavered. It wasn't in her nature to abandon someone to their difficulties even if they'd created them for themselves. The bike juddered as Tina pushed at the dead weight pinning her right leg to the ground. Bush lawyer attacked her with every movement, tearing at her clothing and leaving spiteful scratches on her face. Phoenix dropped the rope onto Mikaere's neck and tightened her stomach ready to dismount. She might spend the rest of her life regretting it, but she couldn't just leave.

Mikaere had other ideas and they didn't include assisting the vitriolic woman glaring at him from beneath the bike. He gave little warning as he whirled back towards the stream and picked up his hooves. His steady trot became an easy canter along the gouged earth and Phoenix scrabbled to keep her seat. He ignored her signals to pull up, gathering speed and lowering his head to negate the rope's pressure on his head collar. Phoenix released a filthy swearword as his front hooves hit the sill of the drop and soil cascaded down like a brown waterfall.

The stream moved beneath them as time stopped and Mikaere achieved enough lift to carry them across its breadth. He fumbled the landing, not anticipating the unseen jagged stones gathered on the other bank. Trying to avoid them at the last minute, he bunny hopped over the obstacles and skidded on the soft ground. Supplejack vine snagged at his fetlocks like sirens, pulling him down further with every step. When he went down on his knees, Phoenix flew off his back and landed in a clump of silver ferns sheltering beneath a wide kauri tree. The ferns cushioned her fall, but the solid tree trunk proved uncompromising. The last thing she remembered was Mikaere's snort of fury as he struggled in the undergrowth, rivulets of blood snaking from his knees.

32

REUBEN'S GRANDAUGHTER

Phoenix couldn't tell if the rain disturbed her or the strange sensation which assailed her right cheek. Her trembling hand contacted something solid. Her words sounded slurred. "Mama!" she called, confident of Hana's ability to explain the horse sharing her pillow. "Mama!"

She groaned against the haze of warm breath which covered her face and showered her in tiny beads of lung vapour. The ground vibrated with the impatient pawing of Mikaere's front hooves. Phoenix's head ached, sending out an arc of pain which encompassed her neck and shoulders. She raised her left hand to her head and her fingers coasted over a painful, raised bump. It joined with the injury from her beach fall to create a crown of pain.

Mikaere snorted again and Phoenix released a yelp of pain as he sank his sharp teeth into the soft skin of her inner thigh. She pushed his face away. "I can't do this anymore," she admitted, her tone defeatist as she raised herself to a sitting position. Congealed blood covered the horse's knees and a scratch over his muzzle looked deep.

"Phoenix!" She tensed as the voice called her name.

"Oh, no!" she groaned. "Not bloody Tina again!"

Mikaere lipped at her hood and almost throttled her in his efforts to haul her up by her sweatshirt. Phoenix braced her spine against the unforgiving kauri tree and pushed herself to a kneeling position. Then she inched her way up the trunk until her feet took her weight. Her arms and legs worked fine, although reluctance dogged her movements as she forced her muscles back into service. She wavered on her feet and reached out to lean her forehead against Mikaere's solid shoulder. "I feel sick," she hissed, leaning forward and facing the soaked undergrowth. She retched but with nothing in her stomach, the action proved futile. Acid burned the back of her throat.

"Phoenix, are you okay?" Tina sounded concerned and Phoenix contemplated the irony of karma.

"I'm fine." She lifted her voice to a shout and winced as pain left a blinding flash which seared her eyeballs.

"Come back across the stream and we'll go back together." Tina sounded hopeful and Phoenix released a hollow laugh.

"No. I'm not doing that again," she conceded. She pressed her nose into Mikaere's coat, inhaling the comforting scent of horse, mountain grass and home. Anger vied with the hopelessness in her breast as she remembered how Tina tried to drive them backwards into the fast-moving water.

A splash alerted her to Tina's persistence. She couldn't discern whether Tina genuinely cared about her welfare or just wanted to continue her persuasion. But another splash told her she had started to cross the stream. "Good luck with that," she said with a sigh.

Phoenix shook her head and blinked away the prevailing fog left by the unconsciousness. "Knocked senseless," she murmured, understanding the phrase. Unable to vault onto Mikaere's broad back while nursing an epic headache, she picked up the trailing rope attached to his head collar and turned away from the stream. She followed the natural curve of the ridge as it arced up a slope. Heavy footsteps took her away from Tina's splashing. Mikaere trailed behind her.

"Help me!" The bush canopy muted Tina's shouts and allowed Phoenix to ignore them. She tamped down the guilt sensations and stuck to her purpose. The refugees needed help and besides, she couldn't trust the genuineness of Tina's demands for assistance.

A wide, open paddock greeted them at the top of the next rise. Rain trickled down Phoenix's face and mingled with the brown and orange soil covering her sweatshirt. She'd used the cuffs of her shirt to wipe the blood from Mikaere's knees and assess the damage. They looked painful but he walked without limping. The rain washed the blood from his face and experience told Phoenix the cut would scar.

Her mouth felt as though cotton wool filled it and she tasted blood. Using her sleeve to wipe her lips, she felt thirst constrict her throat. Falling rain trickled over her tongue as she tilted her head back and allowed herself a moment of rest. Then Phoenix used a wide post to clamber onto Mikaere's back and the sorry pair jogged along the boundary fence, ploughing through the undergrowth along the bush line. She eased Mikaere into a steady canter as soon as his hooves hit firm ground, drawing comfort from Tina's inability to equal their speed.

Cattle lazed at the far side of the nearest paddock, some lying and others standing. Their jaws moved in a continual beat as they chewed. The sea sounded louder at the top of the rise and Phoenix kept it to her right-hand side, sensing her direction as the fence turned and headed south. She followed it, her head sore and her boots waterlogged and heavy from her dip in the stream. A long downhill ended in a farm gate and Mikaere eased into a controlled gallop, his hooves drumming the grass beneath them. The four-beat turned Phoenix's head into a ball of pain. She closed her eyes against the throb of every deadened impact which passed through Mikaere's powerful body and into hers. She opened her eyes and squinted at the gate as they got nearer, alarmed when Mikaere changed his trajectory and followed the next line of fencing. Phoenix raised her right hand and the rope lifted off his neck. She cursed as he ignored her and his feet pounded over the next rise and kept moving south.

As panic bubbled in her chest, she tamped it down and allowed a sense of inevitability to override its whispers of warning. She trusted Mikaere to keep her safe. Holding on to the sudden realisation provided a flicker of hope from within her thudding brain. Her father trusted him and so would she. "Get help, Mikaere," she begged out loud.

She felt like a fool the moment the words passed her lips. Affording the wilful, unpredictable gelding the same notoriety as a film icon pet with fantastic powers of understanding and communication struck her as ridiculous. The snort of derision hurt her nose and ended in a groan of pain. Mikaere's right ear flicked back and forth as though he shared the joke and he arched his neck and shook his head.

"Sorry, boy." Phoenix patted his wide neck as it rocked beneath her with the motion of his gait. "You're every bit as great as Lassie." Mikaere gave a lengthy sigh and continued his journey.

Phoenix's heart sank as his goal became evident. A paddock filled with grazing horses came into view, the dots taking shape as they grew closer. She groaned at the sight of three heavily pregnant mares and four with foals at heel. "Why?" she shouted into the air. "We should have gone through the gate! Please don't tell me you brought me all the way here for this?" Eleven heads rose and eleven pairs of eyes looked in their direction. One of the pregnant mares lifted her head and gave a high-pitched whinny. The mare with the largest foal lifted her tail in invitation and picked up her feet in a majestic trot. Her infant bounced behind her, tail lifted and his face curious. As Mikaere streaked past they turned as a herd and cantered after him in a swirl of hooves and tails. Only the fence separated them as the mares kicked and bucked with the thrill of running for the hell of it. The babies danced behind, filled with excitement and wonder. Their pincer like legs nipped at the ground in jerky movements. Their paddock ended and they braked in a cloud of dust and disappointment.

Then Phoenix saw the house. Hidden in the hollow behind a rise, it might have evaded them in the space of a long blink. Flaking paint and worn boards coated the outside in the guise of neglect. A broken-down Jeep provided a climbing frame for creeper and pumpkin vines, its wheels missing and the axles propped up on house bricks. The wire fence continued around it like an embrace, halting momentarily as though holding its breath to make way for a wooden gate.

Mikaere overshot the gate and his hooves spat gravel and dirt behind him as he skidded to a halt. An official looking barrier closed the road next to the house and nature had encroached onto the degraded surface. Weeds waved from deep cracks. A dirt road headed east from the gate, bordered by more wire fences and paddocks with sparse, brown grass.

"What do you want?" The voice sounded harsh and a cough punctuated the sentence. An old man staggered from the front door and leaned against the frame. Braces dangled either side of his hips as though defeated holding up his trousers. Despite his dishevelled appearance, a red cravat hung at his neck, the knot even and neat. Sun kissed olive arms matched a brown face and a ta moko tattoo covered every available millimetre of his cheeks, chin and forehead. Lips blackened by tattoo ink straightened into a thin line.

Phoenix ran the back of her hand across her mouth and frowned. Rain dripped from the end of her nose. She spared a second of dismay over her appearance. Dirt and ferns covered her hoodie. Blood soaked the collar and cuffs, hers and Mikaere's. Hopelessness budded in her chest as Mikaere snorted and scraped his front hooves in the dirt. "I need help," Phoenix began. "Please will you call the police?"

"What?" The old man worked his feet forward enough to step off the porch. His tattoos gave his warrior's face a formidable appearance as he shuffled towards her. His slippers splashed through puddles and he held one arm up to shield his head from the rain.

Phoenix plugged into Mikaere's easy confidence and pushed her shoulders back. "Ko Phoenix Du Rose ahau," she called, trying a different approach.

The man stopped on the path and cocked his head. His lips parted in surprise. "Āe mārika," he replied. *You don't say.*

"Āe," Phoenix replied. She lifted her voice to reach him and searched inside herself for the strength of her ancestors. "Ko Waikato te mana whenua." She named her tribe and saw the recognition flare in his irises. "E noho ana au kei Rangiriri."

"Du Rose?" His eyelashes fluttered and he ventured closer, his gnarled hands reaching for the gate's rough surface. "Reuben Du Rose of the Waikato iwi once took a stallion from me in a game of poker. An Appaloosa with grey markings on its hind quarters. The bastard." He frowned and then corrected himself with no sign of conscience for his foul language. "Reuben was the bastard, not the horse."

Phoenix held her head high and nodded. "I'm his mokopuna," she declared, claiming her grandfather with pride though he'd died just hours before her birth.

"And you want the police, you say?" Water dribbled from the gate as the old man's clawed hand shifted. Rain spattered against the roof of the dilapidated house. He stared up at Mikaere. "Is this gelding from my Appaloosa?" he demanded. A practised eye roved over Mikaere's noble conformation and he nodded. "Āe, I think he is," he concluded. His lips parted in a smile of pride. He pointed to Mikaere's blue eye. "I breed them with the wall eyes," he said. "Lots of people don't like that in a horse. They want perfection. Mis matching eyes don't fit their image of it." He chuckled and another guttural cough bent his body in two.

Phoenix swallowed. "His mother is Sacha and she came from Methuselah. Mikaere's sire is a mystery."

"Āe! Methuselah!" A delighted grin split the old man's face. The inked patterns on his cheeks creased into a series of alternate lines and swirls. "He is then." Reaching out a hand, he ran experienced fingers over Mikaere's brow. Phoenix frowned and held back the customary warning. Instinct told her this man had met far worse tempers than Mikaere's.

"Please may I use your phone, Matua?" Phoenix used the Māori word for uncle as a sign of respect and the old man sighed.

"You may, Phoenix Du Rose of the Waikato iwi," he said, stepping back from the gate. It opened with a creak and he waved an arm in welcome, the name of her grandfather acting as the entry ticket into his world.

33

MATUA – UNCLE

Mikaere grazed in the old man's garden, tugging at the sparse green shoots with sharp teeth and snatching them from the ground. He inspected the pumpkin leaves wrapped around the old car and blew out a sigh of disgust. Phoenix unclipped the lunge rope but left the head collar in place to avoid drama when she wanted to leave and he didn't.

"He fell heavy?" Matua spoke English as he pointed at Mikaere's knees.

Phoenix nodded. "He went down in the bush. I think it's just bruising and grazes." She looped the lunge rope over her shoulder and followed the old man up the steps onto the porch.

"Phone is there." Matua pointed to a handset fixed to the wall. He gave her a toothless grin. "Looks old but it works."

"Thank you." Phoenix lifted the handset and paused with her finger over the buttons. In her desperation to summon help, she hadn't considered who she should call. Matua scrabbled around in his pantry looking for something. The door hung by one hinge.

"Kei whea te manuka?" he muttered to himself. His gnarled fingers withdrew, clutching a jar of manuka honey. He lifted it in victory and jerked his head towards the front door. "I'll put this on te hōiho," he said. He snagged an ice cream tub from a shelf as he walked past her. Phoenix saw strange bottles of liquid and a rumpled bag of cotton wool balls nestled inside it.

She forced her lips into a smile and gave him a wave. "Good luck with that," she whispered as he shuffled down the steps. She paused for a moment, expecting to see the old man running for his life in the thirty seconds following his exit. When she heard no commotion, she ventured to the door trailing the coiled cable from the phone. It reached almost as far as the threshold and she leaned outside, consumed by curiosity.

Mikaere stood with his hooves square in the centre of a vegetable patch. He chewed a mouthful of carrots he'd yanked up by their leaves. Matua bent double beside him, dabbing at Mikaere's knees with cotton wool and something brown enough to be iodine. The horse blew out a breath of contentment and chewed his carrots with loud crunches as Matua murmured to him.

"Great!" Phoenix sighed. "That damn horse picks his own friends." She stepped back across the room and stared at the numbered buttons in front of her. The receiver stuck to her palm and the coiled cable needed a dose of disinfectant. "Maybe it's just me he hates then." She swallowed, knowing in her heart it wasn't true.

Her fingers shook as she punched the numbers in a memorised order. She held her breath and waited for the call to connect.

"Inspector Singh Johal." Her half-brother's voice sounded clipped and business-like. The irrational urge to cry bubbled into Phoenix's chest on hearing his familiar cadence. She swallowed and her words emerged as though from a mouth filled with mashed potatoes.

"Bo, it's me, Phoenix," she managed. "I'm in trouble. Can you help me?"

"Phoe?" She closed her eyes and imagined his handsome face creasing into lines of concern. "What's happened?" The outside noises of traffic and voices halted as a door closed in the background.

"Talk to me, babe. How can I help?" No fuss, no histrionics, just facts. Phoenix swallowed. She hadn't thought this through and couldn't form a coherent sentence. "Where are you, Phoe? Are you hurt?" His questions unlocked the block in her brain and the answers flowed with more ease.

"I don't know where I am, but I'm not hurt. Well, I fell off Mikaere and banged my head, but I'm okay. I only lost consciousness for a few minutes. I think." Phoenix halted at the sound of Bodie's sharp inhalation. She dived straight in, afraid if she stopped talking she'd struggle to start again. Her head throbbed and her vision blurred when she moved her eyes too fast. "I went to a horse camp, Bo. Mum dropped me there last weekend." She blinked, no longer certain of the day of the week. "We found a barn with a group of refugees in it. They're locked in there. Some of the camp leaders take water and food after dark." Bodie cursed and Phoenix rushed into a summary of her fears. "I ran away on Mikaere and one of them came after me. They're preparing to move the people somewhere else. You need to send your officers there fast. There's a line of broken branches and dead leaves for them to follow to the barn." Phoenix inhaled and stared at a rip in the wallpaper next to the telephone.

Bodie gave a low whistle. "Wait. What? Slow down, Phoe."

But she couldn't. "Mikaere fell and hurt his knees and his face. I found a house and the kaumatua here let me use his phone to call you."

"What's the number?" Bodie interrupted her. "It's showing as private. How will I reach you?"

Phoenix moved her head to look at the telephone. It clung to the wall and dirt and stains covered its once cream surface. But no number. "I don't know. Sorry." She swallowed. "I think it's a stud farm. We rode south along the beach and then up through the bush. It's the first house I found. Mikaere brought me here." Her last sentence sounded hollow and the pressure of tears built behind her eyelids.

Logan would have understood what she meant, but Bodie couldn't. A product of her mother's first marriage, she doubted he'd ever ridden a horse in his life. Her chest hitched and she struggled to keep her composure. "I want my papa," she whispered into the phone. "He'd know what to do."

Silence greeted her. She almost heard Bodie's teeth grinding in his head. His voice carried a trace of irritation when he replied. "I know what to do, Phoe. Let me make some calls and ring you back. Where's the homeowner? Can he tell you the address or phone number?"

"No." Phoenix shook her head even though Bodie couldn't see her. "He's fixing up Mikaere's legs and the cut to his muzzle. I don't want to stop him." A sense of hopelessness settled over her like a cloak and she regretted calling her brother. She should have phoned Logan. "I need to go," she said. Her finger shook as she pressed it over the button to end the call and sat the receiver on its hook. Calling her father seemed futile. She realised he'd ask her the same questions as Bodie.

Phoenix turned and padded outside, her boots making squelching noises on the threadbare carpet. The old man finished spreading manuka honey onto Mikaere's knees and rose with difficulty. He stood for a moment with his palm rested against the horse's shoulder. "You're a fine boy, aren't you?" he murmured. "Out of a mare of Methuselah's, hey? Āe mārika. In't that wonderful to see after all this time."

"Excuse me." Phoenix lifted the hem of her sweatshirt and twisted it in her fingers. Water escaped from the fabric and dripped onto her jeans. "I phoned my brother, but I couldn't tell him the address."

"I thought you wanted the cops." Matua shuffled towards her, the honey pot sitting at an angle in the ice cream container with his medical supplies.

"He is a cop," Phoenix said. "He's an inspector for Counties Manakau District."

Matua nodded. "Is he coming for ya then? How will he take the horse?"

Phoenix squeezed her eyes shut. "I need to tell him where I am before he can do anything, Uncle."

Matua cleared his voice. "If he's at the main cop shop in Papakura, then he's a good hour away from here. Tell him you're on Karekare Road in the Waitakere Ranges." He frowned. The handrail he used to haul himself up the steps to the porch shook under his weight. "Why are you riding around without knowing where you are? Where did you come from?"

"It's a really long story." Phoenix's head wobbled on her neck and pain radiated from the painful bruise. "I came from a camp near Mercury Bay,"

Matua's head jerked back in surprise. "You rode through the bush? Heahea kōtiro! You're lucky you didn't break your neck!"

"I know it was stupid. But I had to get help." Phoenix swallowed and glanced back at the telephone.

"You ran away?" Matua reached out and laid his gnarled fingers over her wrist. "What happened kōtiro? You tell Uncle all about it and I'll decide if I need to break out my shotgun."

34

Matua shuffled about in his kitchen, boiling water on a gas stove to make Phoenix a cup of coffee. He dug in a canister of solidified brown powder while she called Bodie with the address of the camp and her location. "I'm safe," she reassured him. "Matua knew my tupuna tāne Reuben. I'm fine here for now. Please, just stop them hiding the refugees somewhere else."

"Okay." Bodie insisted on speaking to Matua and took the phone number. Phoenix didn't hear what he said to the old man, but she noticed Matua's bushy grey eyebrows rise. He said nothing and hooked the receiver back on its cradle.

Phoenix sipped the strong coffee and winced. A hefty helping of sugar hit the back of her throat like a syrup. "Did he threaten you?" she asked, her tone filled with ready apology. "Papa says he can be a bit of a dick."

Matua laughed. "No, kōtiro. He asked me to keep you safe and not let you go back to the camp."

Phoenix nodded. "Mikaere needs to rest now. How bad are his knees?" She set her coffee on a scarred low table and rose. "What am I thinking? I should have checked him myself."

"He's fine." Matua waved a hand at her. "Drink your coffee and leave him alone. He's made of strong stock and he's enjoying his salad."

Phoenix groaned. "Your veggie patch. I'm so sorry." She sat on a lumpy sofa and picked up the mug. The mixture tasted better with the second cautious sip and then a third. The sugar replenished her energy and the warmth seeped into her bones.

Matua shrugged and patted the rounded stomach protruding through his straining shirt buttons. "I like me boil ups but without the green stuff."

Phoenix shook her head. "I'll replace everything. I'll come back and plant it myself soon." She glanced at the open door and frowned. A familiar sound grew more dominant against the backdrop of Mikaere's contented sighs and the wind sneaking around the eaves. The rain had stopped and an ominous dripping betrayed a leak in the roof somewhere.

A dirt bike appeared at the front gate and coffee slopped over her hand as she panicked. "She's found me!" Phoenix rose on jerky legs. She dumped the coffee on the table and spun in a circle. The tiny house offered nowhere to hide but Phoenix spotted a double bed housed in a room behind the kitchen. She darted towards it, not sure what she'd do once she got there. Her damp socks slipped on the threadbare carpet and she regretted taking her boots off and leaving them just inside the doorway. Pain from her banged head radiated outward and gave her a moment of blurred vision and confusion. A firm grip closed around her wrist.

"Steady, kōtiro," Matua said. His tone sounded even. Its strength worked its way into Phoenix's mind, dampening her fear enough to halt her panicked flight. "Nobody will hurt you," he promised. His brown irises seemed to swirl as he widened his eyes at her. "I'll keep you safe. Not because your brother asked me to, but in the name of your tupuna tāne Reuben. Whānau takes care of whānau in our world."

"Family." Phoenix's body shook as she forced herself to stand still and listen to his words. She gave a jerky nod. "Family takes care of family." Her father's mantra comforted her as her gaze darted towards the front door. The rickety gate ground open. "Who is it?" she demanded.

A man closed the gate behind him and strode along the path. He stopped and stared to his right, confusion shrouding his expression. Deep wrinkles nestled at the corners of his brown eyes and full lips, indicative of a man who laughed often. Red hair burst from beneath a damp Jackaroo hat, droplets of water cascading from the curls to sprinkle the shoulders of his hunter's jacket. "What the hell, Koro?" he shouted. His boot soles ground against the gritty path. Enormous hands like bear paws slapped his thighs in an attitude of exasperation. "If you didn't want to eat the veggies, you just needed to say!"

"Your son?" Phoenix wiped the back of her hand across her muddy cheeks. Tears prickled behind her eyelids and she swallowed to drive them away. "He's angry at Mikaere."

The man stomped up the porch steps and stood in the doorway. His eyes narrowed at the sight of Phoenix. Command rolled off him in waves, the warrior gene reminiscent of Logan Du Rose's ingrained authority. Phoenix felt herself cow before it and hated the instinct to assume a natural subservience. Matua patted her hand and gave her a sideways wink. "Take no notice, kōtiro," he said, his tone a mix of amusement and defiance. "Tāku moko runs the stud business for me." His chuckle rose from his belly. "I gots me a white boy grandson. How about that?" His irises sparkled with pride and his grandson scowled.

"What about the veggies, Koro?"

Phoenix cleared her throat. "I'm sorry. I promised to replace them."

"Your horse?" He appeared as a giant in the doorway, filling the space with his bulk and the force of his personality.

Phoenix nodded again. She held his gaze and forced herself not to blink. His pale skin and red curls reminded her of Mac and she imagined her gentle brother's reaction to her situation. It hadn't occurred to her to question what the boys might have done to create a different outcome. Mac would have observed and acted with decisiveness and clarity. Wiri's lack of fear and tendency towards strategy would have proved far subtler than her confusion, absence of planning, and hasty flight south. Both would have said less and done more.

Matua removed her need to explain, patting the back of her hand and jerking his head towards his grandson. "Sit down Ika. The girl rode for help. She's in trouble. The police are on their way."

"Police?" The man's eyes narrowed further, hooded by his red brows. "Why?" Matua tutted. Ika released a snort of annoyance, but he kicked off his boots and settled into a scruffy armchair near the door. Water speckled the shoulders of his camouflage jacket and his trousers crinkled as he sat. His tone held insistence. "What's going on, Koro?"

The telephone rang. Its bleating call silenced Ika and sent ripples of fear through Phoenix. She tensed as Matua lifted the receiver and shouted into it as though the caller stood just beyond earshot. Ika looked at Phoenix and she saw the slight purse of his lips. "What?" Matua bellowed. "Yes, she's here. What? Yes, you can speak to her." He fought with the tangled coils of the cord to drag the receiver to Phoenix. "It's for you," he said, his voice returning to normal volume. "Your brother."

Bodie's voice crackled as Phoenix held the receiver to her ear. "Phoe?" He repeated her name when she nodded instead of speaking. "Phoe?"

"Yes." She whispered and turned sideways, unnerved by Ika's piercing gaze boring into her face. "How long before you get here?" Her eyes closed as the signal broke. She strained to piece the fractured sentence together. A moment of torturous silence intervened. "Accident? You're in an accident or someone else?"

"Had to stop," Bodie said. A series of crackles killed the rest of the sentence. "Local guys are coming to take control." Another break, but she gleaned it wasn't his accident. Phoenix heard sirens in the background and then understood Bodie's final sentence before the signal cut out and left her with the landline's dial tone. She replaced the receiver back on its cradle and turned to the men.

"My brother stopped to deal with an accident. He said immigration officers are already on their way." Her fingers writhed in front of her. "What have I done?" she whispered. The tears she'd held back so valiantly plunged over the crests of her cheeks and hit the carpet between her feet. "Those poor people. What have I done?"

35

MISUNDERSTANDINGS

Matua drove a brand-new utility vehicle from a run-down garage behind his house. It sat on the grass like a shiny cherry clinging to a child's handmade cake. Ika watched him almost wipe out the chimney breast before claiming the driver's seat. He drove them to the camp with Phoenix fretting in the back seat. She'd convinced the men she needed to see the refugees before the police arrived and assure them of her good intentions. She just didn't know how to explain it in words.

A police cordon blocked the gate to the camp and a guard refused them access. Matua set up a convoluted barrage of political complaints about the British crown's unlawful occupation of New Zealand. He distracted the officer guarding the entrance while Phoenix sneaked through the bush to the barn housing the refugees. She lost her way twice before finding her markers of death and arriving soaking wet and much too late.

"No, no! You don't understand!" Disbelief stunned her into immobility as a police officer emerged from the barn in front of her. He pushed a bedraggled male ahead of him. The man's thin wrists caused the handcuffs to make a sad, clanking sound. When he cleared his throat, Phoenix realised she faced Elephant. She straightened her shoulders and addressed the officer. "You need to wait for my brother!"

"Get back miss," he replied. He raised his hand, palm outward in a universal stop sign. He directed Elephant to a waiting paramedic who lifted a stethoscope from around his neck. His female team member peered around him, looking eager to greet her next customer.

"But you don't understand. These people are being held prisoner!" Her voice rose at the end, emerging as a squeak. "It's not their fault. This isn't right! It's not meant to happen like this!"

"Get back!" Another police officer approached from behind Phoenix, a snarling German Shepherd hauling on its leash. The dog snapped at the next passing refugee, not serious about attacking her but faking it to good effect. Already quiet and cowed, the female prisoner skirted sideways to avoid the dog. She carried a baby and a tiny girl hung from her long skirt.

The realisation hit Phoenix like a rugby slam as she spun in a circle and observed the gathered officers. They'd come prepared. One group wore black clothing and Kevlar vests, black balaclavas covering their features. Their eyes darted left and right in a continual assessment of threat. Heavy guns hung from straps around their torsos. She'd proved Tina right and in doing so defeated the very people she wanted to save from abuse. Instead of bringing them rescue, she'd made their treacherous journey across the ocean utterly pointless.

The regular police officers wore uniforms, but the immigration officers sported street clothes. They made no secret of their jubilation at securing a lucky bust. The police officers brought the refugees out one at a time, not giving them time to adjust their eyes to the grey gloom after the darkness of the barn. The immigration officers smiled at each other over their clipboards.

"What will you do with them?" Phoenix demanded, venturing closer to the barn door. "They're victims. They aren't terrorists!" The police officers ignored her as they progressed into the light, pushing their human spoils ahead of them. Handcuffs clanked in the humid air, forming a cacophony of desperate, musical sounds. "Listen to me!" Phoenix spotted an immigration officer standing to the side of the door. The hinges bent at right angles and the wood hung in splintered curtains. The woman held a clipboard and spoke into a walkie-talkie. A name badge swung from a lanyard around her neck. Phoenix sprang in front of her as she counted off another prisoner. "You don't understand!" she implored. "This isn't why I called the police."

The woman frowned and tossed her blonde ponytail. "You're the informant?" She raised a pencilled eyebrow and cocked her head. Deft fingers flipped a page on her clipboard. "I'll take your statement soon."

"No!" Phoenix backed away, shocked by the unwelcome label. "I'm not an informant! You're meant to help them, not treat them like criminals."

"They are criminals." The officer shook her head and her ponytail bounced against her shoulder. Her face radiated confusion. "Our laws are there for a reason. People can't just take up residence without permission. There's a process."

"They had no choice." Phoenix's chest tightened and severed the rest of her protest.

The officer released a sarcastic laugh. "Well, they didn't just sail to a remote continent like New Zealand by accident." She waved her hand in dismissal. "They're illegal and we'll process them as such. The paramedics will assess them and then we'll take them into custody. Thank you for doing the right thing. Walk back to camp and one of my colleagues will take your statement in a minute."

Phoenix hopped from foot to foot, waving her hands in distress. "But they sailed here by accident." She made the mistake of tapping the officer's shoulder as the woman turned away. "They headed for Australia. They didn't mean to come here."

"Go back to the camp!" She barked the order and shook off Phoenix's hand. Anger flashed in the woman's blue irises. "Do you want me to ask one of the police officers to arrest you for obstructing us in our duty?"

"No!" Phoenix backed until her ankles tangled in supplejack. She staggered and almost fell. "This isn't right."

The officer raised her hand to stop further argument. Her expression softened. "I know this is hard kid. It seems unfair but rules are rules. You did the right thing." She waved her hand towards the path leading back to the camp. Half an hour of continual foot traffic had stamped the bush into submission and created a visible dirt track from the barn.

Phoenix turned, holding her arms out either side of her like a tightrope walker. She picked her way through the supplejack and skirted the group of officers.

36

TUG-OF WAR

Matua and Ika remained at the edge of the camp, held back by armed officers wearing body armour. Phoenix saw their anxious faces peering at her from beside Matua's truck as she crashed from the bush and onto the campground. She raised her hand in a half-hearted wave to signal she was okay, but her wrist felt almost too heavy to lift. She wasn't okay. Exhaustion vied with disappointment and turned her bones to lead. The bruise from her injury tightened her scalp like a tourniquet.

The campers peered through the windows of their cabins, exiled to their bunks by the police officers. They watched with wide eyes as the camp leaders gathered around the dead fire in a sombre huddle. Sitting with their wrists cuffed behind their backs, they made a sorry crowd. They looked so different from the guitar playing, Bible reading group of a few nights ago. The pastor kept his head down, his dog collar hanging lopsided from his black shirt and his hair mussed. Idris barked from a location which echoed the sound. Phoenix looked for signs of Tina and pursed her lips. Maybe she'd drowned in the stream. Would that make her guilty of murder?

"Which is your cabin?" A sharp female voice affected Phoenix like the sound of nails scraping down a blackboard. "You need to wait in it until we've questioned you and given you permission to leave."

Phoenix stared around the cabins, hardly registering the frightened faces watching her from the windows like a silent audience of a mime. "That one." She jabbed a finger towards Grant's bunk at the end of the row. The thought of seeing Kylie, Sharon and the other girls made her stomach roil. They'd demand an explanation and she didn't have the words to justify her actions.

"Wait inside until someone comes for you." The immigration officer tapped Phoenix's shoulder. "The cops will ring your parents once we've finished. Then you can go home."

Phoenix lowered her voice. Her skin crawled as the group around the fire turned as one to eavesdrop. "What will happen to the refugees?"

The woman's lips flattened into a line. "Don't worry about it. Go to your cabin and stay there."

Phoenix nodded. "There's something you should know about the track."

"Kid!" The woman raised her hand, her fingers almost touching Phoenix's nose. Frowning, Phoenix took a step out of range. "Just go to your cabin. An officer will take your statement soon. Please try to be patient."

Phoenix's feet dragged across the grass to Grant's cabin. She ignored the frantic knocking which came from the window of her cabin, too distressed to even look at the girls. They were her responsibility and she'd failed them.

A police officer stood beneath Grant's porch. He spoke into his radio and stepped aside as she passed. Phoenix slipped inside the cabin and he shut the door behind her with a decisive click. Closing her eyes, she leaned back against it and waited for her heart to stop its frantic thudding.

"Happy now?"

She gasped and opened her eyes, pressing her fingers against her mouth. "You scared me." The comment sounded ludicrous after the events of the morning. She'd spent the hours between leaving and returning to the camp perpetually terrified.

Kirwan lay on his stomach on the bottom bunk. He pulled earbuds from his ears and looked up at Phoenix. Music from her parents' era made a tinny echo against his fingers. He shrugged and tossed an expensive mobile phone onto the mattress. "What's happening out there?"

Phoenix frowned and gaped at the shiny phone. She pointed to it and her words sounded stilted. "Where did you get that?" His smirk told her all she needed to know. Phoenix balled her fists by her sides. "You had access to a phone all the time, didn't you?" The words sounded hollow, echoing inside the cabin's wooden structure. "Why?" Tears of anger swirled into a ball in her throat. "Why didn't you tell me?"

Kirwan planted his feet on the floor and his expression grew serious. He spread his hands either side of him. "It's Grant's contingency. He kept it under his mattress. And why do you think? Have you seen what's going on out there?"

"You didn't trust me?" Phoenix swallowed, unable to deny Kirwan's conclusion. She nodded, the action jerky. "Fair enough." Her hands balled into fists. "You called me a hypocrite. It forced me to do something."

Kirwan shook his head and a laugh escaped his lips. "Don't put this on me," he replied. He blinked and rose to tower over her. "Everyone will go to jail for this, Phoenix. The refugees and the camp leaders. This is on you."

"No." Phoenix shook her head and her fingers flexed to reveal her trembling. "This isn't what I wanted."

Kirwan shrugged. He lifted his index finger and bopped the end of her nose. "But it's what you got." His kiss felt rough and devoid of kindness as he pressed his lips to hers. "I kinda liked you," he confessed. He dipped to retrieve the phone and it disappeared into his back pocket. Deft fingers pressed a lighter and a bag of tobacco into a tatty backpack leaned up against the bunk post.

"What are you doing?" Phoenix's eyes widened. "You can't just leave."

"You did." Kirwan gave her a slow smile and a wink. "You just shouldn't have come back here." He flapped his hand in the air. "Curiosity killed the cat and all that."

Phoenix swallowed. He'd laid bare every dirty space in her personality like bleach on a mildewed wall. "I wanted to fix it," she whispered. "I thought I could."

Kirwan snorted. "Fix this? Kid, you're dreaming."

"Take me with you." The overwhelming urge to escape rocked her back on her heels. She didn't think it through, forcing away the rational arguments which made this a terrible, terrible idea.

Kirwan hoisted the backpack onto his shoulder and straightened his jacket. Then he slipped an arm around Phoenix's shoulders. His breath smelled of nicotine as he kissed her forehead. Phoenix dug her fingers into the fabric of his jacket pocket and held on tight, her heart paralysed by a spasm of longing. He kissed one cheek and then the other before releasing her. "See ya, rich girl," he said, his voice husky. Phoenix clutched the weak fabric of his pocket and he pulled away, the pop of the stitching followed by a tearing sound. A rip in the material showed the threadbare lining inside the jacket and she forced her fingers and thumb apart to release him. Tears rolled over her lower lids and plunged onto the wooden floor.

Phoenix closed her eyes and bowed her head as a wave of fresh pain engulfed her. The pounding in her head sent a steady beat to keep pace with her heart. She jumped as a pressure beneath her chin lifted her head and she looked at Kirwan through a haze of tears.

He leaned closer and kindness mingled with regret in his flecked brown irises. "You're too good for me," he whispered. "I don't deserve you." Robbing Phoenix of the chance to protest, he strode across the cabin and slipped through the door. It sealed behind him with a muted click.

Her breath ragged, Phoenix rushed to the window and peered out with hope fading in her heart. Police officers and immigration staff converged on a transit van backing onto the grass in front of the cabins. The strobing police lights seemed like overkill in the natural surroundings, sending blue and red flashes to dance on the wooden buildings. Kirwan had chosen the perfect moment to blend into the canopy as the distracted officers made a plan for transporting the refugees and camp staff to the nearest Auckland police station.

Phoenix didn't have Kirwan's luck and her attempt to follow him ended in failure. She met the sullen gaze of a police officer as he turned back towards the narrow porch. "Hey!" He prodded a finger at the door behind her. "Get back inside, please."

Phoenix ventured out further. She held her hands up in front of her. "You don't understand. I need to speak to my brother. Inspector Singh Johal. I need to speak to Bodie." She swallowed and the action cut her sentence in half and turned it into a stutter.

The officer frowned and shook his head. He glanced towards the van as the first of the male refugees climbed inside and sat heavily on the bench seat. Phoenix bit her lip as one by one, the group settled into their new prison. The officers corralled the few women and children into another van, separating them from husbands and brothers. They appeared cowed and defeated, their limbs scrawny and their clothing soiled. Scarves covered the women's hair, the once bright fabrics muted by wear and hardship. Their dark eyes appeared as bottomless pits of misery in their olive faces.

"Go inside, please. Someone will speak to you soon." The police officer flapped his hands at Phoenix as though shooing an escaped hen back into its pen. Phoenix backed away as he advanced towards her, her boot heel snagging against the door frame and causing her to stumble.

A blood-curdling scream added shock to the sombre scene. It ricocheted off the tree trunks and echoed around the camp, bringing a surge of fear and fury. The immigration officers froze. The armed police lifted their guns and turned as one to the origins of the scream.

Tina stared straight at Phoenix, her eyes gimlet hard and her scratched and bleeding face fixed in a grimace of hatred. Limbs heavy from hours of walking staggered across the camp, their direction as straight as an arrow loosed from a bow. Phoenix gulped and pressed her spine against the door frame as Tina barrelled towards her.

37

SAVAGE

"Happy now?" Tina screeched. Scratched and bleeding fingers balled into fists and her legs continued to propel her up the stairs towards Phoenix in a fierce piston motion. "You stupid little girl! What did you do?"

"That's enough!" The officer held his hands out in front of him. Three others joined him to haul Tina away from Phoenix. Her damp jacket slid beneath their grip, giving her enough time to press her fingers around Phoenix's throat.

"Why?" she snarled, her voice husky and feral. "You've ruined everything!" Her head snapped back as the officers dragged her off the porch and flipped her onto her stomach in the wet grass. "She tried to kill me! I could have drowned!" The officer sitting on her back pressed Tina's face against the dirt and cut off the rest of the sentence. She still screamed accusations at Phoenix, her words muted by the earth.

Phoenix remained glued to the door frame, her head aching and her heart thudding like a jackhammer. Her limbs shook and trembled and she fought to stop herself sinking to the deck without control. The weight of blame rested hard on her shoulders, condemning her well intentioned actions and muddying her perception of right and wrong. The collective stare of the camp leaders burned her skin as they watched from around the empty fire pit. Grant raised an eyebrow at Gus. Their unspoken condemnation warmed her cheeks.

"Stay inside your cabin!" A barked command forced Phoenix to turn her head, believing at first it was meant for her. The rear doors slammed on the vans containing the refugees and the woman with the clipboard waved to the driver. Kylie's face peeked from the girls' cabin door, her eyes wide and blind with fear. She fixed her wooden gaze on Tina's struggling body as the policeman cuffed her wrists and an immigration officer knelt on her back to stop her bucking. Gus and Grant rose at the same moment, seeing the first of the transporters becoming stuck in the mud. Its rear wheels spun, sending a shower of dirt splaying in arcs behind it. The second driver set his wipers moving and spread the sludge across his windscreen.

"Get inside, kid!" The officer spoke to Kylie, his tone filled with exasperation. "Why will none of you do as you're told?"

"Just go around him!" The woman with the clipboard banged on the side of the second van and Phoenix saw the driver's profile through the open passenger window as he nodded. The steering wheel turned beneath white-knuckled fingers and the van lurched to the right. His left headlight missed the back of the first vehicle by centimetres. Sensing his rear wheels slide, he yanked the steering wheel the other way and gunned the engine.

Phoenix imagined time slowing as his passenger turned to glance through the grille between him and their human cargo. The driver nodded at something he said and cranked the gear lever into reverse. The rear wheels gained traction on the patchy grass and the van lurched backwards as he pressed on the gas pedal. Relief flooded the driver's face as the tyres bit into the firmer surface. He reversed as far as Grant's cabin and squealed to a halt. The van rocked as he found first gear and stepped on the gas. But the rear wheels defeated him, digging in too far and spinning. The immigration officer holding the clipboard screwed up her face in exasperation. Rain dripped from her chin as she whacked the side of the van with her clipboard.

An almighty crash in the distance accompanied a shout. A missile hurtled through the canopy with its perilous burden. Phoenix tensed at the familiar sound of the rain laden widow maker slamming into trees as it headed to earth at speed.

"Did you hear that?" The immigration officer shouted to the cop on the deck. He nodded, his chest inflating with his held breath. A small group of immigration officers emerged from the bush. They moved with haste, those at the rear brushing debris from their heads and shoulders.

"That was close," one shouted. "It's like a bomb went off on the track."

While the gathered personnel rushed towards the arrivals, the driver of the second van gunned the engine again and his vehicle slid sideways in the mud. Its rear wheels found solidity beneath their treads, spitting gravel behind the tyres as it lurched forward. He spun the wheel hard and mounted the slope onto the campground's sodden grass. The engine revved as the tyres found traction and the van shot forward. The driver looked down at the gear lever, grinding the engine into second gear. He picked up the pace and cranked into third. He didn't see the slender shape which darted off the porch and dodged around the distracted police officer. She kept moving and he didn't see her. Not at all.

Phoenix held her breath as the top of Kylie's blonde pigtail bounced in front of the stationary van. She opened her mouth to scream a warning, but no sound emerged. Kylie didn't look before she shot from behind the first van's wing, her eyes fixed on Tina's writhing shape beneath the officers. The moving vehicle increased its speed, the driver eager to carry his cargo back to civilisation. He jammed his boot on the gas and his facial muscles sagged as he glanced up at the windscreen framing Kylie's frightened face. The officer in the passenger seat screamed as she was there and then gone. The heavy wheels traversed the obstacle with a bump. His voice rang out high and strangled. Inhuman almost.

38

BROTHERS IN ARMS

"Phoe, Phoe." The voice sounded urgent. Strong fingers took the weight of her body beneath her armpits. She retched again and her empty stomach protested. "That's enough now." His tone sounded gentle and the dented bucket disappeared from in front of her face. Phoenix flapped her hand to bring it back, certain she'd need it again once her mind replayed the sounds she fought to forget. "You're okay, I've got you."

An arm slipped around her shoulders and her cheek rested against a scratchy blue pullover. The institutional scent of Papakura police station enveloped her head with the reminder of dust and old plasterboard. Bodie laid his cheek against the top of her head and Phoenix heard him sigh.

She puffed out an agonising rush of breath. "Kirwan's dead. They killed him. He pushed her out of the way." Her voice sounded flat. Phoenix tuned her mind into the sounds around her. She forced herself to overwrite the thud of Kirwan's head hitting the van's grille and the crunch of his ribs as its weight pressed him into the earth. But the swish of the wind in the trees and the patter of rain on the cabin's tin roof couldn't block out the sounds of Kylie's screaming. "It won't go!" she wailed.

Her fingers scratched at eyes which had seen too much and Bodie clasped her wrists in one of his big hands. He sank onto the floor next to her in his smart uniform trousers, not caring about the fluff balls which attached to the navy fabric. Keeping hold of her wrists, he pushed her hair out of her eyes. "It'll go," he promised. "Eventually, you won't see or hear it anymore. Your mind amplifies things when you're shocked. It adds things you didn't really see or hear as it tries to make sense of what's happened. It'll go, I promise, but it just takes time." Bodie Singh Johal. Always factual and never pulling any punches, not even for his sister.

Phoenix swallowed acidic liquid left over from her vomiting spree. It burned the back of her throat. She kept her eyes closed and the images rolled on repeat. Kylie's misguided adoration of Tina had driven her to act and resulted in Kirwan's death. But where had the tragedy really started? "I shouldn't have told you," she whispered. "I did this. I did it."

"No, you didn't." Bodie stroked her back in gentle, rounded motions. "Immigration were already on their way. They got a call in the early hours of this morning from a woman in Auckland. Her kid arrived home from the camp with a story about a barn full of refugees. Stupid girl hitched a ride with a truck driver."

"Lexi," Phoenix breathed. She'd known the whole time.

The rain grew harder, slapping against the roof like giant tears of shared grief. Phoenix's thoughts muddled in a series of disjointed sentences interspersed by memories and half reached conclusions. Nothing made sense anymore. Not even facts. She struggled against Bodie's grip and he released her left hand. Her fingers coasted over her lips where Kirwan had kissed her. A welcome numbness seeped into her heart as she refused to stop venturing back into her private cupboard of pain. Her physiology took over, fogging the glass of her inner vision and barring the doors back to Kirwan.

"You okay?" Bodie lifted her chin with his index finger and examined her face. He frowned at the scratches covering her cheeks and the blood staining her collar and the front of her sweatshirt. Phoenix nodded and the action reawakened the bruise on the back of her head. Her fingers rose to coast over it and she winced in pain.

Bodie kept the frown fixed in place as he studied her. Flecks of grey had sneaked through his sideburns and the roots of his black fringe since she last saw him. His forties suited him, honing his muscles into a solidity which stretched the fabric over his biceps. Age created an angular quality to his features and promotion had answered his quest for recognition. "I've asked the paramedics to examine you. Something is bleeding."

"I'm fine." Phoenix's words sounded slurred and her stomach gave a threatening lurch. She shivered beneath the weight of Bodie's heavy waterproof balanced over her shoulders, its thermal warmth unable to reach the cold spaces in her heart. His dark eyelashes blinked and then he held her gaze in a show of defiance. The fingers of his left hand beckoned to someone waiting in the doorway. Phoenix closed her eyes against the sight of the paramedic from outside the barn. "Keep them away from me!" she hissed.

Bodie ignored her, rising to his knees and sitting on the nearby bunk to give the paramedic room.

"We need to warm you up, sweetheart." The female medic took her temperature and lifted the jacket to fit the blood pressure cuff over her damp sleeve. She frowned at her instruments and glanced up at Bodie, communicating the results without speaking. "Where's the blood from, Phoenix?"

"She's touching her head. It's coming from inside her hair." Bodie leaned forward and lifted the matted curls away from Phoenix's neck. The medic knelt up for a better look and Phoenix jerked away from them. The jacket slipped from her shoulders and she overbalanced, splaying her fingers against the floorboards at the last moment. A discarded cigarette paper fluttered from beneath the bed as her movement disturbed the air. With it came a flood of memories, pouring into her brain like the filling of a cup. Kirwan laughing and rolling his cigarettes. Kirwan closing his eyes as he took the first drag. His defiance in the face of Tina's ire and then the sound of his bones breaking beneath the heavy tyres.

Phoenix reached for Bodie's hand, burying her cold fingers inside his warm palm. "I want Mama," she whispered, her eyes wide and filled with the threat of unknown monsters. "I want to go home."

39

ROUGH HANDS

Phoenix pulled her face from her pillow at the knock on her door. The swelling on the back of her head sent an ache radiating down her neck. She rubbed her eyes and sat up, acknowledging the tightness in her chest at the thought of interacting with anyone else trying to be helpful. Matua had phoned earlier to speak to her and his gentle probing had felt like a trial. Mikaere had kicked the innards out of his horse box, not understanding the old man and his son's generosity in transporting him to the hotel. Matua had still asked her if she wanted to sell the gelding, offering cash for the feisty beast if she changed her mind.

"Phoe?" Her mother's voice sounded tentative, as though she'd read her daughter's thoughts from beyond the solid wood. She knocked again. "Papa wants you to wait for him by the front door. He'll arrive in about fifteen minutes."

Phoenix sighed in defeat. If Logan Du Rose had summoned her then she couldn't refuse. The instruction sounded mysterious and her curiosity piqued a fraction. She stumbled to her bedroom door and hauled it open, questions already tumbling from her lips. Hana shook her head and held out a tower of laundered clothing. "I don't know what he's planned, Phoe. But the weather is turning." She pushed the bundle into Phoenix's arms and turned away. "Mac cleaned your boots. He left them by the front door."

Glancing down, Phoenix wrinkled her nose. Closing the bedroom door with her heel, she set the clothes on the bed and sifted through them. Her comfiest riding jeans and a sweater slid from the top of the pile. Bodie had liberated her camp clothes after the immigration officers closed the site. One of Lexi's most indecent thongs slithered from beneath Phoenix's underwear. A few stray socks belonging to the girls created a layer of confusion, testimony to Bodie's smash and grab effort.

Hana had darned a hole in the hem of her shorts and Phoenix lifted them to her face and sniffed. The woodsy scent of the camp had gone, replaced by laundry powder and fabric softener. "Like it never happened," she whispered. A dart of pain behind her ribs reaffirmed that it had. Its consequences would hurt for a long while.

"Phoe?" Edin didn't wait for an answer to her knock. She pushed her way into the bedroom and slumped onto the bed. "That little girl keeps ringing. You should talk to her."

Phoenix's body grew rigid and she closed her eyes. "I can't," she whispered. "I can't speak to any of them."

"Sharon. That's her name." Edin examined her nail polish and dark curls tumbled against her shoulders. The Du Rose grey eyes sparkled as she glanced up at Phoenix. Wiri's half-sister smiled, identical full lips curving upwards and dimples creating dents in her cheeks. "She's just worried about you." Their father's high cheekbones and angular features made Wiri handsome and turned Edin into a stunner. She knew it. Wiri didn't yet understand the devastation his looks wrought in the small mountain township. Phoenix doubted he'd care.

"Thanks, but I'm fine." She hauled the sweater over her head and heard the static hiss as it passed across her hair. "I don't want to talk about it." Her mind recreated the accident like a film reel, slowing it down at the point of impact and consuming her inner vision. Kirwan came from nowhere. Kylie became airborne with the grace of a coiled rope. Then the crunch of metal on bone. Phoenix shivered as though an icy hand had run a finger along her spine.

"Okay." Edin shrugged and got to her feet. A mischievous glint appeared in her eyes, reminiscent of Kane Du Rose's more troubled streak. "I told her you'd call her back," she said. Dainty feet took her across the room and the door clicked shut behind her, robbing Phoenix of a suitable retort.

Phoenix groaned and sank onto the bed. She put her head in her hands and rested her elbows on her knees. Kylie had gone back into foster care and Sharon had realised too late that she missed her. Phoenix had listened to her tears and rambling the first few times but couldn't face any more hour-long conversations. Sharon rehashed the week's sorry events at every opportunity. "I can't do this anymore," Phoenix whispered into her hands. "I can't do things just because I should."

Once dressed, Phoenix waited under the porch. The scent of cape daisies shrouded her in perfume from Hana's flower garden. Mac rode around the front garden on the mower, the motor too loud for conversation. He seemed to understand her reluctance to talk, his little acts of service thoughtful and precious. He pointed to her boots and tilted his head to one side in question. Her thumbs-up sign reassured him and caused a wide smile to split his lips. His auburn hair ruffled as he spun the mower to cut another long swathe of grass. The absence of his smile let the darkness encroach a little further around Phoenix's heart. She turned her favourite hat in her hands, her fingers edging their way around the brim in a fruitless march to meet back where they started.

The summer had turned its back on the mountain and left a coolness in its place. Dark clouds scudded overhead. Phoenix clasped her arms around herself as though forming a physical barrier against the inner storm raging in her heart. She heard her father before she saw him, the echo of hooves plodding up the long track to the house. Twin beats hit the ridge and bounced off, telling her he wasn't alone.

Mikaere jerked his head as Phoenix jogged towards them. The indignity of being towed up the mountain on a lead rope had made him crabby. Temper flared behind his blue eye. Logan had continued treating his knees and muzzle with manuka honey. A yellow streak covered Mikaere's cheek where he'd transferred it from rubbing against his leg.

Logan sat astride his white mare, Dove. She kept her ears back against her neck, disliking the proximity of the temperamental gelding within kicking range. Logan gave Phoenix a lazy smile and handed her the rope. "He's no better then," he commented. It was a statement and not a question, referring to the degree of difficulty he'd had catching and then tacking the stubborn horse. He'd met the challenge with his usual brand of calm assurance and the knowledge that his will was stronger than Mikaere's ever would be. Steel girded Logan Du Rose's spine and the huge sigh which Mikaere released showed he knew it.

"He's okay for me." Phoenix rubbed the furry ears and pressed her face against his wiry mane. She fingered the soft leather of the bridle and frowned. "Can't I free ride?" she asked, her tone flat.

"Not where we're going," Logan replied. He tilted the brim of his cowboy hat back enough to sight the clouds. "And it's now or never, kōtiro."

Phoenix felt the hat cord tighten against her voice box as she bounced into the saddle. Mikaere tipped to one side with her weight and planted his feet. Phoenix lifted her offside leg forward and leaned down to tighten his girth. He gave a huge sigh and blew out his stomach like a tight balloon to prevent her hauling the buckle higher. Phoenix groaned and glanced up at the rumble of her father's laughter. "Yep. No better," he concluded.

Logan swung his mare in a perfect arc and set off back towards the gate. He rode one handed, the other resting over his broad thigh. He lifted it to wave to his son and Mac waved back in acknowledgement. Strong shoulders filled out Logan's signature white tee shirt which his wife would curse as she bleached sweat and mud from the fabric later. His jeans fit snug around the instep of his tan cowboy boots. As soon as he passed through the gate, he veered right and with the click of his tongue and a tap of his reins on the mare's neck, disappeared.

"Great," Phoenix grumbled. She slipped her feet into the stirrups and gathered up her reins. Mikaere jogged on the spot, his giant hooves pressing into the grass. He wanted to chase the mare, not because he liked her but because his nature demanded it. His dam's sense of superiority flowed through his veins and he tossed his head as Phoenix kept the reins lifted off his neck. He backed up in temper, gouging clods out of the neat lawn and bunching power into his hind quarters. "Behave!" Phoenix complained. "I don't have the energy for this."

She said the words and heard the truth of them return to her like a hammer blow to the head. Getting out of bed and dressing had taken all her dwindling reserves of enthusiasm for life. Confusion and depression urged her to go back to bed and roll in the sheets with them. Dove's hooves hammered along the boundary fence and Phoenix caught a flash of white as Logan headed deep into the bush. She considered dismounting, shutting the gate and letting Mikaere mow the patch of grass Mac had missed as he'd turned the heavy machine. But her disobedience would disappoint her father. He'd wiped his busy schedule to spend time with her. The realisation sent tears to prick her eyes. She squeezed the bridge of her nose between thumb and forefinger. "At least he's the one person who won't ask me what happened," she told Mikaere. The thought induced a bubble of safety around her heart. Logan knew everything without asking questions. She inhaled and released the breath, refreshed by the thought of spending time with her father.

Mikaere read the sudden change in her seat as her shoulders relaxed. He took it as permission. Dove's hoof beats quieted as Logan turned off the ridge and took a narrow track towards the densest part of the bush. In a flash of stubbornness reminiscent of his mother, Mikaere dug the front edge of his hooves into the lawn and lurched forward, abandoning his training and almost leaving his rider behind him. Phoenix swore as he took off after Logan, his pace reckless and dangerous in the spirit of the pursuit. They both almost fell as he jerked right at the gate, his neck shortening as he made the tight turn and his bare hooves scrabbling in the dust. Phoenix concentrated on not losing her seat, finding herself halfway along the ridge before she dared to release the sharp inhale she'd held since Mikaere bolted. A high-pitched whinny told them which of the tracks to follow and Mikaere careened along until his fear of missing out subsided enough to slow his gait.

Logan waited for them at a fork in the track. He appeared relaxed, the buckle of his reins resting across his thigh as though he had all the time in the world. "Nice of you to join us," he said, his tone steady and his eyes smiling. Phoenix frowned and ignored his sarcasm, angry at him, her horse and herself. She tutted and rolled her eyes, the obedient daughter swapped for someone else's grumpy teenager. Mikaere panted and sweated, the sprint both treacherous and fulfilling. Dove flattened her ears and snaked her neck, reminding him who carried the alpha on their back. Mikaere released a snort which sounded like derision as Logan shortened Dove's reins.

"Papa, where are we going?" Phoenix demanded. Her tone sounded more petulant than she intended.

Logan gave her a wink, the one that made her school friends swoon and giggle behind their hands. "You'll know it when you see it," he replied. He flicked Dove's neck with his reins and set off at a steady trot.

Curiosity occupied Phoenix's mind. She pushed Mikaere after him, allowing the bush to start its healing process on her frayed nerves. The canopy protected her from the biting wind coming up from the south, closing above her like angel wings offering shelter. The air held its own unique scent of greenery and moss. Each new hoof beat churned up comfort and familiarity. It filled her nostrils and soothed her sore heart. She followed her father where he led, trusting him as she always had. The tangata whenua whispered their waiata over her, lending her their wisdom and pressing breathy kisses to warm the top of her bare head.

40

GENTLE MOUTH

The ridge ended before them, the horses keen to keep their hooves away from the edge. A treacherous drop fell like a giant had punched its foot into the mountain top and withdrawn it to leave a wide gully. The ocean peeked from the gaps to both left and right, cutting off this section of the mountain like an island at high tide. Paddock 101. Beautiful to gaze upon, but useless for farming.

Phoenix had never ventured further than this point, the island accessible only by helicopter or by free climbing into the deep, bush coated valley. Then a swim and a treacherous climb up the other side. Only one person had ever made the journey and his bones still lay at the bottom, riddled with cancer and regret. Wiri and Edin's father had chosen his own graveyard, robbing his family of a tangihanga. And sparing them conflict.

Phoenix leaned a palm over the pommel of her saddle and sighed. Dust coated her skin from the ride and leftover sunburn from the camp prickled the bridge of her nose. "Why are we here?" she asked, her voice containing an element of petulance guaranteed to alienate her fiery father. It had crept in of late, the seed sewn as the paramedics shook their heads over Kirwan's body. Flourishing into a full-grown tree in her chest, the anger bubbled and churned beneath the sadness. The sounds of that day returned. Elephant had screamed from the back of the van, his agony palpable. "I'm a trauma surgeon," he begged. "I can help him. Let me help him." He'd remained in the van. Rules were rules. Kirwan had paid the price.

Logan turned to face her and instead of rebuke, his expression held understanding. "What are you thinking?" he demanded.

Phoenix frowned. Confusion replaced all other emotions, and she floundered beneath his grey-eyed gaze. "You weren't supposed to ask questions." Her tone sounded sullen. "It's the only reason I agreed to come."

"Did you agree?" Logan grinned. "I hadn't noticed." A dimple flashed in his cheek and disappeared; an old injury from a fall which left its mark on a body already scarred by his disease.

"I don't ... understand what you're asking." Phoenix's words emerged with a stammer, a new and embarrassing after effect of the camp. It reappeared with stress, fragmenting her thoughts as her tongue tripped over familiar words.

Logan Du Rose released a sigh and leaned forward. His left forearm rested on his thigh as he turned in the saddle. "Your mother thinks you've taken responsibility for everything that happened, Phoe. I want to know why you believe it's your fault."

Phoenix closed her eyes and shook her head. "I can't think about it," she whispered. "I can't think about... anything."

Logan inhaled and settled in the saddle. He slipped his feet from his stirrups and stretched his long legs. "You take your time, kōtiro. I've got all day." Dove let out a sigh and her head drooped until her neck formed a parallel with the earth. Her lower lip wobbled in contentment as the sunshine peeked through the clouds and kissed the whorl of hair which set out from her white forehead to cover her entire body.

"Why... here?" Phoenix ground her teeth against the irritating stutter.

Logan kept his gaze on the bush which coated the side of the strange island. It created the effect of hairy toes and joints as it met the gully at the bottom. Sea water stormed the gap at high tide and cut it off, though only a fool would venture there, anyway. Native punga and a lone kauri clung to the sheer side, their roots embedded somehow in the craggy rock like natural bonsai. "There's something I want to show you. But we need to wait."

"What is it?" Phoenix tugged on the cord of her hat and lifted it onto her head. Her fingers shook on the brim.

"Just wait." Logan cocked his head and his grey eyes bored into her soul. Phoenix felt herself withering and the stutter occupied her head so she couldn't form words.

The sun rose high as it burned off the clouds and denied their gloomy autonomy. Logan hadn't worn a watch for years, using the shadows on the landscape to navigate his days. Tilting his head back, he let the sun's heat touch his cheeks. "Midday," he said, his voice jarring in the stillness. Then silence settled back over them like a cloak.

A radio crackled on the loop of his belt as the disjointed voices of his stock men gave sit reps and locations. Mikaere's giant left hoof pawed the earth as boredom scratched at his psyche. The ball of fire in Phoenix's chest built a scream in the back of her throat. She couldn't contain its force. "It is my fault!" she shouted, her body shaking as the raw truth escaped.

Mikaere jerked backwards in fright and Phoenix scrabbled to grip a tuft of his mane. She saw a flash of sleek equine muscle as she tipped over his shoulder and then the yawning cavern in front of his feet. But her skin burned against the rough seams beneath her armpits and across the back of her neck as her father's strong fingers caught her sweater. He didn't release the fabric until she'd reclaimed her seat and steadied her nerves. His dark left eyebrow remained cocked and a hint of fear sparkled behind his slate grey irises.

"Sorry, sorry." Phoenix gripped the reins in her right hand and ran her left across her face. Only the cord beneath her chin had saved her hat. Her grandmother's hat, the Jillaroo Logan once gave to

Miriam and then to Hana. An accidental heirloom which Phoenix had claimed and kept without asking. Her hat. Its original owner's fate reinforced her moral code. *This is what happens when you break the rules; tragedy disappoints everyone.*

"What are you sorry for, daughter?"

The loaded question attacked the remains of her resolve, Logan's use of the English word both stark and unusual. Phoenix closed her eyes and drew in a shaky breath. "I didn't speak Māori all week," she whispered. "They didn't understand me and it felt like I'd cauterised my soul." She ran a shaking hand over her top lip. "They had rules which made no sense." The shock had created a catharsis and her stutter abated. Words tumbled unfettered from her lips. "They didn't allow boys in girls' cabins, but they ran an illegal smuggling operation. They said grace before breakfast and broke the law after dark."

Logan leaned sideways and prised the reins from her gripping fingers. He pressed his left heel into his mare and she moved sideways to match Mikaere's position in front of the ridge. The gelding tossed his head and Logan poked him in the shoulder with the knuckle of his index finger. "Pack it in," he growled. Mikaere's head tossing ceased, but his ears flicked back and forth in constant assessment of his dwindling control. Logan retained the reins, pulling them over into his left hand. His right arm slipped around his daughter's shoulders. "Horses for courses," he murmured.

Phoenix shook her head. "I never understood that phrase."

Logan shrugged, the action carrying through her body like a Mexican wave. "It means people don't always pick the best tools or course of action to achieve their goal. They go about something the wrong way, like using a racehorse to round up cattle. It can't work. They meant well but messed up the outcome. It was inevitable." He blinked. "There were other means of doing what they wanted. They could have talked to the immigration department about sponsoring refugee families."

Phoenix nodded. She leaned her head against her father's shoulder and closed her eyes. "They were hypocrites," she concluded. "And so am I."

Logan snuffed out a laugh. "Welcome to my world, kid. It's been getting kinda lonely." He turned his head and pressed a kiss to her temple. The scratch of his stubble brought comfort and soothed her soul. Dove snaked her head sideways and pressed her wide nostril over Mikaere's. They bumped noses before she shied away with an ear-splitting screech. Logan relinquished his hold on Phoenix at the last second before the mare jerked sideways. He shook his head as they ended up metres away from the edge of the ridge. "At least she went backwards," he commented, his voice calm. His seat hadn't changed; still rock steady and built from years in the saddle.

Phoenix gathered up Mikaere's reins from where Logan dropped them. The leather felt warm against her fingers. Logan's mare hoisted her tail like a flag and shot her ears forward. His laugh filled the mountain and ricocheted off the ridge to return as an echo. "I'm surrounded by unpredictable females." He tapped Dove's neck with his right rein, opening it to urge her forward but leaving a decent distance between the horses. "Always changing their minds."

"I thought they hated each other," Phoenix commented. She held onto the rest of the sentence, not wanting to hear herself stumble over familiar words.

"Not anymore." Logan raised an eyebrow and wrinkled his nose at Mikaere. He patted Dove's wide neck. "Sorry, girl," he acknowledged. "You're wasting your time. This man has no balls."

"A for effort though," Phoenix breathed, repeating the well-worn phrase of their stock man, David Allen.

The horses settled and peace descended over them. Until Logan spoke. "It's okay, you know," he said, his voice gentle. "It's okay to be faulty."

Phoenix swallowed and shook her head. "Faulty gets you killed," she stated.

Logan's chin jerked back as though she'd struck him. "Where d'you learn rubbish like that?" he exclaimed.

"Poppa Reuben, Uncle Kane, Uncle Nev. Should I keep... going?" Her grey eyes flashed as she faced him. "If you do wrong, it goes wrong. You disappoint everyone." Her teeth clenched in her jaw. "I tried to pick which rules I followed. Now, the refugees are in immigration hell and Kirwan is dead. I disappointed everyone. I didn't mend their situation, I broke it beyond repair."

"Sounds to me like you were the only one following the rules," Logan said. His voice sounded strained as though the situation had gone beyond his control.

Phoenix's eyes flashed with a strange fire. "No, I thought I was. But I didn't know where the line was, Papa. They were showing Christian kindness, and I made a complete mess of it. I should have just left things alone."

"What's your premise?" The question shocked her into silence and halted her stammering rant. Logan raised a wise eyebrow. "What's your premise, Phoe?"

"Always do the right thing," she whispered, certainty leaking through her voice. "Always."

Logan shook his head and his eyes narrowed. "Na uh," he concluded. If he noticed the rage budding in his daughter's face at his denial, he didn't acknowledge it. "That's not your premise, babe. You've built your life on a whole other game board. You're just looking at the outworking."

"Really?" Phoenix snarled. In her anger, she dropped her reins and fixed her hands on her hips. "So, what's my premise then? You tell me!"

Logan smiled at her, though the expression didn't reach his eyes or activate the crow's feet in the corners. His tone sounded sad. "To please people, kōtiro. To fix everything that's broken. You think my whānau came to grief because they didn't follow the rules. You're wearing their shame and disappointment for not doing the right thing, Phoe. But you can't govern your life by carrying the weight of their sins. It's too late to put it all right. You need to stop trying to fix the world."

"What about you?" Phoenix's eyes flashed the colour of an angry sea. "You always fix everything for everyone. They all rely on you."

Logan's dark eyelashes fluttered and he released a deep sigh. "I wish they wouldn't, Phoe. Fixing their messes has led me down some real destructive paths in my lifetime. It's not a strength. It's a flaw. I don't want to see you follow me to a personal hell."

"Is that why we're here?" Phoenix's chin wobbled with the force of holding in her tears. "Because your brother is still down there? He took a poor path and this is the lesson?" A shaking hand pointed at the gully below them. Darkness enfolded it as the straggling bush covered the rocks and hid the bottom from view.

"No." Logan's eyes narrowed and he inhaled. Mikaere stiffened beneath Phoenix's legs as his giant head rose. A low whinny ground from between his lips and a distant answering call met it. Logan lifted his hand and a crooked index finger pointed at the bank opposite them. "That's why."

Phoenix blinked away her tears and peered across the cavern. Sunlight danced across the muscular ribs of a stallion. His black and white mottled coat marked him as an Appaloosa, but his Kaimanawa shaped head and body gave him an odd, chunky physique. He planted his front feet on a raised rock and stared across the distance, ears perked and his body ready to run. Four loose mares grazed nervously on the grassy plateau behind him, nipping at tufts with jerky movements. Mikaere whinnied again and a mare replied. Her bulging stomach carried a late foal. Her markings matched his, the strange black and grey spots almost identical. Phoenix held her breath, gathering up her reins as she sensed Mikaere bunching power in his hind quarters. For a moment of sheer horror, she imagined him pitching over the side of the cliff.

But he wasn't welcome. The stallion objected from a distance, tossing his head and flattening his ears along his neck. He moved from a standstill with a burst of energy, arching his back and kicking up his heels in a show of power and authority. He bounced back from the rock and rounded up his mares, nipping at their hocks and driving them off the plateau and back to wherever they hailed.

Mikaere's lungs blew out a snort of defiance before his body relaxed beneath Phoenix. She lifted a hand to shield her eyes from the bright sunlight and scanned the island opposite for the horses.

"About eleven hectares." Logan answered her unspoken question. "More than enough room for now. He's breeding slow at the moment."

"It's Mikaere's sire," Phoenix whispered. Her face broke into her first smile in days. "It explains his odd colouring. Wow."

Logan nodded. "That's what I wanted you to see," he said. His expression softened, the hard angles of his face lessening. "I don't know how Sacha got across there or how she brought him back. But she did. For you."

"Why me?" Phoenix's voice cracked.

Logan reached across and rested his scarred hand over her writhing fingers. "Because Phoe, you're the best of us. She believed in you. Following the rules and doing the right thing for everyone else is a noble goal until it compromises your own integrity. I should know." He released her and sat up, his feet fitting back into his stirrups with ease. "People do dumb stuff for the best of reasons and you can't control them. Only yourself. I'm proud of who you've become, Phoe. Not disappointed. Stop trying to be perfect and live your own life. My kids are the best thing that ever happened to me. Nothing you did could make me love you any less."

The lump in her throat spread to encase her jaw. She knew one thing he wouldn't tolerate. Wiri. Pain tingled into her temples as pressure grew behind her eyes. Logan Du Rose demonstrated his love; he didn't say the words often. The old Phoenix would have responded in kind, keen not to disappoint him by not returning his affection. The new Phoenix sensed he didn't need to hear the words. He understood. She hoped he'd always understand. As if to reinforce her realisation, Logan gave one of his rare smiles. It offered a view behind the mask and gave her a momentary glimpse of the man her mother adored. Then he ruined it.

"What's that thing Sam's always banging on about in his sermons? Love God and then your neighbour. Just concentrate on those two things and you'll do fine."

Sensing he'd done it on purpose to lighten the gravity of the moment, Phoenix's lips curved into a reluctant smile. "I'm telling Ma you listened to Sam preaching."

Logan snorted and this time, his eyes smiled along with his lips. "Na," he replied, "you won't."

41

LIGHT HANDS

The church echoed the sound of the organ, sending the notes to waver near the vaulted ceiling before crashing over Phoenix's head like a judgement. She bowed forward, her elbows digging into the hard muscles of her thighs. The fragrance of furniture polish and Mrs Randall's colourful floral decoration encased her in familiarity, but it wasn't enough. Phoenix Du Rose sought peace in all the usual places, meeting instead, the cacophony of her own muddled thoughts.

She saw Kirwan's face everywhere. When she touched Mikaere's sleek coat, she remembered their ride along the beach. When she closed her eyes, his hard kisses robbed her of sleep. She couldn't reconcile the sense of aliveness which Kirwan possessed with the narrow casket which had summed up his life. Her mother drove her to his funeral, but she'd baulked at the sight of the girls from her cabin gathered outside the chapel. She'd dressed in her best clothes and they'd driven for an hour, the exercise a complete waste. Phoenix couldn't go inside the simple brick building and they'd returned home in silence. The whump of Kirwan's body hitting the van seemed like a constant echo in her mind, a concerto played as background music to everything she did. Whump. Whump. Whump.

Her brain buzzed with the need to be busy, while her arms and legs refused to engage. Here. Not here. Gone. Just like that. One minute he was grinning at her with that mischievous glint in his eyes and the next second, bleeding from his ears as life slipped from him.

Phoenix blew out a ragged breath and clamped her teeth on her lower lip to halt the threatening tears. She'd thought she had none left after her ride with Logan, but they still appeared from an unknown well hidden deep in her soul.

"Hey, Phoe." Pastor Sam slumped into the pew next to her. "E pewhea ana koe?" His dark fringe flopped forward into his eyes as he bowed his head in prayer. He'd asked her how she felt without expecting an answer she couldn't give. Irrational rage bubbled into her chest as the beast unleashed from the depths of her misery sought someone else to blame. Phoenix ground her teeth and stayed silent. She couldn't trust herself. His flakiness formed the catalyst for the disaster her life had become. If he'd been honest with her from the start, she wouldn't have gone to the camp, never met Kirwan or discovered the refugees. He'd still be alive, biding time to escape the foster care system and find his own crazy-paved path.

Phoenix rose, bursting to her feet with the force of the inner detonation which rocked her mind. Sam's head shot up and his eyes opened, the connection between them familiar but changed. "I'm sorry." He reached for her hand and frowned at the balled fist he found. His fingers clutched her wrist and didn't release it. "I couldn't risk coming with you, Phoenix. There were too many opportunities to be alone. I needed to do the right thing."

Phoenix stared down at him and her lips parted in confusion. "What? But we've been alone hundreds of times." Her eyes widened as the implication hit home. Her girlish crush seemed a lifetime ago and ridiculous beneath the shade of Kirwan's death. "You thought I'd throw myself at you?"

Sam sighed, the motion heavy and laboured. He shook his head and the scales began their devastating slide from over Phoenix's vision. "No," he confessed. "I thought I'd throw myself at you."

Phoenix yanked her wrist away with unnecessary force. Her former adoration drained like murky water down a plug hole. A man sat before her, a faulty, struggling mortal weighed down by the guilt of his own thoughts. He'd let her down to save them both, but it had eaten away at his resolve and weakened him. A single word of encouragement from her would prove his undoing and ruin both their lives and countless others. Phoenix clasped her hands behind her back, moving out of reach of Sam's grasping fingers. She shook her head and swallowed as Wiri's words echoed in her mind. He'd called Sam a smokescreen and she realised the wisdom of his observation. "I allowed myself to love you because I knew nothing could ever happen," she whispered. "I gave you my affection for safekeeping, not for you to use." Her legs trembled as she turned, but somehow her shaky knees carried her to the heavy rimu doors.

Bright sunshine greeted her and the smell of dusty earth. Her heart had shattered in her chest and her fingers bled from holding the shards together in the gap. Nothing would ever be the same again. She couldn't fix this. A sob wracked her chest. She didn't want the responsibility.

Another, more box shaped church at the end of the street seemed to call to her, its simplicity stark against the backdrop of her father's mountain. A statue of the Virgin Mary stood out front, her head bowed and her concrete eyes blind to Phoenix's agony. Beyond the Catholic Church stood the urupā, the square of ground retained by her ancestors for burying their dead. Her feet turned of their own volition and stepped towards it. The urge to sit by her namesake's memorial stone increased, and Phoenix broke into a run. She removed her trainers at the gate and stuffed her socks into their open necks. The heat from the soft grass warmed her soles and travelled through her chilled bones as she took a short cut to avoid the gravel path.

A wide stone commemorated the original Phoenix Du Rose, though her bones lay beneath the kauri tree at the top of Logan's mountain where she died. The list of ancestors began generations before with a litany of Māori names, later joined by French. The wide stone paid lip service to the pakeha's need for remembrance. A few graves dotted the grassy knoll. Miriam Du Rose and Reuben lay together in death as they had in life. Their love affair kept them from burial on the mountain they'd defiled.

Phoenix leaned against the stone and stared up at the sky. Cumulus clouds dotted the azure blueness like fluffy balls of cotton wool. They moved in a slow procession, as though they had all the time they needed to make their journey. Drying her tears on the bottom of her shirt, Phoenix released a sigh laced with pure sadness and regret. "What a mess," she whispered. The rough stone chilled her palm and Phoenix turned sideways to press her cheek against the chiselled letters of her great grandmother's name. "Phoenix Du Rose," she whispered. "I'm here, Kuia."

Powerful arms wrapped around her from behind, hauling her spine against a hard chest. Brawny forearms crossed to form a cage over her heart and contain the wellspring of emotion and hurt. Phoenix looked down at the familiar fingers, the first knuckle of the left pinkie enlarged by a nasty break. The strong nails and work coarsened hands induced a sense of safety and comfort as they clasped in front of her stomach. Wiri's chin rested on top of her head and Phoenix heard him sigh. A gentle peace settled over her in the urupā's silence. The fragile tendrils of mana, which her great grandmother had held back, travelled up through the balls of her feet and lodged in her heart. A surge of strength accompanied it alongside a sliver of hope.

Wiri pressed a kiss to the top of her head. "Are you gonna be okay?" he asked, his tone soft. Phoenix nodded and her curls snagged against his rough chin. His arms flexed around her, sinews and tendons showing in the hard muscles earned through manual labour. But he was more than just brawn. A quick, intelligent brain processed the thoughts beneath his tousled hair. Wiremu was treading water, waiting for something before choosing his path in life. He could do anything, go anywhere. Phoenix's chest clenched at the thought of him being anywhere but at home.

"The boy who died, did you love him?" Wiri's tone held accusation and he cleared his throat as though not wanting the answer. Phoenix swallowed, realising she didn't know, anyway.

"I don't think so," she replied. "No. I knew him less than a week, Wiri." She sighed and pressed her spine against his chest.

"Sorry. It's none of my business." Wiri's shoulders hunched and he released her from his embrace. The motion felt final. He'd aged in the week since Phoenix left, as though the weight of his planned confession had eaten away at him. He stumbled over his next sentence, the words spilling from his lips. "I'm sorry for what I said, Phoe." He ran his tongue over his upper lip and paused. Rarely wrong footed, Wiremu Du Rose appeared utterly lost. "I put you in a terrible position. Your father would kill us both if we tried to take this thing between us further. It's always been there and probably always will. I need to learn to get past it and start living my life." An uncomfortable blush started somewhere inside his tee shirt and ran its course up his neck, his cheeks and into his hair. Phoenix realised she held her breath. Misery rose into her throat again. He was abandoning her. Abandoning them.

She turned to face him, her mind consumed with the need to stop time. The words wouldn't come and her breathing hitched. Silent tears followed, first one and then another until they ran down her olive cheeks in rivulets. They poured from a well in her core she hadn't known existed. Her hand shook as her fingers grappled in the pocket of her shorts. She found it there, the thing which had both confused and comforted her as she'd threaded the pieces together.

Wiri took a step back and Phoenix shivered from his lack of contact, despite the blazing sun. He reached out and the coarse pads of his fingers stroked the tears from her wet cheek. But more arrived, bouncing over his fingers and splashing off in different directions. His thumb strayed over the apex of her cheek before caressing the corner of her trembling lip. His eyes darkened as though chastened, and he withdrew his hand and folded his arms. "Uncle Logan secured me a place up north with the whānau," he said. "I'll do some paid work on their farm until I decide what I want to do with my life." His voice trembled. "Uncle thinks I should go to university. I've asked for a gap year just to think." His grey eyes implored her to understand and he looked away to shield the rush of grief pooling against his grey irises.

Phoenix nodded. She understood, but devastation threatened as the last bastion of her security crashed down around her ears. She'd held onto him like a throwaway crutch, ready to disregard him at the earliest opportunity. He'd leave of his own volition and it served her right. She should have dreaded this terrible possibility, but had been too blind to consider it.

Wiri turned, a fluid action driven by the powerful leg muscles which brought any horse under his control with supernatural ease. His Du Rose genes demanded respect by the same degree as they exhibited mana and authority. But in that moment, Wiremu Du Rose resembled a child cowed by devastation.

Phoenix kept her head bowed and her eyes closed. Her inner vision rode the waves of failure like a stricken surfer out of her depth. She'd tried to be perfect. She believed she'd kept a short account with God, but she hadn't. Beneath the veneer of righteousness, she'd hidden pride and a set of unfair weights and measures. She'd wanted to fix everything, but at any cost. In the last month, the colour grey had seeped through her defences and rendered her incapable of distinguishing between right and wrong. Because somehow, her right and wrong didn't seem to tally with God's.

Wiri turned back one last time, his body governed by paralysis at facing the thing he'd spent a lifetime dreading; separation from Phoenix. His last smile looked hollow. She sensed that without her, he'd become like Tama, moving through empty relationships like a man sampling wine without ever finding the oblivion of intoxication. Wiri reached the gate of the cemetery and bent to wash his hands under the tap. Phoenix sensed the urupā release him from its tapu sacredness as the water gushing over his fingers restored him back to noa, the ordinary. He stood, his spine stiffening into a curve as his stomach suffered from a painful, physical ache. She saw his pain mirror hers. Dragging the ute keys from his pocket, he forced his feet towards the truck parked on the road.

"Wiri!" Phoenix's voice caught in her throat and he almost didn't hear her. She left her trainers by the memorial and ran along the path through the cemetery, her bare feet pounding the gravel without care. Her shorts flapped against her lithe thighs and her grey eyes radiated the terror which lumbered after her like a black cloud. Wiri paused, his heart a roiling ball of fire in his gut. Phoenix reached the gate and skidded to a halt. An arm's-length stood between them, stretching as far as the Pacific Ocean. Her left hand grappled for the gate's wrought iron finial and held on, a life raft in a sea of confusion.

Phoenix glanced at the tap and then at Wiri's rigid stance. Conflict budded in the furrowing of her brow. Tikanga and proper Māori custom meant she needed to wash her hands before leaving the cemetery. She glanced at the still dripping tap and then the devastated face of her cousin.

Wiri stood his ground. A single step would take him across the threshold and back into the urupā. Phoenix expected him to bend to her will and when his feet remained rooted to the pavement, something hot burned behind her irises. He'd spent his life compromising for others and so had she, but this new day marked a fresh set of rules for them both. Phoenix stole one more glance at the tap and then fixed her gaze on the pavement.

That single step cost her everything. Phoenix Du Rose broke something that no one could fix. Her ancestors should have groaned beneath the whenua and the mountain should have cracked as their beloved Du Rose daughter stepped over the tikanga into a life beyond rules and risked the disappointment of others.

That single giant step propelled Phoenix's chin against Wiri's chest. Her balled fists contacted hard muscle and her left hand grappled to bunch the fabric of his tee shirt to hold herself upright. She raised her eyes to his, finding a world of hurt and confusion swirling in the stormy grey of his irises. He caught her elbows and held her, his lifted eyebrow forming the question he wouldn't humiliate himself by asking her again.

Phoenix swallowed and a stray tear from the bottom of the well escaped through the corner of her eye and plunged to its death against Wiri's wrist. Unfurling her right hand, Phoenix exposed her gift. She raised it for his perusal, risking his rejection.

A string of silver plastic hearts formed a circle against her palm. The ratty knot barely kept the beads together, the end frayed and its tension threatening disaster. Phoenix lifted her palm and presented herself to her cousin, the plastic hearts a symbol for her own. A voice in her head warned her she'd left it too late, but the need for honesty made her knees tremble with the relief of catharsis. "I made it for you," she stammered. "At the camp." Her voice wavered and a hitch in her chest cut the sentence in half.

Phoenix lowered her heels to the hot pavement. She pulled Wiri's left hand from beneath her elbow and dropped the bracelet into his palm. Then she closed his fingers around it. Turning, she stepped back over the threshold and onto the burial ground of the town's ngā mate. She warmed beneath their embrace as the wind tossed her hair and the sunshine kissed her damp cheeks dry.

Wiri remained outside the gate, his shattered heart bleeding into his chest cavity. His blank expression gave away nothing as he stared at the sorry gift in his palm. Sadness enveloped Phoenix and she tried to put right at least one of her wrongs. She bent to turn the tap, the rusty head creaking beneath her fingers. Water gushed onto her feet and she watched it for a moment before cupping both palms and letting the freshness of the mountain spring run over her fingers and wrists. The urge to get clean filled her mind and she lifted her hands and tipped their contents over her head. Then she did it again and again until her tee shirt clung to her delicate breasts and the water plastered her curls to her forehead.

Wiri's lips parted and he took a giant breath. His voice sounded cracked and feeble against the gushing of the tap. Phoenix turned as he spoke behind her and her chest hitched with another painful shudder. Wiri stepped back into the cemetery and reached down to turn off the water. His fingers travelled from the tap to Phoenix's drenched hands. He pulled her towards him, cosseting her in an achingly familiar embrace. "You're already clean," he said. "The only person who doesn't know it, is you."

Phoenix gulped and closed her eyes against the sensation of his thumb brushing her cheek. The elastic dangled next to her eye, the beads safe in Wiri's palm. He ran his fingers under her chin and forced her to look at him. He smiled down at her, his grey eyes still stormy but edging towards an ethereal calm. Tilting her chin, he pressed his lips over hers. The chaste kiss defined the start of something tender, filled with hope and redemption.

When he drew back, his lips lingered for a moment above hers. His smile leaked utter sincerity. "I'll come back for you in the spring," he whispered. He swallowed and his perceptive grey eyes stared into her soul as he pressed on the sore at the bitter root of everything. "It doesn't matter about the haemophilia, Phoe. I know why you don't want children and I'm fine with it. I've never lied to you and I won't let you down. Trust me."

Phoenix watched him walk away from her, hearing the same words her father once spoke to her mother. *Trust me.* Wiri climbed into the truck and started the engine, looking over his shoulder before reversing out onto the main road. Phoenix drank in the sight of his chestnut curls and the dimple which flashed in his cheek as he gave her a last, winning smile. When he lifted his hand to wave, she saw the bracelet's elastic dangling from his thumb.

As she abandoned her trainers by the family memorial and stepped out onto the main road to wait for her mother, she wondered how long the gift would last in Wiri's care. Or if the tenuous knot would betray them both and let their fragile hearts fall to the ground like silver beads. And become lost in the cracks of life.

A little help from my friends.

Gosh, reviews, where do I start? I feel like I'm always begging for the things. Most readers (I include myself in this as I read heaps too) don't perhaps understand how incredibly important reviews are to writers. A bad review isn't bad if it highlights something that needs fixing. And a good review isn't just so the author can fluff their feathers and think, 'Well, that's okay then." There's so much more to the process than that.

The store where you made your purchase is a complicated piece of software engineering, and having no reviews can hurt a book just as much as having bad ones. Having no reviews indicates that the book isn't popular and eventually, the store will just stop showing it to customers.

So, I know it's a pain and it takes your valuable time, but I'd love for you to help me stop my work becoming choked in the weeds of the retailers. When I started writing, there were a million books. Now, there are a million released every few months. It's hard to stay afloat and remain visible.

Please consider clicking through to your retailer and leaving a review. I will be so grateful.

About the Author

K T Bowes is a bestselling teen and women's author. Her novel *A Trail of Lies* was the winner of the genre award for Author's Cave in 2014.

K T Bowes is an Englishwoman in exile in New Zealand, swapping rugged cosmopolitan for mountain ranges and terrifying rivers. She lives in the same street as the Māori king and the culture around her is infused into most of her novels.

You can find her hanging out on social media in the following places.

Check in and say hello. Maybe suggest she gets back to writing and stops watching cat videos.

FACEBOOK
https://www.facebook.com/NZauthorKTBowes/
TWITTER
https://twitter.com/ktboweswrites
INSTAGRAM

Other Novels By KT Bowes

The Hana Du Rose Mysteries:
Logan Du Rose novella
Tama Du Rose novella
About Hana
Hana Du Rose
Du Rose Legacy
The New Du Rose Matriarch
One Heartbeat
The Du Rose Prophecy
Du Rose Sons
Du Rose Family Ties
Du Rose Vendetta
Wiremu Du Rose

The Calculated Risk Series:
The Actuary
The Actuary's Wife
The Actuary in Trouble

The Heart of the Actuary

Troubled Series:
Free from the Tracks -FREE digital copy
Sophia's Dilemma
A Trail of Lies
Gone Phishing

Escaping the Back Country NZ Series:
Pirongia's Secret
Deleilah

A Keeper's War Fantasy Trilogy:
Perpetual Winter
The Bee Queen
Hive

Standalone Novels
Artifact
Demons on Her Shoulder
Her Quiet Legacy
All Saints

Glossary of Maori Words and Phrases

Each tribe had its own complete language in the old days, not dialects as the English settlers made everyone believe. The tribes were independent people groups, much as England, Ireland, Scotland and Wales. They didn't use dialects of each other's language. Te Reo is now the nationally accepted native language of New Zealand, embodying much of the heart and sentence structure of the old. That's what I've used in my novels because it's what I've learned. Where I've used Te Reo, I've made sure there's a translation in place right there in the text, either through another character repeating it in English, or just clarifying in the next sentence so you become familiar.

I love this language. I attend a class at our local arts centre every Thursday afternoon and have done for some time. The teacher is a volunteer retired headmaster and his classes typically begin running for 10 weeks and keep going for 6 years. We've become a family as we've greeted each other in a lost tongue each week. Our oldest student is in her eighties and is learning to speak the words she heard at her grandmother's knee but buried through oppression. It's an amazing experience and I feel truly grateful to be part of the Te Reo revival.

This link goes to an awesome resource known as The Maori Dictionary. It speaks the words as well as spelling them for you if you want an audible version.

Things to remember

wh is pronounced as **f**

   ng is pronounced with the g as very faint behind the **n**

GLOSSARY

I've given the definitions as I've used the words.

Some words have different meanings for verb and noun use.

ara line of weaving, way, path, passage.

aroha - noun means love, verb means to love.

hapu - sub tribe, extended family group linked by ancestry.

haraheke - New Zealand flax.

inoi - prayer to God.

iwi - people group, tribe, race. The noun also means 'strength, bone' which is relevant. It's the thing which holds everything together. Logan's **iwi** is the Waikato tribe, but his **hapu** is Ngāpuhi in Northland through family relationships. A famous Ngāpuhi ancestor is Hōne Heke, who kept chopping the English flag down in Russell, Northland when the English refused to honour the Treaty of Waitangi.

kai - noun means food. Verb means 'to eat'. Mac is always hungry.

kia ora - be well, used as a greeting.

karakia - blessing.

kōtiro - girl. Term of affection.

Kuia - elderly woman, grandmother, female elder.

karanga - formal ceremonial call, welcome.

kaumātua - respected elder.

koha - gift, present, offering, nowadays often financial.

marae - gathering place for different tribes.

Matua kēkē -uncle, aunt.

maunga - mountain.

mihi whakatau or mihimihi - This is a greeting during which the male will give his credentials or lineage. Logan's **mihi** involves declaring the landmarks and people which make him Logan Du Rose.

mokopuna/moko - grandchildren, the next generation.

rākau - this is a length of wood or a stick. The noun refers to a challenge stick laid down before distinguished visitors on a marae. It was used as a weapon of war.

raranga weaving.

Tainui - one of the boats which navigated to New Zealand from Polynesia. Most Māori can trace their lineage back to the boat which their ancestors arrived on. They navigated using the stars and came back and forth often over thousands of years. There was no great invasion as the English settlers would have everyone believe. It was small groups of adventurers who arrived over the centuries and stayed. The ancestors of the Waikato tribes arrived at Kawhia on the west coast of New Zealand on the **Tainui.**

tāne - husband, man.

tangata whenua - I've used this as 'people of the land', often Logan's ancestors.

taonga - heirloom, treasure, something of value.

tēna koe - there you are (used as a greeting).

urupā - cemetery, burial ground.

waka - canoe. Latterly it also means 'car, vehicle.'

Whaea noun for mother, aunt, aunty.

whakapapa - noun means genealogy. Verb means to recite a genealogy. There are many ways to do that, either through senior males, including spouses, or single lines of descent. Logan's used to include Alfred, but you saw how that went for him. Because the mitochondria is the energy particle in an ovum before conception, the energy comes through the female line. Female lineage is very important for Māori for this reason. Logan has chosen to rely on his female genealogy in this novel because his male descent has become unreliable.

whānau - noun means family group.

wharenui - big house, often the sleeping house on a marae.

whenua - land, for Logan that means the mountain where his placenta was buried.